SHE BEGAN THE RATHER UNLIKELY STORY OF HER LIFE

"Trans-Temp is not the Great Trans-Temporal Cadre of Heroes and Heroines. It's a study complex for archeologists," Alyx explained. "They fish around blindfold in the past, though they're very careful where and when they fish because they have an unholy horror of even chipping the bottom off a canoe. They stay thirty feet above the top of the sea and twenty feet below it and outside city limits and so on and so on. And they can't even let through anything that's alive.

"Only one day they were fishing in the Bay of Tyre a good forty feet down and they just happened to receive twenty-odd cubic meters of sea-water complete with a small, rather inept Greek thief who had just pinched an expensive chess set from the Prince of Tyre, who between ourselves is no gentleman. They tell me I was attached to a rather large boulder more dead than alive . . . just alive enough to be salvageable, in fact."

THE ADVENTURES OF ALYX

JOANNA RUSS

BAEN
SCIENCE FICTION
BOOKS

THE ADVENTURES OF ALYX

This is a work of fiction. All the characters and events portrayed in this book are fictional, and any resemblance to real people or incidents is purely coincidental.

"Bluestocking" first published as "The Adventuress" in *Orbit 2*, New York, Berkley Books, 1967, copyright © 1967 by Damon Knight; "I Thought She Was Afeard Till She Stroked My Beard" first published as "I Gave Her Sack and Sherry" in *Orbit 2*, New York, Berkley Books, 1967, copyright © 1967 by Damon Knight; "The Barbarian" from *Orbit 3*, New York, Berkley Books, 1968, copyright © 1968 by Damon Knight; *Picnic on Paradise*, New York, Ace Books, 1968, copyright © 1968 by Joanna Russ; and "The Second Inquisition" from *Orbit 6*, New York, Berkley Books, 1970, copyright © 1970 by Damon Knight.

A Baen Book

Baen Publishing Enterprises
260 Fifth Avenue
New York, N.Y. 10001

First Baen printing, November 1986

ISBN: 0-671-65601-5

Cover art by Victoria Poyser

Printed in the United States of America

Distributed by
SIMON & SCHUSTER
TRADE PUBLISHING GROUP
1230 Avenue of the Americas
New York, N.Y. 10020

CONTENTS

BLUESTOCKING

This is the tale of a voyage that is of interest only as it concerns the doings of one small, gray-eyed woman. Small women exist in plenty—so do those with gray eyes—but this woman was among the wisest of a sex that is surpassingly wise. There is no surprise in that (or should not be) for it is common knowledge that Woman was created fully a quarter of an hour before Man, and has kept that advantage to this very day. Indeed, legend has it that the first man, Leh, was fashioned from the sixth finger of the left hand of the first woman, Loh, and that is why women have only five fingers on the left hand. The lady with whom we concern ourselves in this story had all her six fingers, and what is more, they all worked.

In the seventh year before the time of which we speak, this woman, a neat, level-browed, governessy

1

person called Alyx, had come to the City of Ourdh as part of a religious delegation from the hills intended to convert the dissolute citizens to the ways of virtue and the one true God, a Bang tree of awful majesty. But Alyx, a young woman of an intellectual bent, had not been in Ourdh two months when she decided that the religion of Yp (as the hill god was called) was a disastrous piece of nonsense, and that deceiving a young woman in matters of such importance was a piece of thoughtlessness for which it would take some weeks of hard, concentrated thought to think up a proper reprisal. In due time the police chased Alyx's coreligionists down the Street of Heaven and Hell and out the swamp gate to be bitten by the mosquitoes that lie in wait among the reeds, and Alyx—with a shrug of contempt—took up a modest living as pick-lock, a profession that gratified her sense of subtlety. It provided her with a living, a craft and a society. Much of the wealth of this richest and vilest of cities stuck to her fingers but most of it dropped off again, for she was not much awed by the things of this world. Going their legal or illegal ways in this seventh year after her arrival, citizens of Ourdh saw only a woman with short, black hair and a sprinkling of freckles across her milky nose; but Alyx had ambitions of becoming a Destiny. She was thirty (a dangerous time for men and women alike) when this story begins. Yp moved in his mysterious ways, Alyx entered the employ of the Lady Edarra, and Ourdh saw neither of them again—for a while.

Alyx was walking with a friend down the Street of Conspicuous Display one sultry summer's morning when she perceived a young woman, dressed like a jeweler's tray and surmounted with a great coil of red hair, waving to her from the table of a wayside garden-terrace.

"Wonderful are the ways of Yp," she remarked, for although she no longer accorded that deity any respect, yet her habits of speech remained. "There sits a red-headed young woman of no more than seventeen years and with the best skin imaginable, and yet she powders her face."

"Wonderful indeed," said her friend. Then he raised one finger and went his way, a discretion much admired in Ourdh. The young lady, who had been drumming her fingers on the tabletop and frowning like a fury, waved again and stamped one foot.

"I want to talk to you," she said sharply. "Can't you hear me?"

"I have six ears," said Alyx, the courteous reply in such a situation. She sat down and the waiter handed her the bill of fare.

"You are not listening to me," said the lady.

"I do not listen with my eyes," said Alyx.

"Those who do not listen with their eyes as well as their ears," said the lady sharply, "can be made to regret it!"

"Those," said Alyx, "who on a fine summer's morning threaten their fellow-creatures in any way, absurdly or otherwise, both mar the serenity of the day and break the peace of Yp, who," she said, "is mighty."

"You are impossible!" cried the lady. "Impossible!" and she bounced up and down in her seat with rage, fixing her fierce brown eyes on Alyx. "Death!" she cried. "Death and bones!" and that was a ridiculous thing to say at eleven in the morning by the side of the most wealthy and luxurious street in Ourdh,

for such a street is one of the pleasantest places in
the world if you do not watch the beggars. The lady,
insensible to all this bounty, jumped to her feet and
glared at the little pick-lock; then, composing herself
with an effort (she clenched both hands and gritted
her teeth like a person in the worst throes of marsh
fever), she said—calmly—

"I want to leave Ourdh."

"Many do," said Alyx, courteously.

"I require a companion."

"A lady's maid?" suggested Alyx. The lady jumped
once in her seat as if her anger must have an outlet
somehow; then she clenched her hands and gritted
her teeth with doubled vigor.

"I must have protection," she snapped.

"Ah?"

"I'll pay!" (This was almost a shriek.)

"How?" said Alyx, who had her doubts.

"None of your business," said the lady.

"If I'm to serve you, everything's my business.
Tell me. All right, how much?"

The lady named a figure, reluctantly.

"Not enough," said Alyx. "Particularly not knowing how. Or why. And why protection? From whom?
When?" The lady jumped to her feet. "By water?"
continued Alyx imperturbably. "By land? On foot?
How far? You must understand, little one—"

"*Little one!*" cried the lady, her mouth dropping
open. "*Little one!*"

"If you and I are to do business—"

"I'll have you thrashed—" gasped the lady, out of
breath, "I'll have you so—"

"And let the world know your plans?" said Alyx,
leaning forward with one hand under her chin. The

lady stared, and bit her lip, and backed up, and then she hastily grabbed her skirts as if they were sacks of potatoes and ran off, ribbons fluttering behind her. *Wine-colored ribbons*, thought Alyx, *with red hair; that's clever*. She ordered brandy and filled her glass, peering curiously into it where the hot mid-morning sun of Ourdh was suffused into a winy glow, a sparkling, trembling, streaky mass of floating brightness. *To* (she said to herself with immense good humor) *all the young ladies in the world*. "And," she added softly, "great quantities of money."

At night Ourdh is a suburb of the Pit, or that steamy, muddy bank where the gods kneel eternally, making man; though the lights of the city never show fairer than then. At night the rich wake up and the poor sink into a distressed sleep, and everyone takes to the flat, white-washed roofs. Under the light of gold lamps the wealthy converse, sliding across one another, silky but never vulgar; at night Ya, the courtesan with the gold breasts (very good for the jaded taste) and Garh the pirate, red-bearded, with his carefully cultivated stoop, and many many others, all ascend the broad, white steps to someone's roof. Each step carries a lamp, each lamp sheds a blurry radiance on a tray, each tray is crowded with sticky, pleated, salt, sweet . . . Alyx ascended, dreaming of snow. She was there on business. Indeed the sky was overcast that night, but a downpour would not drive the guests indoors; a striped silk awning with gold fringes would be unrolled over their heads, and while the fringes became matted and wet and water spouted into the garden below, ladies would put out their hands (or their heads—but that took a

brave lady on account of the coiffure) outside the
awning and squeal as they were soaked by the warm,
mild, neutral rain of Ourdh. Thunder was another
matter. Alyx remembered hill storms with gravel
hissing down the gullies of streams and paths turned
to cold mud. She met the dowager in charge and that
ponderous lady said:

"Here she is."

It was Edarra, sulky and seventeen, knotting a silk
handkerchief in a wet wad in her hand and wearing a
sparkling blue-and-green bib.

"That's the necklace," said the dowager. "Don't let
it out of your sight."

"I see," said Alyx, passing her hand over her eyes.

When they were left alone, Edarra fastened her
fierce eyes on Alyx and hissed, "Traitor!"

"What for?" said Alyx.

"Traitor! Traitor! Traitor!" shouted the girl. The
nearest guests turned to listen and then turned away,
bored.

"You grow dull," said Alyx, and she leaned lightly
on the roof-rail to watch the company. There was the
sound of angry stirrings and rustlings behind her.
Then the girl said in a low voice (between her teeth),
"Tonight someone is going to steal this necklace."

Alyx said nothing. Ya floated by with her metal
breasts gleaming in the lamplight; behind her, Peng
the jeweler.

"I'll get seven hundred ounces of gold for it!"

"Ah?" said Alyx.

"You've spoiled it," snapped the girl. Together
they watched the guests, red and green, silk on silk
like oil on water, the high-crowned hats and earrings
glistening, the bracelets sparkling like a school of

fish. Up came the dowager accompanied by a land-lord of the richest and largest sort, a gentleman bridegroom who had buried three previous wives and would now have the privilege of burying the Lady Edarra—though to hear him tell it, the first had died of overeating, the second of drinking and the third of a complexion-cleanser she had brewed her-self. Nothing questionable in *that*. He smiled and took Edarra's upper arm between his thumb and finger. He said, "Well, little girl." She stared at him. "Don't be defiant," he said. "You're going to be rich." The dowager bridled. "I mean—even richer," he said with a smile. The mother and the bride-groom talked business for a few minutes, neither watching the girl; then they turned abruptly and disappeared into the mixing, moving company, some of whom were leaning over the rail screaming at those in the garden below, and some of whom were slipping and sitting down involuntarily in thirty-five pounds of cherries that had just been accidentally overturned onto the floor.

"So that's why you want to run away," said Alyx. The Lady Edarra was staring straight ahead of her, big tears rolling silently down her cheeks. "Mind your business," she said.

"Mind yours," said Alyx softly, "and do not insult me, for I get rather hard then." She laughed and fingered the necklace, which was big and gaudy and made of stones the size of a thumb. "What would you do," she said, "if I told you yes?"

"You're impossible!" said Edarra, looking up and sobbing.

"Praised be Yp that I exist then," said Alyx, "for I do ask you if your offer is open. Now that I see your necklace more plainly, I incline towards accepting it—whoever you hired was cheating you, by the way; you can get twice again as much—though that gentleman we saw just now has something to do with my decision." She paused. "Well?"

Edarra said nothing, her mouth open.

"Well, speak!"

"No," said Edarra.

"Mind you," said Alyx wryly, "you still have to find someone to travel with, and I wouldn't trust the man you hired—probably hired—for five minutes in a room with twenty other people. Make your choice. I'll go with you as long and as far as you want, anywhere you want."

"Well," said Edarra, "yes."

"Good," said Alyx. "I'll take two-thirds."

"No!" cried Edarra, scandalized.

"Two-thirds," said Alyx, shaking her head. "It has to be worth my while. Both the gentleman you hired to steal your necklace—and your mother—and your husband-to-be—and heaven alone knows who else—will be after us before the evening is out. Maybe. At any rate, I want to be safe when I come back."

"Will the money—?" said Edarra.

"Money does all things," said Alyx, "and I have long wanted to return to this city, this paradise, this—swamp!—with that which makes power! Come," and she leapt onto the roof-rail and from there into the garden, landing feet first in the loam and ruining a bed of strawberries. Edarra dropped beside her, all of a heap and panting.

"Kill one, kill all, kill devil!" said Alyx gleefully. Edarra grabbed her arm. Taking the lady by the crook of her elbow, Alyx began to run, while behind them the fashionable merriment of Ourdh (the guests were pouring wine down each other's backs) grew fainter and fainter and finally died away.

They sold the necklace at the waterfront shack that smelt of tar and sewage (Edarra grew ill and had to wait outside), and with the money Alyx bought two short swords, a dagger, a blanket, and a round cheese. She walked along the harbor carving pieces out of the cheese with the dagger and eating them off the point. Opposite a fishing boat, a square-sailed, slovenly tramp, she stopped and pointed with cheese and dagger both.

"That's ours," said she. (For the harbor streets were very quiet.)

"Oh, *no!*"

"Yes," said Alyx, "that mess," and from the slimy timbers of the quay she leapt onto the deck. "It's empty," she said.

"No," said Edarra, "I won't go," and from the landward side of the city thunder rumbled and a few drops of rain fell in the darkness, warm, like the wind.

"It's going to rain," said Alyx. "Get aboard."

"No," said the girl. Alyx's face appeared in the bow of the boat, a white spot scarcely distinguishable from the sky; she stood in the bow as the boat rocked to and fro in the wash of the tide. A light across the street, that shone in the window of a waterfront café, went out.

"Oh!" gasped Edarra, terrified, "give me my money!" A leather bag fell in the dust at her feet. "I'm going back," she said, "I'm never going to set foot in that thing. It's disgusting. It's not ladylike."

"No," said Alyx.

"It's *dirty!*" cried Edarra. Without a word, Alyx disappeared into the darkness. Above, where the clouds bred from the marshes roofed the sky, the obscurity deepened and the sound of rain drumming on the roofs of the town advanced steadily, three streets away, then two . . . a sharp gust of wind blew bits of paper and the indefinable trash of the seaside upwards in an unseen spiral. Out over the sea Edarra could hear the universal sound of rain on water, like the shaking of dried peas in a sheet of paper but softer and more blurred, as acres of the surface of the sea dimpled with innumerable little pockmarks. . . .

"I thought you'd come," said Alyx. "Shall we begin?"

Ourdh stretches several miles southward down the coast of the sea, finally dwindling to a string of little towns; at one of these they stopped and provided for themselves, laying in a store of food and a first-aid kit of dragon's teeth and ginger root, for one never knows what may happen in a sea voyage. They also bought resin; Edarra was forced to caulk the ship under fear of being called soft and lazy, and she did it, although she did not speak. She did not speak at all. She boiled the fish over a fire laid in the brass firebox and fanned the smoke and choked, but she never said a word. She did what she was told in silence. Every day bitterer, she kicked the stove and scrubbed the floor, tearing her fingernails, wearing out her skirt; she swore to herself, but without a word, so that when one night she kicked Alyx with her foot, it was an occasion.

"Where are we going?" said Edarra in the dark, with violent impatience. She had been brooding over the question for several weeks and her voice carried

a remarkable quality of concentration; she prodded
Alyx with her big toe and repeated, "I said, where
are we going?"

"Morning," said Alyx. She was asleep, for it was
the middle of the night; they took watches above.
"In the morning," she said. Part of it was sleep and
part was demoralization; although reserved, she was
friendly and Edarra was ruining her nerves.

"Oh!" exclaimed the lady between clenched teeth,
and Alyx shifted in her sleep. "When will we buy
some decent *food?*" demanded the lady vehemently.
"When? When?"

Alyx sat bolt upright. "Go to sleep!" she shouted,
under the hallucinatory impression that it was she
who was awake and working. She dreamed of nothing but work now. In the dark Edarra stamped up
and down. "Oh, wake up!" she cried, "for goodness'
sakes!"

"What do you want?" said Alyx.

"Where are we going?" said Edarra. "Are we going
to some miserable little fishing village? Are we? Well,
are we?"

"Yes," said Alyx.

"Why!" demanded the lady.

"To match your character."

With a scream of rage, the Lady Edarra threw
herself on her preserver and they bumped heads for
a few minutes, but the battle—although violent—was
conducted entirely in the dark and they were tangled
up almost completely in the beds, which were nothing but blankets laid on the bare boards and not the
only reason that the lady's brown eyes were turning
a permanent, baleful black.

"Let me up, you're strangling me!" cried the lady,

and when Alyx managed to light the lamp, bruising her shins against some of the furniture, Edarra was seen to be wrestling with a blanket, which she threw across the cabin. The cabin was five feet across.

"If you do that again, madam," said Alyx, "I'm going to knock your head against the floor!" The lady swept her hair back from her brow with the air of a princess. She was trembling. "Huh!" she said, in the voice of one so angry that she does not dare to say anything. "Really," she said, on the verge of tears.

"Yes, really," said Alyx, "really" (finding some satisfaction in the word), "really go above. We're drifting." The lady sat in her corner, her face white, clenching her hands together as if she held a burning chip from the stove. "No," she said.

"Eh, madam?" said Alyx.

"I won't do anything," said Edarra unsteadily, her eyes glittering. "You can do everything. You want to, anyway."

"Now look here—" said Alyx grimly, advancing on the girl, but whether she thought better of it or whether she heard or smelt something (for after weeks of water, sailors—or so they say—develop a certain intuition for such things), she only threw her blanket over her shoulder and said, "Suit yourself." Then she went on deck. Her face was unnaturally composed.

"Heaven witness my self-control," she said, not raising her voice but in a conversational tone that somewhat belied her facial expression. "Witness it. See it. Reward it. May the messenger of Yp—in whom I do not believe—write in that parchment leaf that holds all the records of the world that I, provoked beyond human endurance, tormented, kicked in the midst of sleep, treated like the off-scourings of a filthy, cheap, sour-beer-producing brewery—"

Then she saw the sea monster.

Opinion concerning sea monsters varies in Ourdh and the surrounding hills, the citizens holding monsters to be the souls of the wicked dead forever ranging the pastureless wastes of ocean to waylay the living and force them into watery graves, and the hill people scouting this blasphemous view and maintaining that sea monsters are legitimate creations of the great god Yp, sent to murder travelers as an illustration of the majesty, the might and the unpredictability of that most inexplicable of deities. But the end result is much the same. Alyx had seen the bulbous face and coarse whiskers of the creature in a drawing hanging in the Silver Eel on the waterfront of Ourdh (the original—stuffed—had been stolen in some prehistoric time, according to the proprietor), and she had shuddered. She had thought, *Perhaps it is just an animal*, but even so it was not pleasant. Now in the moonlight that turned the ocean to a ball of silver waters in the midst of which bobbed the tiny ship, very very far from anyone or anything, she saw the surface part in a rain of sparkling drops and the huge, wicked, twisted face of the creature, so like and unlike a man's, rise like a shadowy demon from the dark, bright water. It held its baby to its breast, a nauseating parody of humankind. Behind her she heard Edarra choke, for that lady had followed her onto the deck. Alyx forced her unwilling feet to the rail and leaned over, stretching out one shaking hand. She said:

"By the tetragrammation of dread,
"By the seven names of God.
"Begone and trouble us no more!"

Which was very brave of her because she did not believe in charms. But it had to be said directly to the monster's face, and say it she did.

The monster barked like a dog.

Edarra screamed. With an arm suddenly nerved to steel, the thief snatched a fishing spear from its place in the stern and braced one knee against the rail; she leaned into the creature's very mouth and threw her harpoon. It entered below the pink harelip and blood gushed as the thing trumpeted and thrashed; black under the moonlight, the blood billowed along the waves, the water closed over the apparition, ripples spread and rocked the boat, and died, and Alyx slid weakly onto the deck.

There was silence for a while. Then she said, "It's only an animal," and she made the mark of Yp on her forehead to atone for having killed something without the spur of overmastering necessity. She had not made the gesture for years. Edarra, who was huddled in a heap against the mast, moved. "It's gone," said Alyx. She got to her feet and took the rudder of the boat, a long shaft that swung at the stern. The girl moved again, shivering.

"It was an animal," said Alyx with finality, "that's all."

The next morning Alyx took out the two short swords and told Edarra she would have to learn to use them.

"No," said Edarra.

"Yes," said Alyx. While the wind held, they fenced up and down the deck, Edarra scrambling resentfully. Alyx pressed her hard and assured her that she would have to do this every day.

"You'll have to cut your hair, too," she added, for no particular reason.

"Never!" gasped the other, dodging.

"Oh, yes, you will!" and she grasped the red braid and yanked; one flash of the blade—

Now it may have been the sea air—or the loss of her red tresses—or the collision with a character so different from those she was accustomed to, but from this morning on it became clear that something was exerting a humanizing influence on the young woman. She was quieter, even (on occasion) dreamy; she turned to her work without complaint, and after a deserved ducking in the sea had caused her hair to break out in short curls, she took to leaning over the side of the boat and watching herself in the water, with meditative pleasure. Her skin, that the pick-lock had first noticed as fine, grew even finer with the passage of the days, and she turned a delicate ivory color, like a half-baked biscuit, that Alyx could not help but notice. But she did not like it. Often in the watches of the night she would say aloud:

"Very well, I am thirty—" (Thus she would soliloquize.) "But what, O Yp, is thirty? Thrice ten. Twice fifteen. Women marry at forty. In ten years I will be forty—"

And so on. From these apostrophizations she returned uncomfortable, ugly, old and with a bad conscience. She had a conscience, though it was not active in the usual directions. One morning, after these nightly wrestlings, the girl was leaning over the rail of the boat, her hair dangling about her face, watching the fish in the water and her own reflection. Occasionally she yawned, opening her pink mouth and shutting her eyes; all this Alyx watched

surreptitiously. She felt uncomfortable. All morning
the heat had been intense and mirages of ships and
gulls and unidentified objects had danced on the
horizon, breaking up eventually into clumps of sea-
weed or floating bits of wood.

"Shall I catch a fish?" said Edarra, who occasionally spoke now.

"Yes—no—" said Alyx, who held the rudder.

"Well, shall I or shan't I?" said Edarra tolerantly.

"Yes," said Alyx, "if you—" and swung the rudder
hard. All morning she had been watching black,
wriggling shapes that turned out to be nothing; now
she thought she saw something across the glittering
water. *One thing we shall both get out of this,* she
thought, *is a permanent squint.* The shape moved
closer, resolving itself into several verticals and a
horizontal; it danced and streaked maddeningly. Alyx
shaded her eyes.

"Edarra," she said quietly, "get the swords. Hand
me one and the dagger."

"What?" said Edarra, dropping a fishing line she
had begun to pick up.

"Three men in a sloop," said Alyx. "Back up against
the mast and put the blade behind you."

"But they might not—" said Edarra with unex-
pected spirit.

"And they might," said Alyx grimly, "they just
might."

Now in Ourdh there is a common saying that if
you have not strength, there are three things which
will serve as well: deceit, surprise and speed. These
are women's natural weapons. Therefore when the
three rascals—and rascals they were or appearances
lied—reached the boat, the square sail was furled

and the two women, like castaways, were sitting idly against the mast while the boat bobbed in the oily swell. This was to render the rudder useless and keep the craft from slewing round at a sudden change in the wind. Alyx saw with joy that two of the three were fat and all were dirty; *too vain*, she thought, *to keep in trim or take precautions*. She gathered in her right hand the strands of the fishing net stretched inconspicuously over the deck.

"Who does your laundry?" she said, getting up slowly. She hated personal uncleanliness. Edarra rose to one side of her.

"You will," said the midmost. They smiled broadly. When the first set foot in the net, Alyx jerked it up hard, bringing him to the deck in a tangle of fishing lines; at the same instant with her left hand—and the left hand of this daughter of Loh carried all its six fingers—she threw the dagger (which had previously been used for nothing bloodier than cleaning fish) and caught the second interloper squarely in the stomach. He sat down, hard, and was no further trouble. The first, who had gotten to his feet, closed with her in a ringing of steel that was loud on that tiny deck; for ninety seconds by the clock he forced her back towards the opposite rail; then in a burst of speed she took him under his guard at a pitch of the ship and slashed his sword wrist, disarming him. But her thrust carried her too far and she fell; grasping his wounded wrist with his other hand, he launched himself at her, and Alyx—planting both knees against his chest—helped him into the sea. He took a piece of the rail with him. By the sound of it, he could not swim. She stood over the rail, gripping her blade until he vanished for the last time. It was over that quickly. Then she perceived Edarra standing over the third man, sword in hand, an incredulous, pleased expression on her face. Blood holds no terrors for a child of Ourdh, unfortunately.

"Look what I did!" said the little lady.

"Must you look so pleased?" said Alyx, sharply. The morning's washing hung on the opposite rail to dry. So quiet had the sea and sky been that it had not budged an inch. The gentleman with the dagger sat against it, staring.

"If you're so hardy," said Alyx, "take that out."

"Do I have to?" said the little girl, uneasily.

"I suppose not," said Alyx, and she put one foot against the dead man's chest, her grip on the knife and her eyes averted; the two parted company and he went over the side in one motion. Edarra turned a little red; she hung her head and remarked, "You're splendid."

"You're a savage," said Alyx.

"But why!" cried Edarra indignantly. "All I said was—"

"Wash up," said Alyx, "and get rid of the other one; he's yours."

"I said you were splendid and I don't see why that's—"

"And set the sail," added the six-fingered picklock. She lay down, closed her eyes, and fell asleep.

Now it was Alyx who did not speak and Edarra who did; she said, "Good morning," she said, "Why do fish have scales?" she said, "I *like* shrimp; they look funny," and she said (once), "I like you," matter-of-factly, as if she had been thinking about the question and had just then settled it. One afternoon they were eating fish in the cabin—"fish" is a cold, unpleasant, slimy word, but sea trout baked in clay with onion, shrimp and white wine is something else again—when Edarra said:

"What was it like when you lived in the hills?" She said it right out of the blue, like that.

"What?" said Alyx.

"Were you happy?" said Edarra.

"I prefer not to discuss it."

"All right, *madam,*" and the girl swept up to the deck with her plate and glass. It isn't easy climbing a rope ladder with a glass (balanced on a plate) in one hand, but she did it without thinking, which shows how accustomed she had become to the ship and how far this tale has advanced. Alyx sat moodily poking at her dinner (which had turned back to slime as far as she was concerned) when she smelled something char and gave a cursory poke into the firebox next to her with a metal broom they kept for the purpose. This ancient firebox served them as a stove. Now it may have been age, or the carelessness of the previous owner, or just the venomous hatred of inanimate objects for mankind (the religion of Yp stresses this point with great fervor), but the truth of the matter was that the firebox had begun to come apart at the back, and a few flaming chips had fallen on the wooden floor of the cabin. Moreover, while Alyx poked among the coals in the box, its door hanging open, the left front leg of the creature crumpled and the box itself sagged forward, the coals inside sliding dangerously. Alyx exclaimed and hastily shut the door. She turned and looked for the lock with which to fasten the door more securely, and thus it was that until she turned back again and stood up, she did not

see what mischief was going on at the other side.
The floor, to the glory of Yp, was smoking in half a
dozen places. Stepping carefully, Alyx picked up the
pail of seawater kept always ready in a corner of the
cabin and emptied it onto the smoldering floor, but
at that instant—so diabolical are the souls of machines—the second front leg of the box followed the
first and the brass door burst open, spewing burning
coals the length of the cabin. Ordinarily not even a
heavy sea could scatter the fire, for the door was too
far above the bed on which the wood rested and the
monster's legs were bolted to the floor. But now the
boards caught not in half a dozen but in half a hundred places. Alyx shouted for water and grabbed a
towel, while a pile of folded blankets against the wall
curled and turned black; the cabin was filled with the
odor of burning hair. Alyx beat at the blankets and the
fire found a cupboard next to them, crept under the
door and caught in a sack of sprouting potatoes,
which refused to burn. Flour was packed next to
them. "Edarra!" yelled Alyx. She overturned a rack
of wine, smashing it against the floor regardless of
the broken glass; it checked the flames while she
beat at the cupboard; then the fire turned and leapt
at the opposite wall. It flamed up for an instant in
a straw mat hung against the wall, creeping upward,
eating down through the planks of the floor, searching out cracks under the cupboard door, roundabout.
The potatoes, dried by the heat, began to wither
sullenly; their canvas sacking crumbled and turned
black. Edarra had just come tumbling into the cabin,
horrified, and Alyx was choking on the smoke of
canvas sacking and green, smoking sprouts, when
the fire reached the stored flour. There was a con-

cussive bellow and a blast of air that sent Alyx staggering into the stove; white flame billowed from the corner that had held the cupboard. Alyx was burned on one side from knee to ankle and knocked against the wall; she fell, full-length.

When she came to herself, she was half lying in dirty seawater and the fire was gone. Across the cabin Edarra was struggling with a water demon, stuffing half-burnt blankets and clothes and sacks of potatoes against an incorrigible waterspout that knocked her about and burst into the cabin in erratic gouts, making tides in the water that shifted sluggishly from one side of the floor to the other as the ship rolled.

"Help me!" she cried. Alyx got up. Shakily she staggered across the cabin and together they leaned their weight on the pile of stuffs jammed into the hole.

"It's not big," gasped the girl, "I made it with a sword. Just under the waterline."

"Stay here," said Alyx. Leaning against the wall, she made her way to the cold firebox. Two bolts held it to the floor. "No good there," she said. With the same exasperating slowness, she hauled herself up the ladder and stood uncertainly on the deck. She lowered the sail, cutting her fingers, and dragged it to the stern, pushing all loose gear on top of it. Dropping down through the hatch again, she shifted coils of rope and stores of food to the stern; patiently fumbling, she unbolted the firebox from the floor. The waterspout had lessened. Finally, when Alyx had pushed the metal box end over end against the opposite wall of the cabin, the water demon seemed to lose his exuberance. He drooped and almost died.

With a letting-out of breath, Edarra released the mass pressed against the hole: blankets, sacks, shoes, potatoes, all slid to the stern. The water stopped. Alyx, who seemed for the first time to feel a brand against the calf of her left leg and needles in her hand where she had burnt herself unbolting the stove, sat leaning against the wall, too weary to move. She saw the cabin through a milky mist. Ballooning and shrinking above her hung Edarra's face, dirty with charred wood and sea slime; the girl said:

"What shall I do now?"

"Nail boards," said Alyx slowly.

"Yes, then?" urged the girl.

"Pitch," said Alyx. "Bail it out."

"You mean the boat will pitch?" said Edarra, frowning in puzzlement. In answer Alyx shook her head and raised one hand out of the water to point to the storage place on deck, but the air drove the needles deeper into her fingers and distracted her mind. She said, "Fix," and leaned back against the wall, but as she was sitting against it already, her movement only caused her to turn, with a slow, natural easiness, and slide unconscious into the dirty water that ran tidally this way and that within the blackened, sour-reeking, littered cabin.

Alyx groaned. Behind her eyelids she was reliving one of the small contretemps of her life: lying indoors ill and badly hurt, with the sun rising out of doors, thinking that she was dying and hearing the birds sing. She opened her eyes. The sun shone, the waves sang, there was the little girl watching her. The sun was level with the sea and the first airs of evening stole across the deck.

Alyx tried to say, "What happened?" and managed only to croak. Edarra sat down, all of a flop.

"You're *talking!*" she exclaimed with vast relief. Alyx stirred, looking about her, tried to rise and thought better of it. She discovered lumps of bandage on her hand and her leg; she picked at them feebly with her free hand, for they struck her somehow as irrelevant. Then she stopped.

"I'm alive," she said hoarsely, "for Yp likes to think he looks after me, the bastard."

"I don't know about *that,*" said Edarra, laughing. "My!" She knelt on the deck, with her hair streaming behind her like a ship's figurehead come to life; she said, "I fixed everything. I pulled you up here. I fixed the boat, though I had to hang by my knees. I pitched it." She exhibited her arms, daubed to the elbow. "Look," she said. Then she added, with a catch in her voice, "I thought you might die."

"I might yet," said Alyx. The sun dipped into the sea. "Long-leggedy thing," she said in a hoarse whisper, "get me some food."

"Here." Edarra rummaged for a moment and held out a piece of bread, part of the ragbag loosened on deck during the late catastrophe. The pick-lock ate, lying back. The sun danced up and down in her eyes, above the deck, below the deck, above the deck. . . .

"Creature," said Alyx, "I had a daughter."

"Where is she?" said Edarra.

Silence.

"Praying." said Alyx at last. "Damning me."

"I'm sorry," said Edarra.

"But you," said Alyx, "are—" and she stopped blankly. She said "You—"

"Me what?" said Edarra.

"Are here," said Alyx, and with a bone-cracking yawn, letting the crust fall from her fingers, she fell asleep.

At length the time came (all things must end and Alyx's burns had already healed to barely visible scars—one looking closely at her could see many such faint marks on her back, her arms, her sides, the bodily record of the last rather difficult seven years) when Alyx, emptying overboard the breakfast scraps, gave a yell so loud and triumphant that she inadvertently lost hold of the garbage bucket and it fell into the sea.

"What is it?" said Edarra, startled. Her friend was gripping the rail with both hands and staring over the sea with a look that Edarra did not understand in the least, for Alyx had been closemouthed on some subjects in the girl's education.

"I am thinking," said Alyx.

"Oh!" shrieked Edarra, "Land! Land!" And she capered about the deck, whirling and clapping her hands. "I can change my dress!" she cried. "Just think! We can eat fresh food! Just think!"

"I was not," said Alyx, "thinking about that." Edarra came up to her and looked curiously into her eyes, which had gone as deep and as gray as the sea on a gray day; she said, "Well, what are you thinking about?"

"Something not fit for your ears," said Alyx. The little girl's eyes narrowed. "Oh," she said pointedly. Alyx ducked past her for the hatch, but Edarra sprinted ahead and straddled it, arms wide.

"I want to hear it," she said.

"That's a foolish attitude," said Alyx. "You'll lose your balance."

"Tell me."

"Come, get away."

The girl sprang forward like a red-headed fury, seizing her friend by the hair with both hands. "If it's not fit for my ears, I want to hear it!" she cried.

Alyx dodged around her and dropped below, to retrieve from storage her severe, decent, formal black clothes, fit for a business call. When she reappeared, tossing the clothes on deck, Edarra had a short sword in her right hand and was guarding the hatch very exuberantly.

"Don't be foolish," said Alyx crossly.

"I'll kill you if you don't tell me," remarked Edarra.

"Little one," said Alyx, "the stain of ideals remains on the imagination long after the ideals themselves vanish. Therefore I will tell you nothing."

"Raahh!" said Edarra, in her throat.

"It wouldn't be proper," added Alyx primly, "if you don't know about it, so much the better," and she turned away to sort her clothes. Edarra pinked her in a formal, black shoe.

"Stop it!" snapped Alyx.

"Never!" cried the girl wildly, her eyes flashing. She lunged and feinted and her friend, standing still, wove (with the injured boot) a net of defense as invisible as the cloak that enveloped Aule the Messenger. Edarra, her chest heaving, managed to say, "I'm tired."

"Then stop," said Alyx.

Edarra stopped.

"Do I remind you of your little baby girl?" she said.

Alyx said nothing.

"I'm not a little baby girl," said Edarra. "I'm eighteen now and I know more than you think. Did I ever tell you about my first suitor and the cook and the cat?"

"No," said Alyx, busy sorting.

"The cook let the cat in," said Edarra, "though she shouldn't have, and so when I was sitting on my suitor's lap and I had one arm around his neck and the other arm on the arm of the chair, he said, 'Darling, where is your *other* little hand?' "

"Mm hm," said Alyx.

"It was the cat, walking across his lap! But he could only feel one of my hands so he thought—" but here, seeing that Alyx was not listening, Edarra shouted a word used remarkably seldom in Ourdh and for very good reason. Alyx looked up in surprise. Ten feet away (as far away as she could get), Edarra was lying on the planks, sobbing. Alyx went over to her and knelt down, leaning back on her heels. Above, the first sea birds of the trip—sea birds always live near land—circled and cried in a hard, hungry mew like a herd of aerial cats.

"Someone's coming," said Alyx.

"Don't care." This was Edarra on the deck, muffled. Alyx reached out and began to stroke the girl's disordered hair, braiding it with her fingers, twisting it round her wrist and slipping her hand through it and out again.

"Someone's in a fishing smack coming this way," said Alyx. Edarra burst into tears.

"Now, now, now!" said Alyx, "why that? Come!" and she tried to lift the girl up, but Edarra held stubbornly to the deck.

"What's the matter?" said Alyx.

"You!" cried Edarra, bouncing bolt upright. "You; you treat me like a baby."

"You are a baby," said Alyx.

"How'm I ever going to stop if you treat me like one?" shouted the girl. Alyx got up and padded over to her new clothes, her face thoughtful. She slipped into a sleeveless black shift and belted it; it came to just above the knee. Then she took a comb from the pocket and began to comb out her straight, silky black hair. "I was remembering," she said.

"What?" said Edarra.

"Things."

"Don't make fun of me." Alyx stood for a moment, one blue-green earring on her ear and the other in her fingers. She smiled at the innocence of this red-headed daughter of the wickedest city on earth; she saw her own youth over again (though she had been unnaturally knowing almost from birth), and so she smiled, with rare sweetness.

"I'll tell you," she whispered conspiratorially, dropping to her knees beside Edarra, "I was remembering a man."

"Oh!" said Edarra.

"I remembered," said Alyx, "one week in spring when the night sky above Ourdh was hung as brilliantly with stars as the jewelers' trays on the Street of a Thousand Follies. Ah! what a man. A big Northman with hair like yours and a gold-red beard—God, what a beard!—Fafnir—no, Fafh—well, something ridiculous. But he was far from ridiculous. He was amazing."

Edarra said nothing, rapt.

"He was strong," said Alyx, laughing, "and hairy,

beautifully hairy. And willful! I said to him, 'Man, if you must follow your eyes into every whorehouse—' And we fought! At a place called the Silver Fish. Overturned tables. What a fuss! And a week later," (she shrugged ruefully) "gone. There it is. And I can't even remember his name."

"Is that sad?" said Edarra.

"I don't think so," said Alyx; "After all, I remember his beard," and she smiled wickedly. "There's a man in that boat," she said, "and that boat comes from a fishing village of maybe ten, maybe twelve families. That symbol painted on the side of the boat—I can make it out; perhaps you can't; it's a red cross on a blue circle—indicates a single man. Now the chances of there being two single men between the ages of eighteen and forty in a village of twelve families is not—"

"A man!" exploded Edarra, "that's why you're primping like a hen. Can I wear your clothes? Mine are full of salt," and she buried herself in the piled wearables on deck, humming, dragged out a brush and began to brush her hair. She lay flat on her stomach, catching her underlip between her teeth, saying over and over "Oh—oh—oh—"

"Look here," said Alyx, back at the rudder, "before you get too free, let me tell you: there are rules."

"I'm going to wear this white thing," said Edarra busily.

"Married men are not considered proper. It's too acquisitive. If I know you, you'll want to get married inside three weeks, but you must remember—"

"My shoes don't fit!" wailed Edarra, hopping about with one shoe on and one off.

"Horrid," said Alyx briefly.

"My feet have gotten bigger," said Edarra, plumping down beside her. "Do you think they spread when I go barefoot? Do you think that's ladylike? Do you think—"

"For the sake of peace, be quiet!" said Alyx. Her whole attention was taken up by what was far off on the sea; she nudged Edarra and the girl sat still, only emitting little explosions of breath as she tried to fit her feet into her old shoes. At last she gave up and sat—quite motionless—with her hands in her lap.

"There's only one man there," said Alyx.

"He's probably too young for you." (Alyx's mouth twitched.)

"Well?" added Edarra plaintively.

"Well what?"

"Well," said Edarra, embarrassed, "I hope you don't mind."

"Oh! I don't mind," said Alyx.

"I suppose," said Edarra helpfully, "that it'll be dull for you, won't it?"

"I can find some old grandfather," said Alyx.

Edarra blushed.

"And I can always cook," added the pick-lock.

"You must be a *good* cook."

"I am."

"That's nice. You remind me of a cat we once had, a very fierce, black, female cat who was a *very* good mother," (she choked and continued hurriedly) "she was a ripping fighter, too, and we just couldn't keep her in the house whenever she—uh—"

"Yes?" said Alyx.

"Wanted to get out," said Edarra feebly. She giggled. "And she always came back pr—I mean—"

"Yes?"

"She was a popular cat."

"Ah," said Alyx, "but old, no doubt."

"Yes," said Edarra unhappily. "Look here," she
added quickly, "I hope you understand that I like
you and I esteem you and it's not that I want to cut
you out, but I *am* younger and you can't expect—"
Alyx raised one hand. She was laughing. Her hair
blew about her face like a skein of black silk. Her
gray eyes glowed.

"Great are the ways of Yp," she said, "and some
men prefer the ways of experience. Very odd of
them, no doubt, but lucky for some of us. I have
been told—but never mind. Infatuated men are bad
judges. Besides, maid, if you look out across the
water you will see a ship much closer than it was
before, and in that ship a young man. Such is life.
But if you look more carefully and shade your red,
red brows, you will perceive—" and here she poked
Edarra with her toe—"that surprise and mercy share
the world between them. Yp is generous." She
tweaked Edarra by the nose.

"Praise God, maid, there be two of them!"

So they waved, Edarra scarcely restraining herself
from jumping into the sea and swimming to the
other craft, Alyx with full sweeps of the arm, standing both at the stern of their stolen fishing boat on
that late summer's morning while the fishermen in
the other boat wondered—and disbelieved—and then
believed—while behind all rose the green land in
the distance and the sky was blue as blue. Perhaps it
was the thought of her fifteen hundred ounces of

gold stowed belowdecks, or perhaps it was only her own queer nature but in the sunlight Alyx's eyes had a strange look, like those of Loh, the first woman, who had kept her own counsel at the very moment of creation, only looking about her with an immediate, intense, serpentine curiosity, already planning secret plans and guessing at who knows what unguessable mysteries. . . .

("You old villain!" whispered Edarra, "we made it!")

But that's another story.

✳ ✳ ✳

I THOUGHT SHE WAS
AFEARD TILL SHE
STROKED MY BEARD

Many years ago, long before the world got into the
state it is in today, young women were supposed to
obey their husbands; but nobody knows if they did
or not. In those days they wore their hair piled foot
upon foot on top of their heads. Along with such
weights they would also carry water in two buckets
at the ends of a long pole; this often makes you slip.
One did; but she kept her mouth shut. She put the
buckets down on the ground and with two sideward
kicks—like two dance steps, flirt with the left foot,
flirt with the right—she emptied the both of them.
She watched the water settle into the ground. Then
she swung the pole upon her shoulder and carried
them home. She was only just seventeen. Her husband and made her do it. She swung the farm door
open with her shoulder and said:

SHE: Here is your damned water.

HE: Where?

SHE: It is beneath my social class to do it and you know it.

HE: You have no social class; only I do, because I am a man.

SHE: *I* wouldn't do it if you were a—

(Here follows something very unpleasant.)

HE: Woman, go back with those pails. Someone is coming tonight.

SHE: Who?

HE: That's not your business.

SHE: Smugglers.

HE: Go!

SHE: Go to hell.

Perhaps he was somewhat afraid of his tough little wife. She watched him from the stairs or the doorway, always with unvarying hatred; that is what comes of marrying a wild hill girl without a proper education. Beatings made her sullen. She went to the water and back, dissecting him every step of the way, separating blond hair from blond hair and cracking and sorting his long limbs. She loved that. She filled the farm water barrel, rooted the maidservant out of the hay and slapped her, and went indoors with her head full of pirates. She spun, she sewed, she shelled, ground, washed, dusted, swept, built fires all that day and once, so full of her thoughts was she that she savagely wrung and broke the neck of an already dead chicken.

Near certain towns, if you walk down to the beach at night, you may see a very queer sight: lights springing up like drifting insects over the water and others answering from the land, and then something bobbing over the black waves to a blacker huddle drawn up at the very margin of the sand. They are at their revenues. The young wife watched her husband sweat in the kitchen. It made her gay to see him bargain so desperately and lose. The maid complained that one of the men had tried to do something indecent to her. Her mistress watched silently from the shadows near the big hearth and more and more of what she saw was to her liking. When the last man was gone she sent the maid to bed, and while collecting and cleaning the glasses and the plates like a proper wife, she said:

"They rooked you, didn't they!"

"Hold your tongue," said her husband over his shoulder. He was laboriously figuring his book of accounts with strings of circles and crosses and licking his finger to turn the page.

"The big one," she said, "what's his name?"

"What's it to you?" he said sharply. She stood drying her hands in a towel and looking at him. She took off her apron, her jacket and her rings; then she pulled the pins out of her black hair. It fell below her waist and she stood for the last time in this history within a straight black cloud.

She dropped a cup from her fingers, smiling at him as it smashed. They say actions speak louder. He jumped to his feet; he cried, "What are you doing!" again and again in the silent kitchen; he shook her until her teeth rattled.

"Leaving you," she said.

He struck her. She got up, holding her jaw. She said, "You don't see anything. You don't know anything."

"Get upstairs," he said.

"You're an animal," she cried, "you're a fool," and

she twisted about as he grasped her wrist, trying to free herself. They insist, these women, on crying, on making demands, and on disagreeing about everything. They fight from one side of the room to the other. She bit his hand and he howled and brought it down on the side of her head. He called her a little whore. He stood blocking the doorway and glowered, nursing his hand. Her head was spinning. She leaned against the wall and held her head in both hands. Then she said:

"So you won't let me go."

He said nothing.

"You can't keep me," she said, and then she laughed; "no, no, you can't," she added, shaking her head, "you just can't." She looked before her and smiled absently, turning this fact over and over. Her husband was rubbing his knuckles.

"What do you think you're up to," he muttered.

"If you lock me up, I can't work," said his wife and then, with the knife she had used for the past half year to pare vegetables, this woman began to saw at her length of hair. She took the whole sheaf in one hand and hacked at it. Her husband started forward. She stood arrested with her hands involved in her hair, regarding him seriously, while without taking his eyes off her, running the tip of his tongue across his teeth, he groped behind the door—he knew there is one thing you can always do. His wife changed color. Her hands dropped with a tumbled rush of hair, she moved slowly to one side, and when he took out from behind the door the length of braided hide he used to herd cattle, when he swung it high in the air and down in a snapping arc to where she—not where she was; where she had been—this extraordinary young woman had leapt half the distance between them and wrested the stock of the whip from him a foot from his hand. He was off balance and fell; with a vicious grimace she brought the stock down short and hard on the top of his head. She had all her wits about her as she stood over him.

But she didn't believe it. She leaned over him, her cut black hair swinging over her face; she called him a liar; she told him he wasn't bleeding. Slowly she straightened up, with a swagger, with a certain awe. *Good lord!* she thought, looking at her hands. She slapped him, called his name impatiently, but when the fallen man moved a little—or she fancied he did—a thrill ran up her spine to the top of her head, a kind of soundless chill, and snatching the vegetable knife from the floor where she had dropped it, she sprang like an arrow from the bow into the night that waited, all around the house, to devour.

Trees do not pull up their roots and walk abroad, nor is the night ringed with eyes. Stones can't speak. Novelty tosses the world upside down, however. She was terrified, exalted, and helpless with laughter. The tree on either side of the path saw her appear for an instant out of the darkness, wild with hurry, straining like a statue. Then she zigzagged between the tree trunks and flashed over the lip of the cliff into the sea.

In all the wide headland there was no light. The ship still rode at anchor, but far out, and clinging to the line where the water met the air like a limpet or a moray eel under a rock, she saw a trail of yellow points appear on the face of the sea: one, two, three, four. They had finished their business. Hasty and out of breath, she dove under the shadow of that black hull, and treading the shifting seas that fetched her up now and again against the ship's side that was too flat and hard to grasp, she listened to the noises overhead: creaking, groans, voices, the sound of feet. Everything was hollow and loud, mixed with the gurgle of the ripples. She thought, *I am going to give them a surprise*. She felt something form within her, something queer, dark, and hard, like the strangeness of strange customs, or the blackened face of the goddess Chance, whose image set up at crossroads looks three ways at once to signify the crossing of influences. Silently this young woman took off her leather belt and wrapped the buckleless end around her right hand. With her left she struck out for the ship's rope ladder, sinking into the water under a mass of bubbles and crosscurrents eddying like hairs drawn across the surface. She rose some ten feet farther on. Dripping seawater like one come back from the dead, with eighteen inches of leather crowned with a heavy brass buckle in her right hand, her left gripping the rope and her knife between her teeth (where else?) she began to climb.

The watch—who saw her first—saw somebody entirely undistinguished. She was wringing the water out of her skirt. She sprang erect as she caught sight of him, burying both hands in the heavy folds of her dress.

"We—ell!" said he.

She said nothing, only crouched down a little by the rail. The leather belt, hidden in her right—her stronger—hand began to stir. He came closer—he stared—he leaned forward—he tapped his teeth with his forefinger. "Eh, a pussycat!" he said. She didn't move. He stepped back a pace, clapped his hands and shouted; and all at once she was surrounded by men who had come crack! out of nothing, sprung in from the right, from the left, shot up from the deck as if on springs, even tumbling down out of the air. She did not know if she liked it.

"Look!" said the watch, grinning as if he had made her up.

Perhaps they had never seen a woman before, or perhaps they had never seen one bare-armed, or with her hair cut off, or sopping wet. They stared as if they hadn't. One whistled, indrawn between his teeth, long and low. "What does she want?" said someone. The watch took hold of her arm and the sailor who had whistled raised both hands over his head and clasped them, at which the crowd laughed.

"She thinks we're hot!"

"She wants some, don't you, honey?"

"Ooh, kiss me, kiss me, dearie!"

"I want the captain!" she managed to get out. All around crowded men's faces: some old, some young, all very peculiar to her eyes with their unaccustomed whiskers, their chins, their noses, their loose collars. It occurred to her that she did not like them a bit. She did not exactly think they were behaving badly, as she was not sure how they ought to behave, but they reminded her uncannily of her husband, of whom she was no longer at all afraid. So when the nearest winked and reached out two hands even huger than the shadow of hands cast on the deck boards, she kicked him excruciatingly in the left knee (he fell down), the watch got the belt buckle round in a circle from underneath (up, always up, especially if you're short), which gave him a cut across the cheek and a black eye; this leaves her left hand still armed and her teeth, which she used. It's good to be able to do several things at once. Forward, halfway from horizon to zenith, still and clear above the black mass of the rigging and the highest mast, burned the constellation of the Hunter, and under that—by way of descent down a monumental fellow who had just that moment sprung on board—frothed and foamed a truly fabulous black beard. She had just unkindly set someone howling by trampling on a tender part (they were in good spirits, most of them, and fighting one another in a heap; she never did admit later to all the things she did in that melee) when the beard bent down over her, curled and glossy as a piece of the sea. Children never could resist that beard. Big one looked at little one. Little one looked at big one. Stars shone over his head. He recognized her at once, of course, and her look, and the pummeling she had left behind her, and the cracked knee, and all the rest of it. "So," he said, "you're a fighter, are you!" He took her hands in his and crushed them, good and hard; she smiled brilliantly, involuntarily.

When she fenced with him (she insisted on fencing with him) she worked with a hard, dry persistence that surprised him. "Well, I have got your—and you have got my teaching," he said philosophically at first, "whatever you may want with *that*," but on the second day out she slipped on soapsuds on the tilting deck ("Give it up, girl, give it up!"), grabbed the fellow who was scrubbing away by the ankles, and brought him down—screaming—on top of the captain. Blackbeard was not surprised that she had tried to do this, but he was very surprised that she had actually brought it off. "Get up," he told her (she was sitting where she fell and grinning). She pulled up her stockings. He chose for her a heavier and longer blade, almost as tall as she ("Huh!" she said, "it's about time"), and held out the blade and the scabbard, one in each hand, both at the same time. She took them, one in each hand, both at the same time.

"By God, you're ambidextrous!" he exclaimed.

"Come on!" she said.

That was a blade that was a blade! She spent the night more or less tangled up in it, as she never yet had with him. Things were still unsettled between them. Thus she slept alone in his bed, in his cabin; thus she woke alone, figuring she still had the best of it. Thus she spurned a heap of his possessions with her foot (the fact that she did not clean the place up in womanly fashion put him to great distress), writhed, stretched, turned over and jumped as a crash came from outside. There was a shuttered window above the bed that gave on the deck. Someone—here she slipped on her shift and swung open the shutter— was bubbling, shouting, singing, sending mountains of water lolloping across the boards. Someone (here she leaned out and twisted her head about to see) naked to the waist in a barrel was taking a bath. Like Poseidon. He turned, presenting her with the black patches under his armpits streaming water, with his hair and beard running like black ink.

"Halloooo!" he roared. She grunted and drew back, closing the shutter. She had made no motion to get dressed when he came in, but lay with her arms under her head. He stood in the doorway, tucking his shirt into his trousers; then this cunning man said, "I came to get something" (looking at her sidewise), and diffidently carried his wet, tightly curled beard past her into a corner of the cabin. He knelt down and burrowed diligently.

"Get what?" said she. He didn't answer. He was rummaging in a chest he had dragged from the wall; now he took out of it—with great tenderness and care—a woman's nightdress, worked all in white lace, which he held up to her, saying:

"Do you want this?"

"No," she said, and meant it.

"But it's expensive," he said earnestly, "it is, look," and coming over to sit on the edge of the bed, he showed the dress to her, for the truth was it was so expensive that he hadn't meant to give it to her at all, and only offered it out of—well, out of—

"I don't want it," she said, a little sharply.

"Do you like jewelry?" he suggested hopefully. He had not got thoroughly dried and water was dripping unobtrusively from the ends of his hair onto the bed; he sat patiently holding the nightgown out by the sleeves to show it off. He said ingenuously, "Why don't you try it on?"

Silence.

"It would look good on you," he said. She said nothing. He laid down the nightgown and looked at her, bemused and wondering; then he reached out and tenderly touched her hair and where it hung down to the point of her small, grim jaw.

"My, aren't you little," he said.

She laughed. Perhaps it was being called little, or perhaps it was being touched so very lightly, but this farm girl threw back her head and laughed until she cried, as the saying is, and then:

"Tcha! It's a bargain, isn't it!" said this cynical girl. He lowered himself onto the floor on his heels; then tenderly folded the nightgown into a lacy bundle, which he smoothed, troubled.

"No, give it to me," she demanded sharply. He looked up, surprised.

"Give it!" she repeated, and scrambling across the bed she snatched it out of his hands, stripped off her shift, and slid the gown over her bare skin. She was compact but not stocky and the dress became her, she walked about the cabin, admiring her sleeves, carrying the train over one arm while he sat back on his heels and blinked at her.

"Well," she said philosophically, "come on." He was not at all pleased. He rose (her eyes followed him), towering over her, his arms folded. He looked at the nightgown, at the train she held, at her arched neck (she had to look up to meet his gaze), at her free arm curved to her throat in a gesture of totally unconscious femininity. He had been thinking, a process that with him was slow but often profound; now he said solemnly:

"Woman, what man have you ever been with before?"

"Oh!" said she startled, "my husband," and backed off a little.

"And where is he?"

"Dead." She could not help a grin.

"How?" She held up a fist. Blackbeard sighed heavily.

Throwing the loose bedclothes onto the bed, he strode to his precious chest (she padded inquisitively behind him), dropped heavily to his knees, and came up with a heap of merchandise: bottles, rings, jingles, coins, scarves, handkerchiefs, boots, toys, half of which he put back. Then, catching her by one

arm, he threw her over his shoulder in a somewhat
casual or moody fashion (the breath was knocked out
of her) and carried her to the center of the cabin,
where he dropped her—half next to and half over a
small table, the only other part of the cabin's furnish-
ings besides the bed. She was trembling all over.
With the same kind of solemn preoccupation he
dumped his merchandise on the table, sorted out a
bottle and two glasses, a bracelet, which he put on
her arm, earrings similarly, and a few other things
that he studied and then placed on the floor. She was
amazed to see that there were tears in his eyes.

"Now, why don't you fight me!" he said emotionally.

She looked at the table, then at her hands.

"Ah!" he said, sighing again, pouring out a glassful
and gulping it, drumming the glass on the table. He
shook his head. He held out his arms and she circled
the table carefully, taking his hands, embarrassed to
look him in the face. "Come," he said, "up here,"
patting his knees, so she climbed awkwardly onto his
lap, still considerably wary. He poured out another
glass and put it in her hand. He sighed, and put
nothing into words; only she felt on her back what
felt like a hand and arched a little—like a cat—with
pleasure; then she stirred on his knees to settle
herself and immediately froze. He did nothing. He
was looking into the distance, into nothing. He might
have been remembering his past. She put one arm
around his neck to steady herself, but her arm felt
his neck most exquisitely and she did not like that,
so she gave it up and put one hand on his shoulder.
Then she could not help but feel his shoulder. It was
quite provoking. He mused into the distance. Sitting
on his lap, she could feel his breath stirring about

her bare face, about her neck—she turned to look at him and shut her eyes; she thought, *What am I doing?* and the blood came to her face harder and harder until her cheeks blazed. She felt him sigh, felt that sigh travel from her side to her stomach to the back of her head, and with a soft, hopeless, exasperated cry ("I don't expect to enjoy this!") she turned and sank, both hands firstmost, into Blackbeard's oceanic beard.

And he, the villain, was even willing to cooperate.

Time passes, even (as they say) on the sea. What with moping about while he visited farmhouses and villages, watching the stars wheel and change overhead as they crept down the coast, with time making and unmaking the days, bringing dinnertime (as it does) and time to get up and what-not—Well, there you are. She spent her time learning to play cards. But gambling and prophecy are very closely allied—in fact they are one thing—and when he saw his woman squatting on deck on the balls of her feet, a sliver of wood in her teeth, dealing out the cards to tell fortunes (cards and money appeared in the East at exactly the same time in the old days) he thought—or thought he saw—or recollected—that goddess who was driven out by the other gods when the world was made and who hangs about still on the fringes of things (at crossroads, at the entrance to towns) to throw a little shady trouble into life and set up a few crosscurrents and undercurrents of her own in what ought to be a regular and predictable business. She herself did not believe in gods and goddesses. She told the fortunes of the crew quite obligingly, as he had taught her, but was much more interested in learning the probabilities of the appearance of any

particular card in one of the five suits*—she had
begun to evolve what she thought was a rather
elegant little theory—when late one day he told her,
"Look, I am going into a town tonight, but you can't
come." They were lying anchored on the coast, facing west, just too far away to see the lights at night.
She said, "Wha'?"

"I am going to town tonight," he said (he was a
very patient man) "and you can't come."

"Why not?" said the woman. She threw down her
cards and stood up, facing into the sunset. The
pupils of her eyes shrank to pinpoints. To her he was
a big, blind rock, a kind of outline; she said again,
"Why not?" and her whole face lifted and became
sharper as one's face does when one stares against
the sun.

"Because you can't," he said. She bent to pick up
her cards as if she had made some mistake in listening, but there he was saying, "I won't be able to take
care of you."

"You won't have to," said she. He shook his head.
"You won't come."

"Of course I'll come," she said.

"You won't," said he.

"The devil I won't!" said she.

He put both arms on her shoulders, powerfully,
seriously, with utmost heaviness and she pulled away
at once, at once transformed into a mystery with a
closed face; she stared at him without expression,
shifting her cards from hand to hand. He said, "Look,
my girl—" and for this got the entire fortunes of the
whole world for the next twenty centuries right in

*ones, tens, hundreds, myriads, tens of myriads

his face.

"Well, well," he said, "I see," ponderously, "I see," and stalked away down the curve of the ship, thus passing around the cabin, into the darkening eastern sky, and out of the picture.

But she did go with him. She appeared, dripping wet and triumphantly smiling, at the door of the little place of business he had chosen to discuss business in and walked directly to his table, raising two fingers in greeting, a gesture that had taken her fancy when she saw it done by someone in the street. She then uttered a word Blackbeard thought she did not understand (she did). She looked with interest around the room—at the smoke from the torches—and the patrons—and a Great Horned Owl somewhat the worse for wear that had been chained by one leg to the bar (an ancient invention)—and the stuffed blowfish that hung from the ceiling on a string: lazy, consumptive, puffed-up, with half its spines broken off. Then she sat down.

"Huh!" she said, dismissing the tavern. Blackbeard was losing his temper. His face suffused with blood, he put both enormous fists on the table to emphasize that fact; she nodded civilly, leaned back on her part of the wall (causing the bench to rock), crossed her knees, and swung one foot back and forth, back and forth, under the noses of both gentlemen. It was not exactly rude but it was certainly disconcerting.

"You. Get out," said the other gentleman.

"I'm not dry yet," said she in a soft, reasonable voice, like a bravo trying to pick a quarrel, and she laid both arms across the table, where they left two dark stains. She stared him in the face as if trying to memorize it—hard enough with a man who made it his business to look like nobody in particular—and the *other gentleman* was about to rise and was reaching for something or other under the table when her gentleman said:

"She's crazy." He cleared his throat. "You sit down," he said. "My apologies. *You* behave," and social stability thus reestablished, they plunged into a discussion she understood pretty well but did not pay much attention to, as she was too busy looking about. The owl blinked, turned his head completely around, and stood on one foot. The blowfish rotated lazily. Across the room stood a row of casks and a mortared wall; next to that a face in the dimness—a handsome face—that smiled at her across the serried tables. She smiled back, a villainous smile full of saltpeter, a wise, nasty, irresponsible, troublemaking smile, at which the handsome face winked. She laughed out loud.

"Shut up," said Blackbeard, not turning round.

He was in a tight place.

She watched him insist and prevaricate and sweat, building all kinds of earnest, openhearted, irresistible arguments with the gestures of his big hands, trying to bully the insignificant other gentleman—and failing—and not knowing it—until finally at the same moment the owl screeched like a rusty file, a singer at the end of the bar burst into wailing quartertones, and Blackbeard—wiping his forehead—said, "All right."

"No, dammit," she cried, "you're ten percent off!"

He slapped her. The other gentleman cleared his throat.

"All right," Blackbeard repeated. The other man nodded. Finishing his wine, drawing on his gloves, already a little bored perhaps, he turned and left. In his place, as if by a compensation of nature, there suddenly appeared, jackrabbited between the tables, the handsome young owner of the face who was not so handsome at close range but dressed fit to kill all the same with a gold earring, a red scarf tucked into his shirt, and a satanic resemblance to her late husband. She looked rapidly from one man to the other, almost malevolently; then she stood rigid, staring at the floor.

"*Well, baby,*" said the intruder.

Blackbeard turned his back on his girl.

The intruder took hold of her by the nape of the neck but she did not move; he talked to her in a low voice; finally she blurted out, "Oh yes! Go on!" (fixing her eyes on the progress of Blackbeard's monolithic back towards the door) and stumbled aside as the latter all but vaulted over a table to retrieve his lost property. She followed him, her head bent, violently flushed. Two streets off he stopped, saying, "Look, my dear, can I please not take you ashore again?" but she would not answer, no, not a word, and all this time the singer back at the tavern was singing away about the Princess Oriana who traveled to meet her betrothed but was stolen by bandits, and how she prayed, and how the bandits cursed, and how she begged to be returned to her prince, and how the bandits said, "Not likely," and how she finally ended it all by jumping into the Bosphorus—in short, art in the good old style with plenty of solid vocal technique, a truly Oriental expressiveness, and innumerable verses.

(She always remembered the incident and maintained for the rest of her life that small producers

should combine in trading with middlemen so as not
to lower prices by competing against each other.)

In the first, faint hint of dawn, as Blackbeard lay
snoring and damp in the bedclothes, his beard spread
out like a fan, his woman prodded him in the ribs
with the handle of his sword; she said, "Wake up!
Something's happening.

"I am," she added. She watched him as he tried to
sit up, tangled in the sheets, pale, enormous, the
black hair on his chest forming with unusual distinct-
ness the shape of a flying eagle. "Wha'?" he said.

"I am," she repeated. Still half asleep, he held out
his arms to her, indicating that she might happen all
over the place, might happen now, particularly in
bed, *he* did not care. "*Wake up!*" she said. He nearly
leapt out of bed, but then perceived her standing
leaning on his sword, the corners of her mouth turned
down. No one was being killed. He blinked, shiv-
ered, and shook his head. "Don't do that," he said
thickly. She let the sword fall with a clatter. He
winced.

"I'm going away," she said very distinctly, "that's
all," and thrusting her face near his, she seized him
by the arms and shook him violently, leaping back
when he vaulted out of the bed and whirling around
with one hand on the table—ready to throw it. That
made him smile. He sat down and scratched his
chest, giving himself every now and then a kind of
shake to wake himself up, until he could look at her
directly in the eyes and ask:

"Haven't I treated you well?"

She said nothing. He dangled one arm between his
knees moodily and rubbed the back of his neck with
the other, so enormous, so perfect, so relaxed, and in

every way so like real life that she could only shrug and fold her arms across her breasts. He examined his feet and rubbed, for comfort, the ankle and the arch, the heel and the instep, stretching his feet, stretching his back, rubbing his fingers over and over and over.

"Damn it, I am cleverer than you!" she exclaimed.

He sighed, meaning perhaps "no," meaning perhaps "I suppose so"; he said, "You've been up all night, haven't you?" and then he said, "My dear, you must understand——" but at that moment a terrific battering shook the ship, propelling the master of it outside, naked as he was, from which position he locked his woman in.

(In those days craft were high, square and slow, like barrels or boxes put out to sea; but everything is relative, and as they crept up on each other, throwing fits every now and again when headed into the wind, creaking and straining at every joist, ships bore skippers who remembered craft braced with twisted rope from stem to stem, craft manned exclusively by rowers, above all craft that invariably—or usually—sank, and they enjoyed the keen sensation of modernity while standing on a deck large enough for a party of ten to dine on comfortably and steering by use of a rudder that no longer required a pole for leverage or broke a man's wrist. Things were getting better. With great skill a man could sail as fast as other men could run. Still, in this infancy of the world, one ship wallowed after another; like cunning sloths one feebly stole up on another; and when they closed—without fire (do you want us to burn ourselves *up*?)—the toothless, ineffectual creatures clung together, sawing dully at each other's

grappling ropes, until the fellows over there got over
here or the fellows over here got over there and
then—on a slippery floor humped like the back of an
elephant and just about as small, amid rails, boxes,
pots, peaks, tar, slants, steps, ropes, coils, masts,
falls, chests, sails and God knows what—they hacked
at each other until most of them died. That they did
very efficiently.

(And the sea was full of robbers.)

Left alone, she moved passively with the motion of
the ship; then she picked up very slowly and looked
into very slowly the hand mirror he had taken for her
out of his chest, brass-backed and decorated with
metal rose-wreaths, the kind of object she had never
in her life seen before. There she was, oddly tilted,
looking out of the mirror, and behind her the room
as if seen from above, as if one could climb down
into the mirror to those odd objects, bright and
reversed, as if one could fall into the mirror, become
tiny, clamber away, and looking back see one's own
enormous eyes staring out of a window set high in the
wall. Women do not always look in mirrors to admire
themselves, popular belief to the contrary. Sometimes they look only to slip off their rings and their
bracelets, to pluck off their earrings, to unfasten
their necklaces, to drop their brilliant gowns, to take
the color off their faces until the bones stand out like
spears and to wipe the hues from around their eyes
until they can look and look at merely naked human
faces, at eyes no longer brilliant and aqueous like the
eyes of angels or goddesses but hard and small as
human eyes are, little control points that are always a
little disquieting, always a little peculiar, because
they are not meant to be looked at but to look, and

then—with a shudder, a shiver—to recover themselves and once again to shimmer, to glow. But some don't care. This one stumbled away, dropped the mirror, fell over the table (she passed her hand over her eyes) and grasped—more by feeling than by sight—the handle of the sword he had given her, thirty or forty—or was it seventy?—years before. The blade had not yet the ironical motto it was to bear some years later: *Good Manners Are Not Enough*, but she lifted it high all the same, and grasping with her left hand the bronze chain Blackbeard used to fasten his treasure chest, broke the lock of the door in one blow.

Such was the strength of iron in the old days.

There is talent and then there is the other thing. Blackbeard had never seen the other thing. He found her after the battle was over with her foot planted on the back of a dead enemy, trying to free the sword he had given her. She did so in one jerky pull and rolled the man overboard with her foot without bothering about him further; she was looking at an ornamented dagger in her left hand, a beautiful weapon with a jeweled handle and a slender blade engraved with scrolls and leaves. She admired it very much. She held it out to him, saying, "Isn't that a beauty?" There was a long gash on her left arm, the result of trying to stop a downward blow with nothing but the bronze chain wrapped around her knuckles. The chain was gone; she had only used it as long as it had surprise value and had lost it somewhere, somehow (she did not quite remember how). He took the dagger and she sat down suddenly on the deck, dropping the sword and running both hands over her hair to smooth it again and again, unaware that her palms left long red streaks. The deck looked as if a tribe of monkeys had been painting on it or as if everyone—living and dead—had smeared himself ritually with red paint. The sun was coming up. He sat down next to her, too winded to speak. With the intent watchfulness (but this will be a millennium or two later) of someone focusing the lens of a microscope, with the noble, arrogant carriage of a tennis star, she looked first around the deck—and then at him—and then straight up into the blue sky.

"So," she said, and shut her eyes.

He put his arm around her; he wiped her face. He stroked the nape of her neck and then her shoulder, but now his woman began to laugh, more and more, leaning against him and laughing and laughing until she was convulsed and he thought she had gone out of her mind. "What the devil!" he cried, almost weeping, "what the devil!" She stopped at that place in the scale where a woman's laughter turns into a shriek; her shoulders shook spasmodically but soon she controlled that too. He thought she might be hysterical so he said, "Are you frightened? You won't have to go through this again."

"No?" she said.

"Never."

"Well," she said, "perhaps I shall all the same," and in pure good humor she put her arms about his neck. There were tears in her eyes—perhaps they were tears of laughter—and in the light of the rising sun the deck showed ever more ruddy and grotesque. *What a mess*, she thought. She said, "It's all right; don't you worry," which was, all in all and in the light of things, a fairly kind goodbye.

"Why the devil," she said with sudden interest,

"don't doctors cut up the bodies of dead people in the schools to find out how they're put together?"

But he didn't know.

Six weeks later she arrived—alone—at that queen among cities, that moon among stars, that noble, despicable, profound, simple-minded and altogether exasperating capital of the world: Ourdh. Some of us know it. She materialized so quietly and expertly out of the dark that the gatekeeper found himself looking into her face without the slightest warning: a young, gray-eyed countrywoman, silent, shadowy, self-assured. She was hugely amused. "My name," she said, "is Alyx."

"Never heard of it," said the gatekeeper, a little annoyed.

"Good heavens," said Alyx, "not yet," and vanished through the gate before he could admit her, with the curious slight smile one sees on the lips of very old statues: inexpressive, simple, classic.

She was to become a classic, in time.

But that's another story.

✳   ✳   ✳

THE BARBARIAN

Alyx, the gray-eyed, the silent woman. Wit, arm, kill-quick for hire, she watched the strange man thread his way through the tables and the smoke toward her. This was in Ourdh, where all things are possible. He stopped at the table where she sat alone and with a certain indefinable gallantry, not pleasant but perhaps its exact opposite, he said:

"A woman—here?"

"You're looking at one," said Alyx dryly, for she did not like his tone. It occurred to her that she had seen him before—though he was not so fat then, no, not quite so fat—and then it occurred to her that the time of their last meeting had almost certainly been in the hills when she was four or five years old. That was thirty years ago. So she watched him very narrowly as he eased himself into the seat opposite, watched him as he drummed his fingers in a lively

Joanna Russ

tune on the tabletop, and paid him close attention when he tapped one of the marine decorations that hung from the ceiling (a stuffed blowfish, all spikes and parchment, that moved lazily to and fro in a wandering current of air) and made it bob. He smiled, the flesh around his eyes straining into folds.

"I know you," he said. "A raw country girl fresh from the hills who betrayed an entire religious delegation to the police some ten years ago. You settled down as a pick-lock. You made a good thing of it. You expanded your profession to include a few more difficult items and you did a few things that turned heads hereabouts. You were not unknown, even then. Then you vanished for a season and reappeared as a fairly rich woman. But that didn't last, unfortunately."

"Didn't have to," said Alyx.

"Didn't last," repeated the fat man imperturbably, with a lazy shake of the head. "No, no, it didn't last. And now," (he pronounced the "now" with peculiar relish) "you are getting old."

"Old enough," said Alyx, amused.

"Old," said he, "old. Still neat, still tough, still small. But old. You're thinking of settling down."

"Not exactly."

"Children?"

She shrugged, retiring a little into the shadow. The fat man did not appear to notice.

"It's been done," she said.

"You may die in childbirth," said he, "at your age."

"That, too, has been done."

She stirred a little, and in a moment a short-handled Southern dagger, the kind carried unobtrusively in sleeves or shoes, appeared with its point buried in the tabletop, vibrating ever so gently.

"It is true," said she, "that I am growing old. My hair is threaded with white. I am developing a chunky look around the waist that does not exactly please me, though I was never a ballet-girl." She grinned at him in the semi-darkness. "Another thing," she said softly, "that I develop with age is a certain lack of patience. If you do not stop making personal remarks and taking up my time—which is valuable—I shall throw you across the room."

"I would not, if I were you," he said.

"You could not."

The fat man began to heave with laughter. He heaved until he choked. Then he said, gasping, "I beg your pardon." Tears ran down his face.

"Go on," said Alyx. He leaned across the table, smiling, his fingers mated tip to tip, his eyes little pits of shadow in his face.

"I come to make you rich," he said.

"You can do more than that," said she steadily. A quarrel broke out across the room between a soldier and a girl he had picked up for the night; the fat man talked through it, or rather under it, never taking his eyes off her face.

"Ah!" he said, "you remember when you saw me last and you assume that a man who can live thirty years without growing older must have more to give—if he wishes—than a handful of gold coins. You are right. I can make you live long. I can insure your happiness. I can determine the sex of your children. I can cure all diseases. I can even" (and here he lowered his voice) "turn this table, or this building, or this whole city to pure gold, if I wish it."

"Can anyone do that?" said Alyx, with the faintest whisper of mockery.

"I can," he said. "Come outside and let us talk. Let me show you a few of the things I can do. I have some business here in the city that I must attend to myself and I need a guide and an assistant. That will be you."

"If you can turn the city into gold," said Alyx just as softly, "can you turn gold into a city?"

"Anyone can do that," he said, laughing: "come along," so they rose and made their way into the cold outside air—it was a clear night in early spring—and at a corner of the street where the moon shone down on the walls and the pits in the road, they stopped.

"Watch," said he.

On his outstretched palm was a small black box. He shook it, turning it this way and that, but it remained wholly featureless. Then he held it out to her and, as she took it in her hand, it began to glow until it became like a piece of glass lit up from the inside. There in the middle of it was her man, with his tough, friendly, young-old face and his hair a little gray, like hers. He smiled at her, his lips moving soundlessly. She threw the cube into the air a few times, held it to the side of her face, shook it, and then dropped it on the ground, grinding it under her heel. It remained unhurt.

She picked it up and held it out to him, thinking:

Not metal, very light. And warm. A toy? Wouldn't break, though. Must be some sort of small machine, though God knows who made it and of what. It follows thoughts! Marvelous. But magic? Bah! Never believed in it before; why now? Besides, this thing too sensible; magic is elaborate, undependable, use-

less. I'll tell him—but then it occurred to her that someone had gone to a good deal of trouble to impress her when a little bit of credit might have done just as well. And this man walked with an almighty confidence through the streets for someone who was unarmed. And those thirty years—so she said very politely:

"It's magic!"

He chuckled and pocketed the cube.

"You're a little savage," he said, "but your examination of it was most logical. I like you. Look! I am an old magician. There is a spirit in that box and there are more spirits under my control than you can possibly imagine. I am like a man living among monkeys. There are things spirits cannot do—or things I choose to do myself, take it any way you will. So I pick one of the monkeys who seems brighter than the rest and train it. I pick you. What do you say?"

"All right," said Alyx.

"Calm enough!" he chuckled. "Calm enough! Good. What's your motive?"

"Curiosity," said Alyx. "It's a monkeylike trait." He chuckled again; his flesh choked it and the noise came out in a high, muffled scream.

"And what if I bite you," said Alyx, "like a monkey?"

"No, little one," he answered gaily, "you won't. You may be sure of that." He held out his hand, still shaking with mirth. In the palm lay a kind of blunt knife which he pointed at one of the white-washed walls that lined the street. The edges of the wall burst into silent smoke, the whole section trembled and slid, and in an instant it had vanished, vanished as completely as if it had never existed, except for a

sullen glow at the raw edges of brick and a pervasive
smell of burning. Alyx swallowed.

"It's quiet, for magic," she said softly. "Have you
ever used it on men?"

"On armies, little one."

So the monkey went to work for him. There seemed
as yet to be no harm in it. The little streets admired
his generosity and the big ones his good humor;
while those too high for money or flattery he won by
a catholic ability that was—so the little pick-lock
thought—remarkable in one so stupid. For about his
stupidity there could be no doubt. She smelled it. It
offended her. It made her twitch in her sleep, like a
ferret. There was in this woman—well hidden away—
an anomalous streak of quiet humanity that abhorred
him, that set her teeth on edge at the thought of
him, though she could not have put into words just
what was the matter. *For stupidity,* she thought, *is
hardly—is not exactly—*

Four months later they broke into the governor's
villa. She thought she might at last find out what this
man was after besides pleasure jaunts around the
town. Moreover, breaking and entering always gave
her the keenest pleasure; and doing so "for nothing"
(as he said) tickled her fancy immensely. The power
in gold and silver that attracts thieves was banal, in
this thief's opinion, but to stand in the shadows of a
sleeping house, absolutely silent, with no object at
all in view and with the knowledge that if you are
found you will probably have your throat cut—! She
began to think better of him. This dilettante passion
for the craft, this reckless silliness seemed to her as
worthy as the love of a piece of magnetite for the

North and South poles—the "faithful stone" they call it in Ourdh.

"Who'll come with us?" she asked, wondering for the fiftieth time where the devil he went when he was not with her, whom he knew, where he lived, and what that persistently bland expression on his face could possibly mean.

"No one," he said calmly.

"What are we looking for?"

"Nothing."

"Do you ever do anything for a reason?"

"Never." And he chuckled.

And then, "Why are you so fat?" demanded Alyx, halfway out of her own door, half into the shadows. She had recently settled in a poor quarter of the town, partly out of laziness, partly out of necessity. The shadows playing in the hollows of her face, the expression of her eyes veiled, she said it again, "Why are you so goddamned fat!" He laughed until he wheezed.

"The barbarian mind!" he cried, lumbering after her in high good humor, "Oh—oh, my dear!—oh, what freshness!" She thought:

That's it! and then

The fool doesn't even know I hate him.

But neither had she known, until that very moment.

They scaled the northeast garden wall of the villa and crept along the top of it without descending, for the governor kept dogs. Alyx, who could walk a taut rope like a circus performer, went quietly. The fat man giggled. She swung herself up to the nearest window and hung there by one arm and a toehold for fifteen mortal minutes while she sawed through the metal hinge of the shutter with a file. Once inside the building (he had to be pulled through the window) she took him by the collar with uncanny accuracy, considering that the inside of the villa was stone dark. "Shut up!" she said, with considerable emphasis.

"Oh?" he whispered.

"I'm in charge here," she said, releasing him with a jerk, and melted into the blackness not two feet away, moving swiftly along the corridor wall. Her fingers brushed lightly alongside her, like a creeping animal: stone, stone, a gap, warm air rising . . . In the dark she felt wolfish, her lips skinned back over her teeth; like another species she made her way with hands and ears. Through them the villa sighed and rustled in its sleep. She put the tips of the fingers of her free hand on the back of the fat man's neck, guiding him with the faintest of touches through the turns of the corridor. They crossed an empty space where two halls met; they retreated noiselessly into a room where a sleeper lay breathing against a dimly lit window, while someone passed in the corridor outside. When the steps faltered for a moment, the fat man gasped and Alyx wrung his wrist, hard. There was a cough from the corridor, the sleeper in the room stirred and murmured, and the steps passed on. They crept back to the hall. Then he told her where he wanted to go.

"What!" She had pulled away, astonished, with a reckless hiss of indrawn breath. Methodically he began poking her in the side and giving her little pushes with his other hand—she moving away, outraged—but all in silence. In the distant reaches of the building something fell—or someone spoke—

and without thinking, they waited silently until the sounds had faded away. He resumed his continual prodding. Alyx, her teeth on edge, began to creep forward, passing a cat that sat outlined in the vague light from a window, perfectly unconcerned with them and rubbing its paws against its face, past a door whose cracks shone yellow, past ghostly staircases that opened up in vast wells of darkness, breathing a faint, far updraft, their steps rustling and creaking. They were approaching the governor's nursery. The fat man watched without any visible horror—or any interest, for that matter—while Alyx disarmed the first guard, stalking him as if he were a sparrow, then the one strong pressure on the blood vessel at the back of the neck (all with no noise except the man's own breathing; she was quiet as a shadow). Now he was trussed up, conscious and glaring, quite unable to move. The second guard was asleep in his chair. The third Alyx decoyed out the anteroom by a thrown pebble (she had picked up several in the street). She was three motionless feet away from him as he stooped to examine it; he never straightened up. The fourth guard (he was in the anteroom, in a feeble glow that stole through the hangings of the nursery beyond) turned to greet his friend—or so thought—and then Alyx judged she could risk a little speech. She said thoughtfully, in a low voice, "That's dangerous, on the back of the head."

"Don't let it bother you," said the fat man. Through the parting of the hangings they could see the nurse, asleep on her couch with her arms bare and their golden circlets gleaming in the lamplight, the black slave in a profound huddle of darkness at the farther door, and a shining, tented basket—the royal baby's royal house. The baby was asleep. Alyx stepped inside—motioning the fat man away from the lamp—and picked the governor's daughter out of her gilt cradle. She went round the apartment with the baby in one arm, bolting both doors and closing the hangings, draping the fat man in a guard's cloak and turning down the lamp so that a bare glimmer of light reached the farthest walls.

"Now you've seen it," she said, "shall we go?"

He shook his head. He was watching her curiously, his head tilted to one side. He smiled at her. The baby woke up and began to chuckle at finding herself carried about; she grabbed at Alyx's mouth and jumped up and down, bending in the middle like a sort of pocket-compass or enthusiastic spring. The woman lifted her head to avoid the baby's fingers and began to soothe her, rocking her in her arms. "Good Lord, she's cross-eyed," said Alyx. The nurse and her slave slept on, wrapped in the profoundest unconsciousness. Humming a little, soft tune to the governor's daughter, Alyx walked her about the room, humming and rocking, rocking and humming, until the baby yawned.

"Better go," said Alyx.

"No," said the fat man.

"Better," said Alyx again. "One cry and the nurse—"

"Kill the nurse," said the fat man.

"The slave—"

"He's dead." Alyx started, rousing the baby. The slave still slept by the door, blacker than the blackness, but under him oozed something darker still in the twilight flame of the lamp. "You did that?" whispered Alyx, hushed. She had not seen him move. He took something dark and hollow, like the shell of a nut, from the palm of his hand and laid it next to the baby's cradle; with a shiver half of awe and half of distaste Alyx put the richest and most fortunate daughter of Ourdh back into her gilt cradle. Then she said:

"Now we'll go."

"But I have not what I came for," said the fat man.

"And what is that?"

"The baby."

"Do you mean to steal her?" said Alyx curiously.

"No," said he, "I mean for you to kill her."

The woman stared. In sleep the governor's daughter's nurse stirred; then she sat bolt upright, said something incomprehensible in a loud voice, and fell back to her couch, still deep in sleep. So astonished was the pick-lock that she did not move. She only looked at the fat man. Then she sat by the cradle and rocked it mechanically with one hand while she looked at him.

"What on earth for?" she said at length. He smiled. He seemed as easy as if he were discussing her wages or the price of pigs; he sat down opposite her and he too rocked the cradle, looking on the burden it contained with a benevolent, amused interest. If the nurse had woken up at that moment, she might have thought she saw the governor and his wife, two loving parents who had come to visit their child by lamplight. The fat man said:

"Must you know?"

"I must," said Alyx.

"Then I will tell you," said the fat man, "not because you must, but because I choose. This little six-months morsel is going to grow up."

"Most of us do," said Alyx, still astonished.

"She will become a queen," the fat man went on, "and a surprisingly wicked woman for one who now looks so innocent. She will be the death of more than one child and more than one slave. In plain fact, she will be a horror to the world. This I know."

"I believe you," said Alyx, shaken.

"Then kill her," said the fat man. But still the pick-lock did not stir. The baby in her cradle snored, as infants sometimes do, as if to prove the fat man's opinion of her by showing a surprising precocity; still the pick-lock did not move, but stared at the man across the cradle as if he were a novel work of nature.

"I ask you to kill her," said he again.

"In twenty years," said she, "when she has become so very wicked."

"Woman, are you deaf? I told you—"

"In twenty years!" In the feeble light from the lamp she appeared pale, as if with rage or terror. He leaned deliberately across the cradle, closing his hand around the shell or round-shot or unidentifiable object he had dropped there a moment before; he said very deliberately:

"In twenty years you will be dead."

"Then do it yourself," said Alyx softly, pointing at the object in his hand, "unless you had only one?"

"I had only one."

"Ah, well then," she said, "here!" and she held out to him across the sleeping baby the handle of her dagger, for she had divined something about this man in the months they had known each other; and when he made no move to take the blade, she nudged his hand with the handle.

"You don't like things like this, do you?" she said.

"Do as I say, woman!" he whispered. She pushed the handle into his palm. She stood up and poked him deliberately with it, watching him tremble and sweat; she had never seen him so much at a loss. She moved round the cradle, smiling and stretching out her arm seductively. "Do as I say!" he cried.

"Softly, softly."

"You're a sentimental fool!"

"Am I?" she said. "Whatever I do, I must feel; I can't just twiddle my fingers like you, can I?"

"Ape!"

"You chose me for it."

Do as I say!

"Sh! You will wake the nurse." For a moment both stood silent, listening to the baby's all-but-soundless breathing and the rustling of the nurse's sheets. Then he said, "Woman, your life is in my hands."

"Is it?" said she.

"I want your obedience!"

"Oh no," she said softly, "I know what you want. You want importance because you have none; you want to swallow up another soul. You want to make me fear you and I think you can succeed, but I think also that I can teach you the difference between fear and respect. Shall I?"

"Take care!" he gasped.

"Why?" she said. "Lest you kill me?"

"There are other ways," he said, and he drew himself up, but here the pick-lock spat in his face. He let out a strangled wheeze and lurched backwards, stumbling against the curtains. Behind her Alyx heard a faint cry; she whirled about to see the governor's nurse sitting up in bed, her eyes wide open.

"Madam, quietly, quietly," said Alyx, "for God's sake!"

The governor's nurse opened her mouth.

"I have done no harm," said Alyx passionately, "I swear it!" But the governor's nurse took a breath with the clear intention to scream, a hearty, healthy, full-bodied scream like the sort pick-locks hear in nightmares. In the second of the governor's nurse's shuddering inhalation—in that split second that would mean unmentionably unpleasant things for Alyx, as Ourdh was not a kind city—Alyx considered launching herself at the woman, but the cradle was between. It would be too late. The house would be roused in twenty seconds. She could never make it to a door—or a window—not even to the garden, where the governor's hounds could drag down a stranger in two steps. All those thoughts flashed through the pick-lock's mind as she saw the governor's nurse inhale with that familiar, hideous violence; her knife was still in her hand; with the smooth simplicity of habit it slid through her fingers and sped across the room to bury itself in the governor's nurse's neck, just above the collarbone in that tender hollow Ourdhian poets love to sing. The woman's open-mouthed expression froze on her face; with an "uh!" of surprise she fell forward, her arms hanging limp over the edge of the couch. A noise came from her throat. The knife had opened a major pulse, and in the blood's slow, powerful, rhythmic tides across sheet and slippers and floor Alyx could discern a horrid similarity to the posture and appearance of the black slave. One was hers, one was the fat man's. She turned and hurried through the curtains into the anteroom, only noting that the soldier blindfolded and bound in the corner had managed patiently to work loose the thongs around two of his fingers with his teeth. He must have been at it all this time. Outside in the hall the darkness of the house was as undisturbed as if the nursery were that very Well of Peace whence the gods first drew (as the saying is) the dawn and the color—but nothing else—for the eyes of women. On the wall someone had written in faintly shining stuff, like snail-slime, the single word *Fever*.

But the fat man was gone.

Her man was raving and laughing on the floor when she got home. She could not control him—she could only sit with her hands over her face and shudder—so at length she locked him in and gave the key to the old woman who owned the house, saying, "My husband drinks too much. He was perfectly sober when I left earlier this evening and now look at him. Don't let him out."

Then she stood stock-still for a moment, trembling and thinking: of the fat man's distaste for walking, of his wheezing, his breathlessness, of his vanity that surely would have led him to show her any magic vehicle he had that took him to whatever he called home. He must have walked. She had seen him go out the north gate a hundred times.

She began to run.

To the south Ourdh is built above marshes that will engulf anyone or anything unwary enough to try to cross them, but to the north the city peters out into sand dunes fringing the seacoast and a fine monotony of rocky hills that rise to a countryside of sandy scrub, stunted trees and what must surely be the poorest farms in the world. Ourdh believes that these farmers dream incessantly of robbing travelers, so nobody goes there, all the fashionable world frequenting the great north road that loops a good fifty miles to avoid this region. Even without its stories the world would have no reason to go here; there is nothing to see but dunes and weeds and now and then a shack (or more properly speaking, a hut) resting on an outcropping of rock or nesting right on the sand like a toy boat in a basin. There is only one landmark in the whole place—an old tower hardly even fit for a wizard—and that was abandoned nobody knows how long ago, though it is only twenty minutes' walk from the city gates. Thus it was natural that Alyx (as she ran, her heart pounding in her side) did not notice the stars, or the warm night-wind that stirred the leaves of the trees, or indeed the very path under her feet; though she knew all the paths for twenty-five miles around. Her whole mind was on that tower. She felt its stones stick in her throat. On her right and left the country flew by, but she seemed not to move; at last, panting, and trembling, she crept through a nest of tree-trunks no thicker than her wrist (they were very old and very tough) and sure enough, there it was. There was a light shining halfway between bottom and top. Then someone looked out, like a cautious householder out of an attic, and the light went out.

Ah! thought she, and moved into the cover of the trees. The light—which had vanished—now reappeared a story higher and so on, higher and higher, until it reached the top. It wobbled a little, as if held in the hand. So this was his country seat! Silently and with great care, she made her way from one pool of shadow to another. One hundred feet from the tower she circled it and approached it from the northern side. A finger of the sea cut in very close to the base of the building (it had been slowly falling into the water for many years) and in this she first waded and then swam, disturbing the faint, cold radiance of the starlight in the placid ripples. There was no moon. Under the very walls of the tower she stopped and listened; in the darkness under the sea she felt along the rocks; then, expelling her breath and kicking upwards, she rushed head-down; the water closed round, the stone rushed past and she struggled up into the air. She was inside the walls.

And so is he, she thought. For somebody had cleaned the place up. What she remembered as choked with stone rubbish (she had used the place for purposes of her own a few years back) was bare and neat and clean; all was square, all was orderly, and someone had cut stone steps from the level of the water to the most beautifully precise archway in the world. But of course she should not have been able to see any of this at all. The place should have been in absolute darkness. Instead, on either side of the arch was a dim glow, with a narrow beam of light going between them; she could see dancing in it the dust-motes that are never absent from this earth, not even from air that has lain quiet within the rock of a wizard's mansion for uncountable years. Up to her neck in the ocean, this barbarian woman then stood very quietly and thoughtfully for several minutes. Then she dove down into the sea again, and when she came up her knotted cloak was full of the tiny crabs that cling to the rocks along the seacoast of Ourdh. One she killed and the others she suspended

captive in the sea; bits of the blood and flesh of the
first she smeared carefully below the two sources of
that narrow beam of light; then she crept back into
the sea and loosed the others at the very bottom
step, diving underwater as the first of the hurrying
little creatures reached the arch. There was a brilliant flash of light, then another, and then darkness.
Alyx waited. Hoisting herself out of the water, she
walked through the arch—not quickly, but not without nervousness. The crabs were pushing and quar-
reling over their dead cousin. Several climbed over
the sources of the beam, *pulling*, she thought, *the
crabs over his eyes*. However he saw, he had seen
nothing. The first alarm had been sprung.

Wizards' castles—and their country residences—
have every right to be infested with all manner of
horrors, but Alyx saw nothing. The passage wound
on, going fairly constantly upward, and as it rose it
grew lighter until every now and then she could see
a kind of lighter shape against the blackness and a
few stars. These were windows. There was no sound
but her own breathing and once in a while the complaining rustle of one or two little creatures she had
inadvertently carried with her in a corner of her
cloak. When she stopped she heard nothing. The fat
man was either very quiet or very far away. She
hoped it was quietness. She slung the cloak over her
shoulder and began the climb again.

Then she ran into a wall.

This shocked her, but she gathered herself together and tried the experiment again. She stepped
back, then walked forward and again she ran into a
wall, not rock but something at once elastic and
unyielding, and at the very same moment someone

said (as it seemed to her, inside her head) *You cannot get through*.

Alyx swore, religiously. She fell back and nearly lost her balance. She put out one hand and again she touched something impalpable, tingling and elastic; again the voice sounded close behind her ear, with an uncomfortable, frightening intimacy as if she were speaking to herself: *You cannot get through.* "Can't I!" she shouted, quite losing her nerve, and drew her sword; it plunged forward without the slightest resistance, but something again stopped her bare hand and the voice repeated with idiot softness, over and over *You cannot get through. You cannot get through—*

"Who are you!" said she, but there was no answer. She backed down the stairs, sword drawn, and waited. Nothing happened. Round her the stone walls glimmered, barely visible, for the moon was rising outside; patiently she waited, pressing the corner of her cloak with her foot, for as it lay on the floor one of the crabs had chewed his way to freedom and had given her ankle a tremendous nip on the way out. The light increased.

There was nothing there. The crab, who had scuttled busily ahead on the landing of the stair, seemed to come to the place himself and stood here, fiddling. There was absolutely nothing there. Then Alyx, who had been watching the little animal with something close to hopeless calm, gave an exclamation and threw herself flat on the stairs—for the crab had begun to climb upward between floor and ceiling and what it was climbing on was nothing. Tears forced themselves to her eyes. Swimming behind her lids she could see her husband's face, appearing first in one place, then in another, as if frozen on the black box the fat man had showed her the first day they met. She laid herself on the stone and cried. Then she got up, for the face seemed to settle on the other side of the landing and it occurred to her that she must go through. She was still crying. She took off one of her sandals and pushed it through the something-nothing (the crab still climbed in the air with perfect comfort). It went through easily. She grew nauseated at the thought of touching the crab and the thing it climbed on, but she put one hand involuntarily over her face and made a grab with the other (*You cannot* said the voice). When she had got the struggling animal thoroughly in her grasp, she dashed it against the rocky side wall of the tunnel and flung it forward with all her strength. It fell clattering twenty feet further on.

The distinction then, she thought, *is between life and death,* and she sat down hopelessly on the steps to figure this out, for the problem of dying so as to get through and yet getting through without dying, struck her as insoluble. Twenty feet down the tunnel (the spot was in darkness and she could not see what it was) something rustled. It sounded remarkably like a crab that had been stunned and was now recovering, for these animals think of nothing but food and disappointments only seem to give them fresh strength for the search. Alyx gaped into the dark. She felt the hairs rise on the back of her neck. She would have given a great deal to see into that spot, for it seemed to her that she now guessed at the principle of the fat man's demon, which kept out any conscious mind—as it had spoken in hers—but perhaps would let through . . . She pondered. This cynical woman had been a religious enthusiast before circumstances forced her into a drier way of thinking; thus it was that she now slung her cloak ahead of her on the ground to break her fall and leaned deliberately, from head to feet, into the horrid, springy net she could not see. Closing her eyes and pressing the fingers of both hands over an artery in the back of her neck, she began to repeat to herself a formula that she had learned in those prehistoric years, one that has to be altered slightly each time it is repeated—almost as effective a self-hypnotic device as counting backward. And the voice, too, whispering over and over *You cannot get through, you cannot get through—cannot—cannot—*

Something gave her a terrific shock through teeth, bones and flesh, and she woke to find the floor of the landing tilted two inches from her eyes. One knee was twisted under her and the left side of her face ached dizzily, warm and wet under a cushion of numbness. She guessed that her face had been laid open in the fall and her knee sprained, if not broken.

But she was through.

She found the fat man in a room at the very top of the tower, sitting in a pair of shorts in a square of light at the end of a corridor; and, as she made her way limping towards him, he grew (unconscious and busy) to the size of a human being, until at last she stood inside the room, vaguely aware of blood along her arm and a stinging on her face where she had tried to wipe her wound with her cloak. The room was full of machinery. The fat man (he had been jiggling some little arrangement of wires and blocks on his lap) looked up, saw her, registered surprise and then broke into a great grin.

"So it's you," he said.

She said nothing. She put one arm along the wall to steady herself.

"You are amazing," he said, "perfectly amazing. Come here," and he rose and sent his stool spinning away with a touch. He came up to where she stood, wet and shivering, staining the floor and wall, and for a long minute he studied her. Then he said softly:

"Poor animal. Poor little wretch."

Her breathing was ragged. She glanced rapidly about her, taking in the size of the room (it broadened to encompass the whole width of the tower) and the four great windows that opened to the four winds, and the strange things in the shadows: multitudes of little tables, boards hung on the walls, knobs and switches and winking lights innumerable. But she did not move or speak.

"Poor animal," he said again. He walked back and surveyed her contemptuously, both arms akimbo, and then he said, "Do you believe the world was once a lump of rock?"

"Yes," she said.

"Many years ago," he said, "many more years than your mind can comprehend, before there were trees—or cities—or women—I came to this lump of rock. Do you believe that?"

She nodded.

"I came here," said he gently, "in the satisfaction of a certain hobby, and I made all that you see in this room—all the little things you were looking at a moment ago—and I made the tower, too. Sometimes

I make it new inside and sometimes I make it look old. Do you understand that, little one?"

She said nothing.

"And when the whim hits me," he said, "I make it new and comfortable and I settle into it, and once I have settled into it I begin to practice my hobby. Do you know what my hobby is?" He chuckled.

"My hobby, little one," he said, "came from this tower and this machinery, for this machinery can reach all over the world and then things happen exactly as I choose. Now do you know what my hobby is? My hobby is world-making. I make worlds, little one."

She took a quick breath, like a sigh, but she did not speak. He smiled at her.

"Poor beast," he said, "you are dreadfully cut about the face and I believe you have sprained one of your limbs. Hunting animals are always doing that. But it won't last. Look," he said, "look again," and he moved one fat hand in a slow circle around him. "It is I, little one," he said, "who made everything that your eyes have ever rested on. Apes and peacocks, tides and times" (he laughed) "and the fire and the rain. I made you. I made your husband. Come," and he ambled off into the shadows. The circle of light that had rested on him when Alyx first entered the room now followed him, continually keeping him at its center, and although her hair rose to see it, she forced herself to follow, limping in pain past the tables, through stacks of tubing and wire and between square shapes the size of stoves. The light fled always before her. Then he stopped, and as she came up to the light, he said:

"You know, I am not angry at you."

Alyx winced as her foot struck something, and grabbed her knee.

"No, I am not," he said. "It has been delightful— except for tonight, which demonstrates, between ourselves, that the whole thing was something of a mistake and shouldn't be indulged in again—but you must understand that I cannot allow a creation of mine, a paring of my fingernail, if you take my meaning, to rebel in this silly fashion." He grinned. "No, no," he said, "that I cannot do. And so" (here he picked up a glass cube from the table in back of him) "I have decided" (here he joggled the cube a little) "that tonight—why, my dear, what is the matter with you? You are standing there with the veins in your fists knotted as if you would like to strike me, even though your knee is giving you a great deal of trouble just at present and you would be better employed in supporting some of your weight with your hands or I am very much mistaken." And he held out to her— though not far enough for her to reach it—the glass cube, which contained an image of her husband in little, unnaturally sharp, like a picture let into crystal. "See?" he said. "When I turn the lever to the right, the little beasties rioting in his bones grow ever more calm and that does him good. A great deal of good. But when I turn the lever to the left—"

"Devil!" said she.

"Ah, I've gotten something out of you at last!" he said, coming closer. "At last you know! Ah, little one, many and many a time I have seen you wondering whether the world might not be better off if you stabbed me in the back, eh? But you can't, you know. Why don't you try it?" He patted her on the shoulder. "Here I am, you see, quite close enough to

you, peering, in fact, into those tragic, blazing eyes—
wouldn't it be natural to try and put an end to me?
But you can't, you know. You'd be puzzled if you
tried. I wear an armor plate, little beast, that any
beast might envy, and you could throw me from a
ten-thousand-foot mountain, or fry me in a furnace,
or do a hundred and one other deadly things to me
without the least effect. My armor plate has *in-er-
tial dis-crim-in-a-tion*, little savage, which means that
it lets nothing too fast and nothing too heavy get
through. So you cannot hurt me at all. To murder
me, you would have to strike me, but that is too fast
and too heavy and so is the ground that hits me
when I fall and so is fire. Come here."

She did not move.

"Come here, monkey," he said. "I'm going to kill
your man and then I will send you away; though
since you operate so well in the dark, I think I'll
bless you and make that your permanent condition.
What do you think you're doing?" for she had put
her fingers to her sleeve; and while he stood, smiling
a little with the cube in his hand, she drew her
dagger and fell upon him, stabbing him again and
again.

"There," he said complacently, "do you see?"

"I see," she said hoarsely, finding her tongue.

"Do you understand?"

"I understand," she said.

"Then move off," he said, "I have got to finish,"
and he brought the cube up to the level of his eyes.
She saw her man, behind the glass as in a refracting
prism, break into a multiplicity of images; she saw
him reach out grotesquely to the surface; she saw his
fingertips strike at the surface as if to erupt into the

air; and while the fat man took the lever between
thumb and forefinger and—prissily and precisely, his
lips pursed into wrinkles, prepared to move it all the
way to the left—

She put her fingers in his eyes and then, taking
advantage of his pain and blindness, took the cube
from him and bent him over the edge of a table in
such a way as to break his back. This all takes place
inside the body. His face worked spasmodically, one
eye closed and unclosed in a hideous parody of a
wink, his fingers paddled feebly on the tabletop and
he fell to the floor.

"My dear!" he gasped.

She looked at him expressionlessly.

"Help me," he whispered, "eh?" His fingers flut-
tered. "Over there," he said eagerly, "medicines.
Make me well, eh? Good and fast. I'll give you half."

"All," she said.

"Yes, yes, all," he said breathlessly, "all—explain
all—fascinating hobby—spend most of my time in
this room—get the medicine—"

"First show me," she said, "how to turn it off."

"Off?" he said. He watched her, bright-eyed.

"First," she said patiently, "I will turn it all off.
And then I will cure you."

"No," he said, "no, no! Never!" She knelt down
beside him.

"Come," she said softly, "do you think I want to
destroy it? I am as fascinated by it as you are. I only
want to make sure you can't do anything to me,
that's all. You must explain it all first until I am
master of it, too, and then we will turn it on."

"No, no," he repeated suspiciously.

"You must," she said, "or you'll die. What do you

think I plan to do? I have to cure you, because otherwise how can I learn to work all this? But I must be safe, too. Show me how to turn it off."

He pointed, doubtfully.

"Is that it?" she said.

"Yes," he said, "but—".

"*Is that it?*"

"Yes, but—no—wait!" for Alyx sprang to her feet and fetched from his stool the pillow on which he had been sitting, the purpose of which he did not at first seem to comprehend, but then his eyes went wide with horror, for she had got the pillow in order to smother him, and that is just what she did.

When she got to her feet, her legs were trembling. Stumbling and pressing both hands together as if in prayer to subdue their shaking, she took the cube that held her husband's picture and carefully—oh, how carefully!—turned the lever to the right. Then she began to sob. It was not the weeping of grief, but a kind of reaction and triumph, all mixed; in the middle of that eerie room she stood, and threw her head back and yelled. The light burned steadily on. In the shadows she found the fat man's master switch, and leaning against the wall, put one finger—only one—on it and caught her breath. Would the world end? She did not know. After a few minutes' search she found a candle and flint hidden away in a cupboard and with this she made herself a light; then, with eyes closed, with a long shudder, she leaned— no, sagged—against the switch, and stood for a long moment, expecting and believing nothing.

But the world did not end. From outside came the wind and the sound of the sea-wash (though louder now, as if some indistinct and not quite audible humming had just ended) and inside fantastic shadows leapt about the candle—the lights had gone out. Alyx began to laugh, catching her breath. She set the candle down and searched until she found a length of metal tubing that stood against the wall, and then she went from machine to machine smashing, prying, tearing, toppling tables and breaking controls. Then she took the candle in her unsteady hand and stood over the body of the fat man, a phantasmagoric lump on the floor, badly lit at last. Her shadow loomed on the wall. She leaned over him and studied his face, that face that had made out of agony and death the most appalling trivialities. She thought:

Make the world? You hadn't the imagination. You didn't even make these machines; that shiny finish is for customers, not craftsmen, and controls that work by little pictures are for children. You are a child yourself, a child and a horror, and I would ten times rather be subject to your machinery than master of it.

Aloud she said:

"Never confuse the weapon and the arm," and taking the candle, she went away and left him in the dark.

She got home at dawn and, as her man lay asleep in bed, it seemed to her that he was made out of the light of the dawn that streamed through his fingers and his hair, irradiating him with gold. She kissed him and he opened his eyes.

"You've come home," he said.

"So I have," said she.

"I fought all night," she added, "with the Old Man of the Mountain," for you must know that this demon is a legend in Ourdh; he is the god of this world who dwells in a cave containing the whole world in little, and from his cave he rules the fates of men.

"Who won?" said her husband, laughing, for in the sunrise when everything is suffused with light it is difficult to see the seriousness of injuries.

"I did!" said she. "The man is dead." She smiled, splitting open the wound on her cheek, which began to bleed afresh. "He died," she said, "for two reasons only: because he was a fool. And because we are not."

She added, "I'll tell you all about it."

But that's another story.

PICNIC ON PARADISE

She was a soft-spoken, dark-haired, small-boned woman, not even coming up to their shoulders, like a kind of dwarf or miniature—but that was normal enough for a Mediterranean Greek of nearly four millennia ago, before super-diets and hybridization from seventy colonized planets had turned all humanity (so she had been told) into Scandinavian giants. The young lieutenant, who was two meters and a third tall, or three heads more than herself, very handsome and ebony-skinned, said "I'm sorry, ma'am, but I cannot believe you're the proper Trans-Temporal Agent; I think—" and he finished his thought on the floor, his head under one of his ankles and this slight young woman (or was she young? Trans-Temp did such strange things sometimes!) somehow holding him down in a position he could not get out of without hurting himself to excruciation. She let him go. She

sat down on the balloon-inflated thing they provided
for sitting on in these strange times, looking curiously at the super-men and super-women, and said,
"I am the Agent. My name is Alyx," and smiled. She
was in a rather good humor. It still amused her to
watch this whole place, the transparent columns the
women wore instead of clothing, the parts of the
walls that pulsated in and out and changed color, the
strange floor that waved like grass, the three-dimen-
sional vortices that kept springing to life on what
would have been the ceiling if it had only stayed in
one place (but it never did) and the general air of
unhappy, dogged, insistent, sad restlessness. "A little bit of home," the lieutenant had called it. He had
seemed to find particular cause for nostalgia in a
lime-green coil that sprang out of the floor whenever
anybody dropped anything, to eat it up, but it was
"not in proper order" and sometimes you had to fight
it for something you wanted to keep. The people
moved her a little closer to laughter. One of them
leaned toward her now.

"Pardon me," said this one effusively—it was one
of the ladies— "but is that face yours? I've heard
Trans-Temp does all sorts of cosmetic work and I
thought they might—"

"Why yes," said Alyx, hoping against hope to be
impolite. "Are those breasts yours? I can't help
noticing—"

"Not at all!" cried the lady happily. "Aren't they
wonderful? They're Adrian's. I mean they're by
Adrian."

"I think that's enough," said the lieutenant.

"Only we *rather wondered*," said the lady, elevating her indigo brows at what she seemed to have

taken as an insult, "why you keep yourself so covered
up. Is it a tribal rite? Are you deformed? Why don't
you get cosmetic treatment; you could have asked for
it, you know, I mean I think you could—" but here
everybody went pale and turned aside, just as if she
had finally managed to do something offensive and
All I did, she thought, *was take off my shift*.

One of the nuns fell to praying.

"All right, Agent," said the lieutenant, his voice a
bare whisper, "we believe you. Please put on your
clothes.

"Please, Agent," he said again, as if his voice were
failing him, but she did not move, only sat naked and
cross-legged with the old scars on her ribs and belly
showing in a perfectly natural and expectable way,
sat and looked at them one by one: the two nuns, the
lady, the young girl with her mouth hanging open
and the iridescent beads wound through three feet of
hair, the bald-headed boy with some contraption
strapped down over his ears, eyes and nose, the
artist and the middle-aged political man, whose right
cheek had begun to jump. The artist was leaning
forward with his hand cupped under one eye in the
old-fashioned and nearly unbelievable pose of someone
who has just misplaced a contact lens. He blinked
and looked up at her through a flood of mechanical
tears.

"The lieutenant," he said, coughing a little, "is
thinking of anaesthetics and the lady of surgery—I
really think you had better put your clothes back
on, by the way—and as to what the others think I'm
not so sure. I myself have only had my usual trouble
with these damned things and I don't really mind—"

"Please, Agent," said the young officer.

"But I don't think," said the artist, massaging one eye, "that you quite understand the effect you're creating."

"None of *you* has anything on," said Alyx.

"You have on your history," said the artist, "and we're not used to that, believe me. Not to history. Not to old she-wolves with livid marks running up their ribs and arms, and not to the idea of fights in which people are neither painlessly killed nor painlessly fixed up but linger on and die—slowly—or heal—slowly.

"Well!" he added, in a very curious tone of voice, "after all, we may all look like that before this is over."

"Buddha, no!" gasped a nun.

Alyx put her clothes on, tying the black belt around the black dress. "You may not look as bad," she said a bit sourly. "But you will certainly smell worse."

"And I," she added conversationally, "don't like pieces of plastic in people's teeth. I think it disgusting."

"Refined sugar," said the officer, "one of our minor vices," and then, with an amazed expression, he burst into tears.

"Well, well," muttered the young girl, "we'd better get on with it."

"Yes," said the middle-aged man, laughing nervously, " 'People for Every Need,' you know," and before he could be thoroughly rebuked for quoting the blazon of the Trans-Temporal Military Authority (Alyx heard the older woman begin lecturing him on the nastiness of calling anyone even by insinuation a thing, an agency, a means or an instrument, *anything* but a People, or as she said "a People People") he began to lead the file toward the door, with the girl coming next, a green tube in the middle of her mouth, the two nuns clinging together in shock, the bald-headed boy swaying a little as he walked, as if to unheard music, the lieutenant and the artist—who lingered.

"Where'd they pick you up?" he said, blinking again and fingering one eye.

"Off Tyre," said Alyx. "Where'd they pick *you* up?"

"We," said the artist, "are rich tourists. Can you believe it? Or refugees, rather. Caught up in a local war. A war on the surface of a planet, mind you; I don't believe I've heard of that in my lifetime."

"I have," said Alyx, "quite a few times," and with the lightest of light pushes she guided him toward the thing that passed for a decent door; the kind of thing she had run through, roaring with laughter, time after time at her first day at Trans-Temp, just for the pleasure of seeing it open up like a giant mouth and then pucker shut in an enormous expression of disgust.

"Babies!" she said.

"By the way," called back the artist, "I'm a flat-color man. What was your profession?"

"Murderer," said Alyx, and she stepped through the door.

"Raydos is the flat-color man," said the lieutenant, his feet up on what looked gratifyingly like a table. "Used to do wraparounds and walk-ins—very good walk-ins, too, I have a little education in that line myself—but he's gone wild about something called pigment on flats. Says the other stuff's too easy."

"Flats whats?" said Alyx.

"I don't know, any flat surface, I suppose," said the lieutenant. "And he's got those machines in his eyes which keep coming out, but he won't get retinotherapy. Says he likes having two kinds of vision. Most of us are born myopic nowadays, you know."

"I wasn't," said Alyx.

"Iris," the lieutenant went on, palming something and then holding it to his ear, "is pretty typical, though: young, pretty stable, ditto the older woman— oh yes, her name's Maudey—and Gavrily's a conamon, of course."

"Conamon?" said Alyx, with some difficulty.

"Influence," said the lieutenant, his face darkening a little. "Influence, you know. I don't like the man. That's too personal an evaluation, of course, but damn it, I'm a decent man. If I don't like him, I say I don't like him. He'd honor me for it."

"Wouldn't he kick your teeth in?" said Alyx.

"How much did they teach you at Trans-Temp?" said the lieutenant, after a pause.

"Not much," said Alyx.

"Well, anyway," said the lieutenant, a little desperately, "you've got Gavrily and he's a conamon, then Maudey—the one with the blue eyebrows, you know—"

"Dyed?" asked Alyx politely.

"Of course. Permanently. And the wienie—"

"Well, well!" said Alyx.

"You know," said the lieutenant, with sarcastic restraint, "you can't drink that stuff like wine. It's distilled. Do you know what distilled means?"

"Yes," said Alyx. "I found out the hard way."

"All right," said the lieutenant, jumping to his

feet, "all right! A wienie is a wienie. He's the one with the bald head. He calls himself Machine because he's an idiotic adolescent rebel and he wears that—that Trivia on his head to give himself twenty-four hours a day of solid nirvana, station NOTHING, turns off all stimuli when you want it to, operates psionically. We call it a Trivia because that's what it is and because forty years ago it was a Tri-V and I *despise* bald young inexistential rebels who refuse to relate!"

"Well, well," she said again.

"And the nuns," he said, "are nuns, whatever that means to you. It means nothing to me; I am not a religious man. You have got to get them from here to there, 'across the border' as they used to say, because they had money and they came to see Paradise and Paradise turned into—" He stopped and turned to her.

"You know all this," he said accusingly.

She shook her head.

"Trans-Temp—"

"Told me nothing."

"Well," said the lieutenant, "perhaps it's best. Perhaps it's best. What we need is a person who knows nothing. Perhaps that's exactly what we need."

"Shall I go home?" said Alyx.

"Wait," he said harshly, "and don't joke with me. Paradise is the world you're on. It's in the middle of a commercial war. I said commercial war; I'm military and I have nothing to do here except get killed trying to make sure the civilians are out of the way. That's what you're for. You get them" (he pressed something in the wall and it turned into a map; she recognized it instantly, even though there were no sea-monsters and no four winds puffing at the corners, which was rather a loss) "from here to here," he said. "B is a neutral base. They can get you off-planet."

"Is that all?"

"No, that's not all. Listen to me. If you want to exterminate a world, you blanket it with hell-bombs and for the next few weeks you've got a beautiful incandescent disk in the sky, very ornamental and very dead, and that's that. And if you want to strip-mine, you use something a little less deadly and four weeks later you go down in heavy shielding and dig up any damn thing you like, and *that's* that. And if you want to colonize, we have something that kills every form of animal and plant life on the planet and then you go down and cart off the local flora and fauna if they're poisonous or use them as mulch if they're usable. But you can't do any of that on Paradise."

She took another drink. She was not drunk.

"There is," he said, "every reason not to exterminate Paradise. There is every reason to keep her just as she is. The air and the gravity are near perfect, but you can't farm Paradise."

"Why not?" said Alyx.

"Why not?" said he. "Because it's all up and down and nothing, that's why. It's glaciers and mountains and coral reefs; it's rainbows of inedible fish in continental slopes; it's deserts, cacti, waterfalls going nowhere, rivers that end in lakes of mud and skies—and sunsets—and that's all it is. That's *all*." He sat down.

"Paradise," he said, "is impossible to colonize, but it's still too valuable to mess up. It's too beautiful." He took a deep breath. "It happens," he said, "to be a tourist resort."

Alyx began to giggle. She put her hand in front of her mouth but only giggled the more; then she let go and hoorawed, snorting derisively, bellowing, weeping with laughter.

"That," said the lieutenant stiffly, "is pretty ghastly." She said she was sorry.

"I don't know," he said, rising formally, "just what they are going to fight this war with. Sound on the buildings, probably; they're not worth much; and for the people every nasty form of explosive or neuronic hand-weapon that's ever been devised. But no radiation. No viruses. No heat. Nothing to mess up the landscape or the ecological balance. Only they've got a net stretched around the planet that monitors everything up and down the electromagnetic spectrum. Automatically, each millisecond. If you went out in those mountains, young woman, and merely sharpened your knife on a rock, the sparks would bring a radio homer in on you in fifteen seconds. No, less."

"Thank you for telling me," said she, elevating her eyebrows.

"No fires," he said, "no weapons, no transportation, no automatic heating, no food processing, nothing airborne. They'll have some infrared from you but they'll probably think you're local wildlife. But by the way, if you hear anything or see anything overhead, we think the best thing for all of you would be to get down on all fours and pretend to be yaks. I'm not fooling."

"Poseidon!" said she, under her breath.

"Oh, one other thing," he said. "We can't have induction currents, you know. Might happen you'll have to give up everything metal. The knife, please."

She handed it over, thinking *If I don't get that back—*

"Trans-Temp sent a synthetic substitute, of course," the lieutenant went on briskly. "And crossbows—same stuff—and packs, and we'll give you all the irradiated food we can get you. And insulated suits."

"And ignorance," said she. His eyebrows went up.

"Sheer ignorance," she repeated. "The most valuable commodity of all. Me. No familiarity with mechanical transportation or the whatchamacallits. Stupid. Can't read. Used to walking. Never used a compass in my life. Right?"

"Your skill—" he began.

From each of her low sandals she drew out what had looked like part of the ornamentation and flipped both knives expertly at the map on the wall—both hands, simultaneously—striking precisely at point A and point B.

"You can have those, too," she said.

The lieutenant bowed. He pressed the wall again. The knives hung in a cloudy swirl, then in nothing, clear as air, while outside appeared the frosty blue sky, the snowy foothills drawing up to the long, easy swelling crests of Paradise's oldest mountain chain— old and easy, not like some of the others, and most unluckily, only two thousand meters high.

"By God!" said Alyx, fascinated, "I don't believe I've ever seen snow before."

There was a sound behind her, and she turned. The lieutenant had fainted.

They weren't right. She had palmed them a hundred times, flipped them, tested their balance, and they weren't right. Her aim was off. They felt soapy. She complained to the lieutenant, who said you couldn't expect exactly the same densities in synthetics, and sat shivering in her insulated suit in the shed, nodding now and again at the workers assembling their packs, while the lieutenant appeared and disappeared into the walls, a little frantically. "Those are just androids," said Iris good-humoredly. "Don't nod to them. Don't you think it's *fun?*"

"Go cut your hair," said Alyx.

Iris's eyes widened.

"And tell that other woman to do the same," Alyx added.

"Zap!" said Iris cryptically, and ambled off. It was detestably chilly. The crossbows impressed her, but she had had no time to practice with them (*Which will be remedied by every one of you bastards*, she thought) and no time to get used to the cold, which all the rest of them seemed to like. She felt stupid. She began to wonder about something and tried to catch the lieutenant by the arm, cursing herself in her own language, trying to think in her own language and failing, giving up on the knives and finally herding everyone outside into the snow to practice with the crossbows. The wienie was surprisingly good. He stayed at it two hours after the others drifted off, repeating and repeating; Iris came back with her cut hair hanging around her face and confided that she had been named after part of a camera; the lieutenant's hands began to shake a little on each appearance; and Machine became a dead shot. She stared at him. All the time he had kept the thing he wore on his head clamped over ears and eyes and nose. "He can see through it if he wants to," said Iris. Maudey was talking earnestly in a corner with Gavrily, the middle-aged politician, and the whole thing was taking on the air of a picnic. Alyx grew exasperated. She pinched a nerve in the lieutenant's arm the next time he darted across the shed and stopped him, he going "aaah!" and rubbing his arm; he said, "I'm very sorry, but—" She did it again.

"Look here," she said, "I may be stupid, but I'm not that stupid—"

"Sorry," he said, and was gone again, into one of the walls, right into one of the walls.

"He's busy," said Raydos, the flat-color man. "They're sending someone else through and he's trying to talk them out of it."

"Joy," said Alyx.

"Have you noticed," said Raydos, "how your vocabulary keeps expanding? That's the effect of hypnotic language training; they can't give you the whole context consciously, you see, only the sectors where the languages overlap so you keep coming up against these unconscious, 'buried' areas where a sudden context triggers off a whole pre-implanted pattern. It's like packing your frazzle; you always remember where it is when you need it, but of course it's always at the bottom. You'll be feeling rather stupid for a few days, but it'll wear off."

"A frazzle?" said Maudey, drifting over. "Why, I imagine she doesn't even know what a frazzle is."

"I told you to cut your hair," said Alyx.

"A frazzle," said Gavrily, "is the greatest invention of the last two centuries, let me assure you. Only in some cities, of course; they have a decibel limit on most. And of course it's frazzle*s*, one for each ear; they neutralize the sound-waves, you know, absolute silence, although" (he went on and everybody giggled) "I have had them used against *me* at times!"

"I would use one against your campaigns all the

time," said Iris, joining them. "See, I cut my hair! Isn't it *fun?*" and with a sudden jerk she swung her head down at Alyx to show her short, silver hair, swinging it back and forth and giggling hysterically while Gavrily laughed and tried to catch at it. They were all between two and two-and-a half meters tall. It was intolerable. They were grabbing at Iris's hair and explaining to each other about the different frazzles they had used and the sound-baffles of the apartments they had been in, and simulated forests with walls that went *tweet-tweet* and how utterly lag it was to install free-fall in your bathroom (if only you could afford it) and take a bath in a bubble, though you must be careful not to use *too* large a bubble or you might suffocate. She dove between them, unnoticed, into the snow where Machine practiced shooting bolts at a target, his eyes hooded in lenses, his ears muffled, his feet never moving. He was on his way to becoming a master. There was a sudden rise in the excited gabble from inside, and turning, Alyx saw someone come out of the far wall with the lieutenant, the first blond person she had seen so far, for everyone except the lieutenant seemed to be some kind of indeterminate, mixed racial type, except for Maudey and Iris, who had what Alyx would have called a dash of the Asiatic. Everyone was a little darker than herself and a little more pronounced in feature, as if they had crossbred in a hundred ways to even out at last, but here came the lieutenant with what Alyx would have called a freak Northman, another giant (she did not give a damn); and then left him inside and came out and sat down on the outside bench.

"Lieutenant," said Alyx, "why are you sending me on this picnic?"

He made a vague gesture, looking back into the shed, fidgeting like a man who has a hundred things to do and cannot make up his mind where to start.

"An explorer," said the lieutenant, "amateur. Very famous."

"Why don't you send them with him and stop this nonsense, then!" she exploded.

"It's not nonsense," he said. "Oh, no."

"Isn't it? A ten-day walk over those foothills? No large predators? An enemy that doesn't give a damn about us? A path a ten-year-old could follow. An explorer right to hand. *And how much do I cost?*"

"Agent," said the lieutenant, "I know civilians," and he looked back in the shed again, where the newcomer had seized Iris and was kissing her, trying to get his hands inside her suit while Gavrily danced around the couple. Maudey was chatting with Raydos, who made sketches on a pad. "Maybe, Agent," said the lieutenant, very quietly, "I know how much you cost, and maybe it is very important to get these people out of here before one of them is killed, and maybe, Agent, there is more to it than that when you take people away from their—from their electromagnetic spectrum, shall we say. That man" (and he indicated the blond) "has never been away from a doctor and armor and helpers and vehicles and cameras in his life." He looked down into the snow. "I shall have to take their drugs away from them," he said. "They won't like that. They are going to walk on their own feet for two hundred and forty kilometers. That may be ten days to you but you will see how far you get with them. You cost more than you think,

Agent, and let me tell you something else" (here he lifted his face intently) "which may help you to understand, and that is, Agent, that this is the first time the Trans-Temporal Authority—which is a military authority, thanks be for that—has ever transported anyone from the past for any purpose whatsoever. And that was accidental—I can't explain that now. All this talk about Agents here and Agents there is purely mythological, fictional, you might say, though why people insist on these silly stories I don't know, for there is only one Agent and that is the first and the last Agent and that, Agent—is you. But don't try to tell them. They won't believe you."

"Is that why you're beginning with a picnic?" said Alyx.

"It will not be a picnic," he said and he looked at the snow again, at Machine's tracks, at Machine, who stood patiently sending bolt after bolt into the paint-sprayed target, his eyes and nose and ears shut to the whole human world.

"What will happen to you?" said Alyx, finally.

"I?" said the young officer. "Oh, I shall die! but that's nothing to you," and he went back into the shed immediately, giving instructions to what Iris had called androids, clapping the giant Northerner on the back, calling Alyx to come in. "This is Gunnar," he said. They shook hands. It seemed an odd custom to Alyx and apparently to everyone else, for they sniggered. He flashed a smile at everyone as the pack was fitted onto his back. "Here," he said, holding out a box, "*Cannabis*," and Iris, making a face, handed over a crumpled bundle of her green cylinders. "I hope I don't have to give these up," said Raydos quietly, stowing his sketchbook into his pack;

"They are not power tools, you know," and he watched dispassionately while Maudey argued for a few minutes, looked a bit sulky and finally produced a tiny, ornate orange cylinder. She took a sniff from it and handed it over to the lieutenant. Iris looked malicious. Gavrily confessed he had nothing. The nuns, of course, said everybody, had nothing and would not carry weapons. Everyone had almost forgotten about them. They all straggled out into the snow to where Machine was picking up the last of his bolts. He turned to face them, like a man who would be contaminated by the very air of humankind, nothing showing under the hood of his suit but his mouth and the goggled lenses and snout of another species.

"I must have that, too," said Alyx, planting both feet on the ground.

"Well, after all," said Maudey, "you can't expect—"

"Teach the young fellow a lesson!" said Gavrily.

"Shall I take it off?" remarked the amateur explorer (*And actor*, thought Alyx) striding forward, smile flashing while Machine bent slowly for the last of his bolts, fitting it back into the carrying case, not looking at anyone or hearing anything, for all she knew, off on station N-O-T-H-I-N-G twenty-four hours each Earth day, the boy who called himself Machine because he hated the lot of them.

"If you touch him," said Alyx evenly, "I shall kill you," and as they gasped and giggled (Gunnar gave a rueful smile; he had been outplayed) she walked over to him and held out her hand. The boy took off his Trivia and dropped it into the snow; the showing of any face would have been a shock but his was completely denuded of hair, according (she supposed) to the fashion he followed: eyebrows, eyelashes and scalp, and his eyes were a staring, brilliant, shattering, liquescent blue. "You're a good shot," she said. He was not interested. He looked at them without the slightest emotion. "He hardly *ever* talks," said Maudey. They formed a straggling line, walking off toward the low hills and Alyx, a thought suddenly coming to her, said off-handedly before she knew it, "You're mother and daughter, aren't you?"

The entire line stopped. Maudey had instantly turned away, Iris looked furiously angry, Gunnar extremely surprised and only Raydos patiently waited, as usual, watching them all. Machine remained Machine. The nuns were hiding their mouths, shocked, with both hands.

"I thought—"

"If you must—"

"Don't you ever—!"

The voices came at her from all sides.

"Shut up," she said, "and march. I'll do worse yet." The column began again. "Faster," she said. "You know," she added cruelly, carefully listening for the effect of her words, "one of you may die." Behind her there was a stiffening, a gasp, a terrified murmur at such bad, bad taste. "Yes, yes," she said, hammering it in, "one of us may very well die before this trip is over," and quickened her pace in the powdery snow, the even, crisp, shallow snow, as easy to walk in as if put down expressly for a pleasure jaunt, a lovely picnic under the beautiful blue heaven of this best of all possible tourist resorts. "Any of us," she repeated carefully, "any one of us at all," and all of a sudden she thought *Why, that's true. That's very true.* She sighed. "Come on," she said.

*   *   *

At first she had trouble keeping up with them;
then, as they straggled and loitered, she had no
trouble at all; and finally they had trouble keeping
up with her. The joking and bantering had stopped.
She let them halt fairly early (the lieutenant had
started them out—wisely, she thought—late in the
afternoon) under an overhanging rock. Mountains so
old and smooth should not have many caves and
outflung walls where a climbing party can rest, but
the mountains of Paradise had them. The late, late
shadows were violet blue and the sunlight going up
the farthest peaks went up like the sunlight in a
children's book, with a purity and perfection of color
changing into color and the snow melting into cobalt
evening which Alyx watched with—

Wonder. Awe. Suspicion. But nobody was about.
However, they were making trouble when she got
back. They were huddled together, rather irritable,
talking insatiably as if they had to make up for their
few silent hours in the afternoon's march. It was ten
degrees below freezing and would not drop much
lower at this time of year, the lieutenant had prom-
ised, even though there might be snow, a fact (she
thought) for which they might at least look properly
thankful.

"Well?" she said, and everyone smiled.

"We've been talking," said Maudey brightly. "About
what to do."

"What to do what?" said Alyx.

"What to do next," said Gavrily, surprised. "What
else?"

The two nuns smiled.

"We think," said Maudey, "that we ought to go

much more slowly and straight across, you know,
and Gunnar wants to take photographs—"

"Manual," said the explorer, flashing his teeth.

"And not through the mountains," said Maudey.
"It's so up-and-down, you know."

"And *hard*," said Iris.

"And we voted," said Maudey, "and Gunnar won."

"Won what?" said Alyx.

"Well, *won*," said Gavrily, "you know."

"Won what?" repeated Alyx, a little sharply; they
all looked embarrassed, not (she thought, surprised)
for themselves but for her. Definitely for her.

"They want Gunnar to lead them." No one knew
who had spoken. Alyx looked from one to the other
but they were as surprised as she; then she whirled
around sharply, for it was Machine who had spoken,
Machine who had never before said one word. He
squatted in the snow, his back against the rock,
looking past them. He spoke precisely and without
the slightest inflection.

"Thank you," said Alyx. "Is that what you all want?"

"Not I," said Raydos.

"I do," said Maudey.

"And I do," said Iris. "I think—"

"I do," said Gavrily.

"We think—" the nuns began.

She was prepared to blast their ears off, to tell
them just what she thought of them. She was shaking
all over. She began in her own language, however,
and had to switch clumsily into theirs, trying to
impress upon them things for which she could not
find words, things for which she did not believe the
language had words at all: that she was in charge of
them, that this was not a pleasure party, that they

might die, that it was her job to be responsible for
them, and that whoever led them, or how, or why,
or in what way, was none of their business. She kept
saying it over and over that it was none of their
business.

"Oh, everything is everybody's business," said
Gavrily cheerfully, as if her feeling that way were
quite natural, quite wrong and also completely irrelevant, and they all began to chat again. Gunnar came
up to her sympathetically and took hold of her hands.
She twisted in his grasp, instinctively beginning a
movement that would have ended in the pit of his
stomach, but he grasped each of her wrists, saying
"No, no, you're not big enough," and holding her
indulgently away from him with his big, straight,
steady arms. He had begun to laugh, saying "I know
this kind of thing too, you see!" when she turned in
his grip, taking hold of his wrists in the double hold
used by certain circus performers, and bearing down
sharply on his arms (he kept them steady for just
long enough, thinking he was still holding her off)
she lifted herself up as if on a gate, swung under his
guard and kicked him right under the arch of the
ribs. Luckily the suit cushioned the blow a little. The
silence that followed—except for his gasping—was
complete. They had never, she supposed, seen Gunnar
on the ground that way before. Or anyone else. Then
Maudey threw up.

"I am sorry," said Alyx, "but I cannot talk to you.
You will do as I say," and she walked away from
them and sat down near Machine, whose eyes had
never left the snow in front of him, who was making
furrows in it with one hand. She sat there, listening
to the frightened whispers in back of her, knowing

she had behaved badly and wanting to behave even worse all over again, trembling from head to foot with rage, knowing they were only children, cursing herself abominably—and the Trans-Temporal Authority—and her own idiot helplessness and the "commercial war," whatever that might be, and each one of her charges, individually and collectively, until the last of the unfamiliar stars came out and the sky turned black. She fell asleep in her wonderful insulated suit, as did they all, thinking *Oh, God, not even keeping a watch,* and not caring; but she woke from time to time to hear their secure breathing, and then the refrain of a poem came to her in the language of Phoenician Tyre, those great traders who had gone even to the gates of Britain for tin, where the savages painted themselves blue and believed stones to be sacred, not having anything else, the poor bastards. The refrain of the poem was *What will become of me?* which she changed to *What will become of them?* until she realized that nothing at all would become of them, for they did not have to understand her. *But I,* she thought, *will have to understand them.*

And then, sang the merchants of Tyre, that great city, *what, O God, will become of me?*

She had no trouble controlling them the next day; they were much too afraid of her. Gunnar, however, plainly admired her and this made her furious. She was getting into her stride now, over the easy snow, getting used to the pack resting on some queer contraption not on her back but on her hips, as they all did, and finding the snow easy to walk over. The sun of Paradise shone in an impossibly blue sky, which she found upsetting. But the air was good; the air was wonderful. She was getting used to walking. She took to outpacing them, long-legged as they were, and sitting in the snow twenty meters away, cross-legged like a monk, until they caught up, then watching them expressionlessly—like a trail-marker—until they passed her, casting back looks that were far from pleasant; and then repeating the whole thing all over again. After the noon meal she stopped that; it was too cruel. They sat down in the middle of a kind of tilted wasteland—it was the side of a hill but one's up-and-down got easily mixed in the mountains—and ate everything in the plastic bags marked Two-B, none of it dried and all of it magnificent; Alyx had never had such food in her life on a trip before: fruits and spicy little buns, things like sausages, curls of candy that sprung round your finger and smelled of ginger, and for drinking, the bags you filled with snow and hung inside your suit to melt. Chilly, but efficient. She ate half of everything and put the rest back, out of habit. With venomous looks, everybody else ate everything. "She's tinier than we are," Gunnar said, trying to smooth things over, "and I'm sure there's more than enough!" Alyx reached inside her suit and scratched one arm. "There may not be enough," she said, "can't tell," and returned the rest to her pack, wondering why you couldn't trust adults to eat one meal at a time without marking it with something. She could not actually read the numbers. But perhaps it was a custom or a ritual. *A primitive ritual,* she thought. She was in much better spirits. *A primitive ritual,* she repeated to herself, *practiced through inveterate and age-old superstition.* She dearly longed to play with the curly candy again. She sud-

denly remembered the epigram made one Mediterranean evening by the Prince of Tyre on the palace
roof over a game of chess and began spontaneously to
tell it to them, with all that had accompanied it: the
sails in the bay hanging disembodied and white like
the flowers in the royal garden just before the last
light goes, the smell of the bay at low tide, not as
bad as inlanders think but oddly stimulating, bringing to one's mind the complex processes of decay and
life, the ins and outs of things, the ins and outs of
herself who could speak six dialects from the gutter
to the palace, and five languages, one of them the
old Egyptian; and how she had filched the rather
valuable chess set later, for the Tyrians were more
than a little ostentatious despite their reputation for
tough-mindedness, odd people, the adventurers, the
traders, the merchants of the Mediterranean, halfway in their habits between the cumbersome digni-
ties of royal Egypt and the people of Crete, who
knew how to live if anyone ever had, decorating
their eggshell-thin bowls with sea-creatures made
unbelievably graceful or with musicians lying in beds
of anemones and singing and playing on the flute.
She laughed and quoted the epigram itself, which
had been superb, a double pun in two languages,
almost a pity to deprive a man like that of a chess set
worth—

Nobody was listening. She turned around and
stared at them. For a moment she could not think,
only smell and stare, and then something shifted
abruptly inside her head and she could name them
again: Gunnar, Machine, Raydos, Maudey, Iris,
Gavrily, the two nuns. She had been talking in her
own language. They shambled along, leaning forward

against the pull of the hip-packs, ploughing up the snow in their exhaustion, these huge, soft people to whom one could not say anything of any consequence. Their faces were drawn with fatigue. She motioned them to stop and they toppled down into the snow without a word, Iris's cheek right in the cold stuff itself and the two nuns collapsed across each other in a criss-cross. They had worn, she believed, a symbol on a chain around their necks something like the symbol . . . but she did not want to fall back into her own speech again. She felt extremely stupid. "I am sorry that you're tired," she said.

"No, no," muttered Gunnar, his legs straight out in the snow, staring ahead.

"We'll take a break," she said, wondering where the phrase had come from all of a sudden. The sun was hardly halfway down in the sky. She let them rest for an hour or more until they began to talk; then she forced them to their feet and began it all again, the nightmare of stumbling, slipping, sliding, the unmistakable agonies of plodding along with cramped legs and a drained body, the endless pull of the weight at one's back. . . . She remembered what the lieutenant had said about people deprived of their electromagnetic spectrum. Long before night-fall she stopped them and let them revive while she scouted around for animal tracks—or human tracks—or anything—but found nothing. Paradise was a winter sportsman's—well, paradise. She asked about animals, but nobody knew for certain or nobody was telling, although Gunnar volunteered the information that Paradise had not been extensively mapped. Maudey complained of a headache. They ate again, this time from a bag marked Two-C, still with nothing dried (*Why carry all that weight in water?* Alyx thought, remembering how the desert people would ride for weeks on nothing but ground wheat), stowed empty, deflated Two-C into their packs and lay down—right in the middle of a vast, empty snow-field. It gave them all the chills. Alyx lay a little apart, to let them talk about her as she was sure they would, and then crept closer. They were talking about her. She made a face and retreated again. A little later she got them up and into the hills above until at sunset it looked as if they would have to sleep in the open. She left them huddled together and went looking about for a cave, but found nothing, until, coming around the path at the edge of a rather sharp drop, she met Machine coming the other way.

"What the devil—!" she exclaimed, planting herself in his way, arms akimbo, face tilted up to look into his.

"Cave," he said blandly and walked up the side of the hill with his long legs, around above her, and down on to the path. He even got back to the others faster than she did, though sweat was running from under his hood.

"All right," said Alyx as she rejoined them, "it's found a cave," but she found them all standing up ready to go, most yawning, all trying not to stagger, and Gunnar beaming heartily in a way that made her wish she had hit him lower down, much lower down, when she had the chance. *Professional*, she thought. "He told us," said Maudey with her head in the air, "before you came," and the troop of them marched— more or less—after the bald-headed boy, who had found a shallow depression in the rock where they could gather in relative comfort. If there had been a wind, although there was no wind on Paradise, the place would have sheltered them; if it had been snowing, although it was not snowing on Paradise, the place would have protected them; and if anyone had been looking for them, although apparently no one was, the place would have afforded a partial concealment. They all got together; they sat down; some of them threw back their hoods; and then they began to talk. They talked and talked and talked. They discussed whether Maudey had behaved impatiently towards Iris, or whether Iris had tried to attract Gunnar, or whether the nuns were participating enough in the group interaction, with due allowance made for their religious faith, of course, and whether the relationship between Raydos and Gunnar was competitive, and what Gavrily felt about the younger men, and whether he wanted to sleep with Iris, and on and on and on about how they felt about each other and how they ought to feel about each other and how they had felt about each other with an insatiability that stunned Alyx and a wealth of detail that fascinated her, considering that all these interactions had been expressed by people staggering with fatigue, under a load of eleven kilos per person, and exposed to a great deal of unaccustomed exercise. She felt sorry for Machine. She wished she had a Trivia herself. She lay at the mouth of the cave until she could not stand it; then she retreated to the back and lay on her stomach until her elbows galled her; then she took off into the snow in front of the cave where there was a little light and lay on her back, watching the strange stars.

"We do it all the time, I'm afraid," said a man's

voice beside her. *Raydos*, she thought instantly. *Machine would have said "they."*

"It doesn't—" he went on, "it doesn't mean—well, it doesn't mean anything, really. It's a kind of habit."

She said nothing.

"I came out," he said, "to apologize for us and to ask you about the watch. I've explained it to the others. I will take the first watch.

"I have read about such things," he added proudly.

Still she said nothing.

"I wish you would repeat to me," he went on slowly, and she realized he was trying to talk simply to her, "what you said this morning in the other language."

"I can't," she said, and then she added, feeling stupid, "the witty saying of . . . of the Prince of Tyre."

"The epigram," he said patiently.

"Epigram," she repeated.

"What did the Prince of Tyre say?"

"He said," she translated, feeling her way desperately, "that in any . . . time . . . any time you . . . have something, whatever tendencies—whatever factors in a situation you have, whatever of these can—can unpredict—"

"Can go wrong," said he.

"Can go wrong," she parroted, caught halfway between two worlds. "Can wrong itself. It—" but here the man beside her burst into such a roar of laughter that she turned to look at him.

"The proverbial Third Law," he said. "Whatever can go wrong, will," and he burst into laughter again. He was big, but they were all big; in the faint glimmer of the snow-field . . .

His hood was back; his hair was pale.

Gunnar.

Alone once more, she lay several meters farther out with her arms wrapped about herself, thinking a bit savagely that the "witty saying" of His Highness had been expressed in two words, not five, both of them punning, both rhymed and each with a triple internal assonance that exactly contrasted with the other.

Damned barbarians! She snapped to herself, and fell asleep.

The next day it began to snow, the soft, even snow of Paradise, hiding their footprints and the little bags of excrement they buried here and there. The insulated suits were ingenious. Her people began to talk to her, just a little, condescendingly but trying to be affable, more and more cheerful as they neared Point B, where they would need her no more, where she could dwindle into a memory, an anecdote, a party conversation: "Did you know, I once met the most *fascinating*—" They really had very little imagination, Alyx thought. In their place she would be asking everything: where she came from, who she was, how she lived, about the desert people who worshiped the wind god, what the Tyrians ate, their economic system, their families, their beliefs, their feelings, their clothes, the Egyptians, the Minoans, how the Minoans made those thin, dyed bowls, how they traded ostrich eggs and perfumes from Egypt, what sort of ships they sailed, how it felt to rob a house, how it felt to cut a throat. . . . But all they did was talk about themselves.

"You ought to have cosmetic surgery," said Maudey. "I've had it on my face and my breasts. It's ingenious. Of course I had a good doctor. And you have to be careful dyeing eyebrows and eyelashes, although the genetic alterations are usually pretty stable. But they might *spread,* you know. Can you imagine having a *blue forehead?*"

"I ran away from home," said Iris, "at the age of fifteen and joined a Youth Core. Almost everyone has Youth Cores, although mine wasn't a delinquent Youth Core and some people will tell you that doesn't count. But let me tell you, it changed my life. It's better than hypnotic psychotherapy. They call it a Core because it forms the core of your adolescent rebellion, don't you see, and I would have been nobody without it, absolutely nobody, it changed my whole life and all my values. Did you ever run away from home?"

"Yes," said Alyx. "I starved."

"Nobody starves any more," said Iris. "A Youth Core to fit each need. I joined a middle-status Youth Core. Once you're past fourteen you needn't drag—um—your family into everything. We forget about that. It's much better."

"Some people call me a Conamon," said Gavrily, "but where would we be without them? There are commercial wars and wars; you know all about that. The point is there are no more wars. I mean real wars. That would be a terrible thing. And if you get caught in a commercial war, it's your own fault, you see. Mixed interests. Mixed economy. I deal in people. Sounds bad, doesn't it? Some people would say I manage people, but *I* say I help them. I work *with* them. I form values. Can you imagine what it would be like without us? No one to bring your group interests to. No one to mediate between you and the army or you and business or you and government. Why, there wouldn't *be* any local government, really, though of course I'm not Gov; I'm Con. Mixed interests. It's the only way."

"Wrap-arounds!" said Raydos contemptuously. "Anybody can build a wrap-around. Simplest thing in the world. The problem is to recover the purity of the medium—I hope I'm not boring you—and to recover the purity of the medium you have to withdraw within its boundaries, not stretch them until they crack. I've done environments until I'm sick of them. I want something you can walk around, not something that walks around you. Lights geared to heartbeats, drug combinations, vertigo—I'm through with all that; it's mere vulgarity. Have you ever tried to draw something? Just draw something? Wait a minute; stand still." (And he sketched a few lines on a piece of paper.) "There! *That's* avant-garde for you!"

"The consciousness," said the nuns, speaking softly one after the other, "must be expanded to include the All. That is the only true church. Of course, that is what *we* believe. We do not wish to force our beliefs on others. We are the ancient church of consciousness and Buddha, nearly six hundred years old; I do hope that when we get back you'll attend a service with us. Sex is only part of the ceremony. The drugs are the main part. Of course we're not using them now, but we do carry them. The lieutenant knew we would never touch them. Not while there's the possibility of violence. The essence of violence violates consciousness while the consciousness of expanded consciousness correlates with the essence of the All which is Love, extended Love and the deepening and expanding of experience implied by the consciousness-expanded consciousness."

"You *do* understand," they chorused anxiously, "don't you?"

"Yes," said Alyx, "perfectly."

Gunnar talked passionately about electronics.

"Now there must be some way," he said, "to neutralize this electromagnetic watch-grid they've set up or to polarize it. Do you think polarization would ring the alarm? It might be damn fun! We're only behaving like parts of the landscape now—you *will* stop me if you don't understand, won't you—but there must be regions in the infra-bass where the shock waves—damn! Paradise doesn't have faults and quakes—well, then, the ultra-hard—they must have the cosmic rays down to the twentieth place—somehow— If I had only brought—you know, I think I could rig up some kind of interference—of course they'd spot that—but just think of the equipment—"

Machine said nothing at all. She took to walking with Machine. They walked through the soft, falling snow of Paradise in absolute silence under a sky that dropped feathers like the sky in a fairy tale, like a sky she had never seen before that made endless pillows and hummocks of the rounded stones of Paradise, stones just large enough to sit on, as if someone had been before them all the way providing armchairs and tables. Machine was very restful. On the tenth day she took his arm and leaned against him briefly; on the eleventh day he said:

"Where do you come from?"

"I come," she said softly, "from great cities and palaces and back-alleys and cemeteries and rotten ships."

"And where," she added, "do you come from?"

"Nowhere!" said Machine—and he spat on the snow.

On the sixteenth day of their ten-day journey they found Base B. Everyone had been excited all day— "picnicky" Alyx called it. Maudey had been digging her fingers into her hair and lamenting the absence of something called an electric tease; Gavrily was poking both women, a little short of breath; and Gunnar displayed his smile—that splendid smile—a little too often to be accounted for by the usual circumstances and laughed a good deal to himself.

"Oh golly, oh gosh, oh golly, oh golly, oh gosh!" sang Iris.

"Is that what they taught you at your Core?" said Raydos dryly.

"Yes," said Iris sniffishly. "*Do* you mind?" and she went on singing the words while Raydos made a face. "Didn't you go to a Core?" said Iris and when Raydos informed her that he had gone to a School (whatever that was) instead, Iris sang "Oh golly, oh gosh" so loud that Alyx told her to stop.

"Animals don't sing," said Alyx.

"Well, I hope you're not being moralistic—" Iris began.

"Animals," said Alyx, "don't sing. People sing. People can be caught. People can be killed. Stop singing."

"But we're so near," said Gunnar.

"Come on," said Gavrily. He began to run. Maudey was shepherding the nuns, chattering excitedly; everything was there—the line of boulders, the hill, a little dip in the snow, up another hill (a steep one this time) and there was Base B. Everybody could go home now. It was all over. They ran up to the top of the hill and nearly tumbled over one another in confusion, Gavrily with his arms spread out against the sky, one of the nuns fallen on one knee and Iris nearly knocking Maudey over.

Base B was gone. In the little dell where there should have been a metal shed with a metal door leading underground, to safety, to home, to the Army, to a room where the ceiling whirled so familiarly ("a little bit of home") and coiled thingamajigs which ate whatever you dropped on the grassy floor, there was no metal shed and no metal door. There was something like a splotch of metal foil smashed flat and a ragged hole in the middle of it, and as they watched, something indeterminate came out of the hole. There was a faint noise in the sky.

"Scatter!" cried Alyx. "Down on your knees!" and as they stood there gaping, she slammed the three nearest across the face and then the others so that when the air vehicle—no one looked up to get a clear view of it—came barreling over the horizon, they were all down on their hands and knees, pretending to be animals. Alyx got down just in time. When the thing had gone, she dared to look into the dell again, where the indeterminate thing had split into four things, which stood at the edges of an exact square while a box the size of a small room floated slowly down between them. The moment it landed they burrowed into it, or were taking it apart; she could not tell. "Lie flat," said Alyx softly. "Don't talk. Gunnar, use your binoculars." *No decent knife,* she thought wryly, *not even a fire, but these marvelous things we do have.*

"I don't see—" began Iris spiritedly.

"Shut up," said Alyx. He was focusing the binoculars. She knew about lenses because she had learned to do it with her own pair. Finally he took them away from his eyes and stared for a few moments into the snow. Then he said, "You can stand up now."

"Is it safe?" cried one of the nuns. "Can we go down now?"

"The snow makes it hard to see," said Gunnar slowly, "but I do not think so. No, I do not think so. Those are commercial usuforms, unpacking a food storage container. They are not Army. Army never uses commercial equipment."

"I think," he said, "that Base B has been taken," and he began quite openly and unashamedly to cry. The snow of Paradise (for it had begun to snow) fell on his cheeks and mingled with his tears, fell as beautifully as feathers from pillows, as if Hera were shaking out the feather quilts of Heaven while the amateur explorer cried and the seven people who had looked to him as their last hope looked first at each other—but there was no help there—and finally—hesitantly—but frightened, oh were they frightened!—at Alyx.

"All right," she said, "it's my show."

"Come on, come on!" she snapped, with all the contempt she could muster, "what's the matter with the lot of you? You're not dead; you're not paralyzed; look alive, will you? I've been in tighter spots than this and I've come out; you there" (she indicated Machine) "pinch them awake, will you! Oh, *will* you snap out of it!" and she shook Gunnar violently, thinking him the most likely to have already recovered. He, at least, had cried. She felt surrounded by enormous puppies.

"Yes—yes—I'm all right," he said at last.

"Listen," she said, "I want to know about those things. When will there be another air vehicle?"

"I don't know," he said.

"How long will it take them to unpack, unload, whatever?".

"About . . . about an hour, I think," he said.

"Then there won't be another box for an hour," she said. "How far can they see?"

"See?" said Gunnar helplessly.

"How far can they perceive, then?" persisted Alyx. "Perceive, you idiot, look, see, hear, touch—what the devil, you know what I mean!"

"They—they perceive," said Gunnar slowly, taking a deep breath, "at about three meters. Four meters. They're meant for close work. They're a low form."

"How do you kill them?"

He indicated the center of his chest.

"Can we do it with a crossbow?" she said.

"Ye-es," he said, "very close range, but—"

"Good. If one of them goes, what happens?"

"I'm not sure," he said, sitting up abruptly. "I think nothing would happen for a few seconds. They've—" (he lifted the binoculars to his eyes again) "they've established some kind of unloading pattern. They seem to be working pretty independently. That model—if it is that model—would let one of them lie maybe fifteen-twenty seconds before radioing down for a removal . . . Perhaps longer. They might simply change the pattern."

"And if all four went dead?"

"Why, nothing would happen," he said, "nothing at all. Not—not for about half an hour. Maybe more. Then they'd begin to wonder downstairs why the stuff wasn't coming in. But we do have half an hour."

"So," said Alyx, "you come with me. And Machine. And—"

"I'll come!" said Iris, clasping her hands nervously. Alyx shook her head. "If you're discriminating against me," said Iris wonderingly, "because I'm a *girl*—"

"No, dear, you're a lousy shot," said Alyx. "Gunnar, you take that one; Machine, that one; I take two. All of you! If they fall and nothing happens, you come down that slope like hell and if something does happen, you go the other way twice as fast! We need food. I want dried stuff, light stuff; you'll recognize it, I won't. Everything you can carry. And keep your voices down. Gunnar, what's—"

"Calories," said Machine.

"Yes, yes, lots of that," said Alyx impatiently, "that—that stuff. Come on," and she started down the slope, waving the other two to circle the little dell. Piles of things—they could not see very well through the falling snow—were growing on each side of the box. The box seemed to be slowly collapsing. The moving things left strange tracks, half-human, half-ploughed; she crossed one of them where a thing had wandered up the side of the hollow for some reason of its own. She hoped they did not do that often. She found her bare hands sweating on the stock of the bow, her gloves hanging from her wrists; *if only they had been men!* she thought, and not things that could call for help in a silent voice called radio, or fall down and not be dead, or you didn't know whether they were dead or not. Machine was in position.

Gunnar raised his bow. They began to close in silently and slowly until Gunnar stopped; then she sighted on the first and shot. They were headless, with a square protuberance in the middle of the "chest" and an assemblage of many coiled arms that ended in pincers, blades, hooks, what looked like plates. It went down, silently. She turned for the second, carefully reloading the bow, only to find Machine waving and grinning. He had got two. The fourth was also flat on the ground. They ran towards the big box, Alyx involuntarily closing her eyes as she passed the disabled things; then they leaned against the big box, big as a room. Piles of boxes, piles of plastic bladders, bags, cartons, long tubes, stoppers, things that looked like baby round cheese. She waved an arm in the air violently. The others came running, skidding, stumbling down the slope. They began to pick up things under Gunnar's direction and stuff them into each other's packs, whispering a little, talking endlessly, while Alyx squatted down in the snow and kept her bow trained dead-steady on that hole in the ground. There was probably not much sense in doing so, but she did it anyway. She was convinced it was the proper thing to do. Someone was enthusiastically stuffing something into her pack; "Easy, easy," she said, and sighted on that hole in the ground, keeping her aim decent and listening for any improper sounds from above or below until someone said in her ear, "We're done," and she took off immediately up the slope, not looking back. It took the others several minutes to catch up with her. *Thank God it's snowing!* she thought. She counted them. It was all right.

"Now!" she gasped. "We're going into the moun-

tains. Double quick!" and all the rest of the day she
pushed them until they were ready to drop, up into
the foothills among the increasingly broken rocks
where they had to scramble on hands and knees and
several people tore holes in their suits. The cold got
worse. There were gusts of wind. She took them the
long way round, by pure instinct, into the worst kind
of country, the place where no one trying to get
anywhere—or trying to escape—would go, in a
strange, doubled, senseless series of turns and re-
turns, crossing their path once, up over obstacles
and then in long, leisurely curves on the flattest part
of the hills. She kept carefully picturing their relation to the abandoned Base B, telling herself *They'll
know someone was there*; and then repeating obses-
sively *Part of the landscape, part of the landscape*
and driving them all the harder, physically shoving
them along, striking them, prodding them, telling
them in the ugliest way she could that they would
die, that they would be eaten, that their minds would
be picked, that they would be crippled, deformed,
tortured, that they would die, that they would die,
die, die, and finally that she would kill them herself
if they stopped, if they stopped for a moment, kill
them, scar their faces for life, disembowel them, and
finally she had to all but torture them herself, bruise
them and pinch them in the nerves she alone knew
about until it was less painful to go on than to be
goaded constantly, to be terrified, to be slapped and
threatened and beaten. At sundown she let them
collapse out in the open and slept immediately herself. Two hours later she woke up. She shook Gunnar.

"Gunnar!" she said. He came awake with a kind of
convulsive leap, struggling horribly. She put an arm

around him, crawling tiredly through the snow and leaned against him to quiet him. She felt herself slipping off again and jerked awake. He had his head in both hands, pressing his temples and swinging his head from side to side.

"Gunnar!" she said, "you are the only one who knows anything about this place. Where do we go?"

"All right, all right," he said. He was swaying a little. She reached under the cuff of his suit and pinched the skin on the inside of his forearm; his eyes opened and he looked at her.

"Where . . . what?" he said.

"Where do we go? Is there any neutral area in this—this place?"

"One moment," he said, and he put his head in his hands again. Then he looked up, awake. "I know," he said, "that there is a control Embassy somewhere here. There is always at least one. It's Military, not Gov; you wouldn't understand that but it doesn't matter. We'd be safe there."

"Where is it?" she said.

"I think," he said, "that I know where it is. It's nearer the Pole, I think. Not too far. A few hours by aircraft, I think. Three hours."

"How long," said she, "on foot?"

"Oh," he said, slipping down into the snow onto one arm, "maybe—maybe twice this. Or a little more. Say five hundred kilometers."

"How long," said she insistently, "is that?"

"Oh not much," he said, yawning and speaking fuzzily. "Not much . . . two hours by aircraft." He smiled. "You might have heard it called," he said, "three hundred *miles*, I think. Or a little less." And he rolled over on his side and went to sleep.

Well, that's not so bad, she thought, half asleep, forgetting them all for the moment and thinking only of herself. *Fourteen, fifteen days, that's all. Not bad.* She looked around. Paradise had begun to blow up a little, covering the farthest of her charges with drifts of snow: eight big, fit people with long, long legs. *Oh God of Hell!* she thought suddenly. *Can I get them to do ten miles a day? Is it three hundred miles? A month? Four hundred? And food—!* so she went and kicked Machine awake, telling him to keep the first watch, then call Iris, and have Iris call her.

"You know," she said, "I owe you something."

He said nothing, as usual.

"When I say 'shoot one,' " said Alyx, "I mean shoot one, not two. Do you understand?"

Machine smiled slightly, a smile she suspected he had spent many years in perfecting: cynical, sullen, I-can-do-it-and-you-can't smile. A thoroughly nasty look. She said:

"You stupid bastard, I might have killed you by accident trying to make that second shot!" and leaning forward, she slapped him backhanded across the face, and then the other way forehand as a kind of afterthought because she was tired. She did it very hard. For a moment his face was only the face of a young man, a soft face, shocked and unprotected. Tears sprang to his eyes. Then he began to weep, turning his face away and putting it down on his knees, sobbing harder and harder, clutching at his knees and pressing his face between them to hide his cries, rocking back and forth, then lying on his face with his hands pressed to his eyes, crying out loud to the stars. He subsided slowly, sobbing, calming down, shaken by less and less frequent spasms of tears, and finally was quiet. His face was wet. He lay back in the snow and stretched out his arms, opening his hands loosely as if he had finally let go of something. He smiled at her, quite genuinely. He looked as if he loved her. "Iris," he said.

"Yes, baby," she said, "Iris," and walked back to her place before anything else could happen. There was a neutral place up there—somewhere—if they could find it—where they would be taken in—if they could make it—and where they would be safe—if they could get to it. If they lived.

And if only they don't drown me between the lot of them, she thought irrationally. And fell asleep.

Paradise was not well mapped, as she found out the next morning with Gunnar's help. He did not know the direction. She asked him about the stars and the sun and the time of year, doing some quick calculating, while everyone else tumbled the contents of their packs into the snow, sorting food and putting it back with low-toned remarks that she did not bother to listen to. The snow had lightened and Paradise had begun to blow up a little with sharp gusts that made their suit jackets flap suddenly now and again.

"Winter has begun," said Alyx. She looked sharply at the explorer. "How cold does it get?"

He said he did not know. They stowed back into their packs the detail maps that ended at Base B (*Very efficient,* she thought) because there was no place to bury them among the rocks. They were entirely useless. The other members of the party were eating breakfast—making faces—and Alyx literally had to stand over them while they ate, shutting

each bag or box much against the owner's will, even
prying those big hands loose (though they were all
afraid of her) and then doling out the food she had
saved to all of them. The cold had kept it fairly fresh.
She told them they would be traveling for three
weeks. She ate a couple of handfuls of some dried
stuff herself and decided it was not bad. She was
regarded dolefully and sulkily by seven pairs of angry
eyes.

"Well?" she said.

"It tastes like—like crams," said Iris.

"It's junk," said Gavrily gravely, "dried breakfast
food. Made of grains. And some other things."

"Some of it's hard as rocks," said Maudey.

"That's starch," said Raydos, "dried starch kernels."

"I don't know what dried starch kernels is," said
Maudey with energy, "but I know what it tastes like.
It tastes like—"

"You will put the dried kennels," said Alyx, "or
anything else that is hard-as-rocks in your water bottles, where it will stop being hard as rocks. Double
handful, please. That's for dinner."

"What do we eat for lunch?" said Iris.

"More junk," said Raydos. "No?"

"Yes," said Alyx. "More junk."

"Kernels," said Raydos, "by the way," and they all
got up from the ground complaining, stiff as boards
and aching in the joints. She told them to move
about a bit but to be careful how they bent over;
then she asked those with the torn suits whether
they could mend them. Under the skin of the suits
was something like thistledown but very little of it,
and under that a layer of something silver. You could
really sleep in the damn things. People were apply-

ing tape to themselves when there was a noise in the air; all dropped heavily to their hands and knees, some grunting—though not on purpose—and the aircraft passed over in the direction of what Alyx had decided to call the south. The equator, anyway. Far to the south and very fast. *Part of the landscape*, she thought. She got them to their feet again, feeling like a coal-heaver, and praised them, saying they had been very quick. Iris looked pleased. Maudey, who was patching up an arm, did not appear to notice; Gavrily was running a tape-strip down the shoulder of one of the nuns and the other was massaging Raydos's back where he had apparently strained something in getting up or down. He looked uncomfortable and uncaring. Gunnar had the professional smile on his face. *My dog*, she thought. Machine was relieving himself off to one side and kicking snow over the spot. He then came over and lifted one cupped hand to his forehead, as if he were trying to take away a headache, which she did not understand. He looked disappointed.

"That's a salute," said Raydos. He grimaced a little and moved his shoulders.

"A what?" said she.

"Army," said Raydos, moving off and flexing his knees. Machine did it again. He stood there expectantly so she did it, too, bringing up one limp hand to her face and down again. They stood awkwardly, smiling at one another, or not perhaps awkwardly, only waiting, until Raydos stuck his tall head over her shoulder and said, "Army salute. He admires the army. I think he likes you," and Machine turned his back instantly, everything going out of his face.

I cannot, thought Alyx, *tell that bum to shut up*

*merely for clearing up a simple point. On the other
hand, I cannot possibly—and if I have to keep restraining myself—I will not let—I cannot, will not,
will not let that interfering fool—*

Iris burst into pure song.

"OH, SHUT UP!" shouted Alyx, "FOR GOD'S
SAKE!" and marshaled them into some kind of line,
abjuring them for Heaven's sake to hurry up and be
quiet. She wished she had never gotten into this.
She wished three or four of them would die and
make it easier for her to keep track of them. She
wished several would throw themselves off cliffs. She
wished there were cliffs they could throw themselves off of. She was imagining these deaths in detail
when one of them loomed beside her and an arm slid
into hers. It was Raydos.

"I won't interfere again," he said, "all right?" and
then he faded back into the line, silent, uncaring, as
if Machine's thoughts had somehow become his own.
Perhaps they were swapping minds. It occurred to
her that she ought to ask the painter to apologize to
the boy, not for interfering, but for talking about him
as if he weren't there; then she saw the two of them
(she thought it was them) conferring briefly together.
Perhaps it had been done. She looked up at the
bleary spot in the sky that was the sun and ran down
the line, motioning them all to one side, telling them
to keep the sun to their left and that Gunnar would
show them what constellations to follow that night, if
it was clear. Don't wander. Keep your eyes open.
Think. Watch it. Machine joined her and walked
silently by her side, his eyes on his feet. Paradise,
which had sloped gently, began to climb, and they
climbed with it, some of them falling down. She

went to the head of the line and led them for an hour, then dropped back to allow Gunnar, the amateur mountain-climber, to lead the way. She discussed directions with him. The wind was getting worse. Paradise began to show bare rock. They stopped for a cold and miserable lunch and Alyx saw that everyone's bow was unsprung and packed, except for hers; "Can't have you shooting yourselves in the feet," she said. She told Gunnar it might look less suspicious if. "If," he said. Neither finished the thought. They tramped through the afternoon, colder and colder, with the sun receding early into the mountains, struggled on, climbing slopes that a professional would have laughed at. They found the hoofprints of something like a goat and Alyx thought *I could live on this country for a year*. She dropped back in the line and joined Machine again, again silent, unspeaking for hours. Then suddenly she said:

"What's a pre-school conditioning director?"

"A teacher," said Machine in a surprisingly serene voice, "of very small children."

"It came into my mind," she said, "all of a sudden, that I was a *pre-school conditioning director*."

"Well, you are," he said gravely, "aren't you?"

He seemed to find this funny and laughed on and off, quietly, for the rest of the afternoon. She did not.

That was the night Maudey insisted on telling the story of her life. She sat in the half-gloom of the cave they had found, clasping her hands in front of her, and went through a feverish and unstoppable list of her marriages: the line marriage, the double marriage, the trial marriage, the period marriage, the group marriage. Alyx did not know what she was talking about. Then Maudey began to lament her troubles with her unstable self-image and at first Alyx thought that she had no soul and therefore no reflection in a mirror, but she knew that was nonsense; so soon she perceived it was one of *their points* (by then she had taken to classifying certain things as *their points*) and tried not to listen, as all gathered around Maudey and analyzed her self-image, using terms Trans-Temp had apparently left out of Alyx's vocabulary, perhaps on purpose. Gunnar was especially active in the discussion. They crowded around her, talking solemnly while Maudey twisted her hands in the middle, but nobody touched her; it occurred to Alyx that although several of them had touched herself, they did not seem to like to get too close to one another. Then it occurred to her that there was something odd in Maudey's posture and something unpleasantly reminiscent in the breathiness of her voice; she decided Maudey had a fever. She wormed her way into the group and seized the woman by the arm, putting her other hand on Maudey's face, which was indeed unnaturally hot.

"She's sick," said Alyx.

"Oh no," said everybody else.

"She's got a fever," said Alyx.

"No, no," said one of the nuns, "it's the drug."

"What—drug?" said Alyx, controlling her temper. How these people could manage to get into such scrapes—

"It's Re-Juv," said Gavrily. "She's been taking Re-Juv and of course the withdrawal symptoms don't come on for a couple of weeks. But she'll be all right."

"It's an unparalleled therapeutic opportunity," said the other nun. Maudey was moaning that nobody cared about her, that nobody had ever paid any attention to her, and whereas other people's dolls were normal when they were little, hers had only had a limited stock of tapes and could only say the same things over and over, just like a person. She said she had always known it wasn't real. No one touched her. They urged her to integrate this perception with her unstable self-image.

"Are you going," said Alyx, "to let her go on like that *all night*?"

"We wouldn't think of stopping her," said Gavrily in a shocked voice and they all went back to talking. "Why wasn't your doll alive?" said one of the nuns in a soft voice. "Think, now; tell us, why do you feel—" Alyx pushed past two of them to try to touch the woman or take her hand, but at this point Maudey got swiftly up and walked out of the cave.

"Eight gods and seven devils!" shouted Alyx in her own language. She realized a nun was clinging to each arm.

"Please don't be distressed," they said, "she'll come back," like twins in unison, only one actually said "She'll return" and the other "She'll come back." Voices pursued her from the cave, everlastingly those damned voices; she wondered if they knew how far an insane woman could wander in a snowstorm. Insane she was, drug or no drug; Alyx had seen too many people behave too oddly under too many different circumstances to draw unnecessary distinctions. She found Maudey some thirty meters along the rockface, crouching against it.

"Maudey, you must come back," said Alyx.

"Oh, I know *you*," said Maudey, in a superior tone.

"You will get lost in the snow," said Alyx softly, carefully freeing one hand from its glove, "and you won't be comfortable and warm and get a good night's sleep. Now come along."

Maudey smirked and cowered and said nothing.

"Come back and be comfortable and warm," said Alyx. "Come back and go to sleep. Come, dear; come on, dear," and she caught Maudey's arm with her gloved hand and with the other pressed a blood vessel at the base of her neck. The woman passed out immediately and fell down in the snow. Alyx kneeled over her, holding one arm back against the joint, just in case Maudey should decide to get contentious. *And how,* she thought, *do you get her back now when she weighs twice as much as you, clever one?* The wind gave them a nasty shove, then gusted in the other direction. Maudey was beginning to stir. She was saying something louder and louder; finally Alyx heard it.

"I'm a living doll," Maudey was saying, "I'm a living doll, I'm a living doll, I'm a living doll!" interspersed with terrible sobs.

They do tell the truth, thought Alyx, *sometimes.* "You," she said firmly, "are a woman. A woman. A woman."

"I'm a doll!" cried Maudey.

"You," said Alyx, "are a woman. A woman with dyed hair. A silly woman. But a woman. A woman!"

"No I'm not," saud Maudey stubbornly, like an older Iris.

"Oh, you're a damned fool!" snapped Alyx, peering nervously about and hoping that their voices would not attract anything. She did not expect people, but she knew that where there are goats or things like goats there are things that eat the things that are like goats.

"Am I damned?" said Maudey. "What's damned?"

"Lost," said Alyx absently, and slipping her gloved hand free, she lifted the crossbow from its loop on her back, loaded it and pointed it away at the ground. Maudey was wiggling her freed arm, with an expression of pain. "You hurt me," she said. Then she saw the bow and sat up in the snow, terrified, shrinking away.

"Will you shoot me, will you shoot me?" she cried.

"Shoot you?" said Alyx.

"You'll shoot me, you hate me!" wailed Maudey, clawing at the rock-face. "You hate me, you hate me, you'll kill me!"

"I think I will," said Alyx simply, "unless you go back to the cave."

"No, no, no," said Maudey.

"If you don't go back to the cave," said Alyx carefully, "I am going to shoot you," and she drove the big woman in front of her, step by step, back along the narrow side of the mountain, back on her own tracks that the snow had already half-obliterated, back through Paradise to the opening of the cave. She trained the crossbow on Maudey until the woman stepped into the group of people inside; then she stood there, blocking the entrance, the bow in her hand.

"One of you," she said, "tie her wrists together."

"You are doing incalculable harm," said one of the nuns.

"Machine," she said, "take rope from your pack. Tie that woman's wrists together and then tie them to Gavrily's feet and the nuns' feet and Iris's. Give them plenty of room but make the knots fast."

"I hear and obey," said Raydos dryly, answering for the boy, who was apparently doing what she had told him to.

"You and Raydos and I and Gunnar will stand watch," she said.

"What's there to watch, for heaven's sake," muttered Iris. Alyx thought she probably did not like being connected to Maudey in any way at all, not even for safety.

"Really," said Gavrily, "she would have come back, you know! I think you might try to understand that!"

"I would have come back," said Maudey in a surprisingly clear and sensible tone, "of course I would have come back, don't be silly," and this statement precipitated such a clamor of discussion, vilification, self-justification and complaints that Alyx stepped outside the cave with her blood pounding in her ears and her hands grasping the stock of the crossbow. She asked the gods to give her strength, although she did not believe in them and never had. Her jaws felt like iron; she was shaking with fury.

Then she saw the bear. It was not twenty meters away.

"Quiet!" she blared. They went on talking loudly.

"QUIET!" she shouted, and as the talk died down to an injured and peevish mutter, she saw that the bear—if it was a bear—had heard them and was slowly, curiously, calmly, coming over to investigate. It seemed to be grayish-white, like the snow, and longer in the neck than it should be.

"Don't move," she said very softly, "there is an animal out here," and in the silence that followed she saw the creature hesitate, swaying a little or lumbering from side to side. It might very well pass them by. It stopped, sniffed about and stood there for what seemed three or four minutes, then fell clumsily on to all fours and began to move slowly away.

Then Maudey screamed. Undecided no longer, the animal turned and flowed swiftly towards them, unbelievably graceful over the broken ground and the sharply sloping hillside. Alyx stood very still. She said, "Machine, your bow," and heard Gunnar whisper "Kill it, kill it, why don't you kill it!" The beast was almost upon her. At the last moment she knelt and sent a bolt between its eyes; then she dropped down automatically and swiftly, rolling to one side, dropping the bow. She snatched her knives from both her sleeves and threw herself under the swaying animal, driving up between the ribs first with one hand and then the other. The thing fell on her immediately like a dead weight; it was too enormous, too heavy for her to move; she lay there trying to breathe, slowly blacking out and feeling her ribs begin to give way. Then she fainted and came to to find Gunnar and Machine rolling the enormous carcass off her. She lay, a swarm of black sparks in front of her eyes. Machine wiped the beast's blood off her suit—it came off absolutely clean with a handful of snow— and carried her like a doll to a patch of clean snow where she began to breathe. The blood rushed back to her head. She could think again.

"It's dead," said Gunnar unsteadily, "I think it died at once from the bolt."

"Oh you devils!" gasped Alyx.

"*I* came out at once," said Machine, with some

relish. "He didn't." He began pressing his hands
rhythmically against her sides. She felt better.

"The boy—the boy put a second bolt in it," said
Gunnar, after a moment's hesitation. "I was afraid,"
he added. "I'm sorry."

"Who let that woman scream?" said Alyx.

Gunnar shrugged helplessly.

"Always know anatomy," said Machine, with astonishing cheerfulness. "You see, the human body is
a machine. I know some things," and he began to
drag the animal away.

"Wait," said Alyx. She found she could walk. She
went over and looked at the thing. It was a bear but
like none she had ever seen or heard of: a white bear
with a long, snaky neck, almost four meters high if it
had chosen to stand. The fur was very thick.

"It's a polar bear," said Gunnar.

She wanted to know what that was.

"It's an Old Earth animal," he said, "but it must
have been adapted. They usually live in the sea, I
think. They have been stocking Paradise with Old
Earth animals. I thought you knew."

"*I did not know*," said Alyx.

"I'm—I'm sorry," he said, "but I never—never
thought of it. I didn't think it would matter." He
looked down at the enormous corpse. "Animals do
not attack people," he said. Even in the dim light
she could see his expression; he knew that what he
had said was idiotic.

"Oh no," she said deliberately, "oh no, of course
not," and kneeling beside the corpse she extracted
both her knives, cleaned them in the snow and put
them back in the sheaths attached to her forearms
under the suit. Convenient not to have water rust

the blades. She studied the bear's claws for a few minutes, feeling them and trying as well as she could to see them in the dim light. Then she sent Machine into the cave for Raydos's artists' tools, and choosing the small, thin knife that he used to sharpen his pencils (some day, she thought, she would have to ask him what a pencils was) she slashed the animal's belly and neck, imitating the slash of claws and disguising the wounds made by her knives. She had seen bears fight once, in a circus, and had heard tales of what they did to one another. She hoped the stories had been accurate. With Raydos's knife she also ripped open one of the animal's shoulders and attempted to simulate the bite of its teeth, being careful to open a main artery. The damned thing had such a layer of fat that she had trouble getting to it. When cut, the vessel pumped slowly; there was not the pool of blood there should be, but *What the devil*, she thought, *no one may ever find it and if they do, will they be able to tell the difference? Probably not*. They could dig out the bolts tomorrow. She cleaned Raydos' knife, returned it to Machine and went back to the cave.

No one said a word.

"I have," said Alyx, "just killed a bear. It was eleven feet high and could have eaten the lot of you. If anyone talks loud again, any time, for any reason, I shall ram his unspeakable teeth down his unspeakable throat."

Maudey began to mutter, sobbing a little.

"Machine," she said, "make that woman stop," and she watched, dead tired, while Machine took something from his pack, pressed it to Maudey's nose, and laid her gently on the floor. "She'll sleep," he said.

"That was not kindly done," remarked one of the nuns.

Alyx bit her own hand; she bit it hard, leaving marks; she told Machine, Raydos and Gunnar about the watch; she and they brought more snow into the cave to cushion the others, although the wind had half done their job for them. Everyone was quiet. All the same, she put her fingers in her ears but that pushed her hood back and made her head get cold; then she rolled over against the cave wall. Finally she did what she had been doing for the past seventeen nights. She went out into the snow and slept by herself, against the rock wall two meters from the drop, with Machine nearby, dim and comforting in the falling snow. She dreamed of the sun of the Tyrian seas, of clouds and ships and Mediterranean heat—and then of nothing at all.

The next morning when the East—she had decided to call it the East—brightened enough to see by, Alyx ended her watch. It had begun to clear during the night and the sky was showing signs of turning a pale winter blue, very uncomfortable-looking. She woke Gunnar, making the others huddled near him stir and mutter in their sleep, for it had gotten colder, too, during the night, and with Gunnar she sat down in the snow and went over the contents of their two packs, item by item. She figured that what they had in common everyone would have. She made him explain everything: the sunglasses, the drugs that slowed you down if you were hurt, the bottle Machine had used that was for unconsciousness in cases of pain, the different kinds of dried foods, the binoculars, a bottle of something you put on wounds to make new flesh (it said "nuflesh" and she tried to memorize the letters on it), the knives, the grooved barrel of the crossbow (but that impressed her greatly), the water containers, the suit-mending tape, fluff you could add to your suit if you lost fluff from it and a coil of extremely thin, extremely strong rope that she measured by solemnly telling it out from her outstretched hand to her nose and so on and so on and so on until she had figured the length. Gunnar seemed to find this very funny. There was also something that she recognized as long underwear (though she did not think she would bring it to anybody's attention just yet) and at the bottom a packet of something she could not make head or tail of; Gunnar said it was to unfold and clean yourself with.

"Everyone's used theirs up," said he, "I'm afraid."

"A ritual, no doubt," said she, "in this cold. I told them they'd stink."

He sat there, wrinkling his brow for a moment, and then he said:

"There are no stimulants and there are no euphorics."

She asked what those were and he explained. "Ah, a Greek root," she said. He started to talk about how worried he was that there were no stimulants and no euphorics; these should have been included; they could hardly expect them to finish a weekend without them, let alone a seven-weeks' trip; in fact, he said, there was something odd about the whole thing. By now Alyx had ambled over to the dead bear and was digging the bolts out of it; she asked him over her shoulder, "Do *they* travel by night or day?"

"They?" he said, puzzled, and then "Oh, them! No, it makes no difference to them."

"Then it will make no difference to us," she said, cleaning the bolts in the snow. "Can they follow our tracks at night?"

"Why not?" said he, and she nodded.

"Do you think," said he, after a moment's silence, "that they are trying something out on us?"

"They?" she said. "Oh, them! Trans-Temp. Possibly. Quite possibly." *But probably not*, she added to herself, *unfortunately*. And she packed the bolts neatly away.

"*I* think," said Gunnar, skirting the bear's carcass where the blood still showed under the trodden snow, "that it is very odd that we have nothing else with us. I'm inclined to—" (*Good Lord, he's nervous*, she thought) "I'm inclined to believe," he said, settling ponderously in a clean patch of snow and leaning towards her so as to make himself heard, for he was speaking in a low voice, "that this is some kind of experiment. Or carelessness. Criminal carelessness. When we get back—" and he stopped, staring into the snow.

"If we get back," said Alyx cheerfully, getting to her feet, "you can lodge a complaint or declare a tort, or whatever it is you do. Here," and she handed him a wad of fluff she had picked out of her pack.

"What I should have done last night," she said, "half-obliterating our tracks around the carcass so they don't look so damned human. With luck" (she glanced up) "the snow won't stop for an hour yet."

"How can you tell?" said he, his mouth open.

"Because it is still coming down," said Alyx, and she gave him a push in the back. She had to reach up to do it. He bent and the two of them backed away, drawing the wads of fluff across the snow like brooms. It worked, but not well.

"How about those nuns," said Alyx. "Don't they have some damned thing or other with them?"

"Oh, you have to be careful!" he said in a whisper. "You have to be careful about *that!*" and with this he worked his way to the mouth of the cave.

The sleepers were coming out.

Waking up by themselves for the first time, they filed out of the cave and stood in a row in the opening staring down at the corpse of the animal they had not even seen the night before. She suspected the story had gotten around. *Twenty handspans*, she thought, *of bear*. The nuns started back, making some kind of complicated sign on their foreheads and breasts. Raydos bowed admiringly, half ironically. The two older people were plainly frightened, even though Maudey had begun to crane forward for a better look; suddenly her whole body jerked and she flung out one arm; she would have overbalanced herself and fallen if Gavrily had not caught her. "After-effects," he said.

"How long do these go on?" said Alyx, a little wearily.

"A couple of days," he said quickly, holding on to the frightened woman, "only a couple of days. They get better."

"Then take care of her until they do," said Alyx, and she was about to add the usual signal for the morning (COME ON!) when a voice somewhere above her head said:

"Agent?"

It was Iris, that great lolloping girl, almost as high as the bear, looking down at her with the unfathomable expression of the very young, twisting and twisting a lock of silver hair that had escaped from her hood. She was really very pretty.

"Agent," blurted Iris, her eyes big, "will you teach me how to shoot?"

"Yes, my dear," said Alyx, "indeed I will."

"Come on!" she bawled then. They came on.

Later in the morning, when she allowed them to stop and eat the soggiest of their protein and dried starch kernels for breakfast, one of the nuns came up to her, squatted gracefully in the snow and made the complicated sign thrice: once on her own forehead, once on her own breast and once in the air between her and the little woman who had shot the bear.

"Violence," said the nun earnestly, "is deplorable. It is always deplorable. It corrupts love, you see, and love is the expansion of consciousness while violence is the restriction of love so that violence, which restricts love and consciousness, is always bad, as consciousness is always good and the consciousness of the All is the best and only good, and to restrict what may lead to the consciousness of the All is unwise and unkind. Therefore to die is only to merge with the All so that actually violence is not justifiable in the postponing of death, as we must all die, and dying is the final good if it is a dying into the All and not a dying away from it, as in violence.

"But," she said, "the recognition of consciousness and the value of expression of consciousness go hand in hand; there is no evil in expressing the impulses of the nature of consciousness, so that there can be no evil in action and action is not violence. Action is actually an expansion of the consciousness, as one becomes more aware of one's particular true nature and thence slowly more aware of one's ultimate all-embracing Nature which unites one with the All. Action is therefore a good. It is not, of course, the same thing as the true religion, but some of us go the slow path and some the quick, and who will attain Enlightenment first? Who knows? What is, is, as the sage said: One way is not another. I hope you will attend our services when we return home."

"Yes," said Alyx. "Indeed I will." The tall lady made the sign again, this time on Alyx's forehead and breast, and went sedately back to her breakfast.

And that, thought Alyx, *is the damndest way of saying Bravo that I have ever heard!*

She decided to teach them all to shoot, including the nuns. It was understood, of course, that the nuns would shoot only bears.

Later in the afternoon, when the snow had stopped and before visibility became bad, she lined all of them up on a relatively level snow-field, assigning the two nuns to Gunnar, Gavrily and Raydos to Machine and herself teaching Iris. Maudey rested, a little dazed from the nervous spasms that had been shaking her all day, though perfectly clear in her mind. Most of them tired of the business after the first hour, except for Raydos, who seemed to enjoy handling the new thing again, and Iris, who kept saying "Just a little more, just a little more; I'm not good enough." When Machine laughed at her, she loftily explained that it was "rather like dancing."

"Which you have never done for pleasure, I am sure," she added.

During the late afternoon they slogged up an ever-narrowing path between cliffs, towards what Gunnar swore was a pass in the mountains. It seemed, however, as if these mountains had no pass but only plateaus; no, not plateaus, only peaks; that even the peaks had no down but only up, and on and on they kept in the red light of the setting winter sun, holding the glare always to the proper side of them, plodding up a steeper and steeper path until the red light turned purple and dim, and died, until each of them saw the other as a dim hulk marching in front of him.

She called a halt. They sat down. For the first time during the whole trip they bunched together, actually touching body to body, with only Maudey a little away from them, for she was still having her trouble. (Alyx had one of the nuns put her to sleep and the spasms stopped instantly.) It was very cold, with the stars splendid, icy points and the whole tumbled waste of jagged rock shining faintly around them. They did not, as they usually did, begin to analyze the events of the day, but only half-sat, half-lay in silence, feeling the still air around them drain away their warmth, which (Iris said) "seemed to flow right up into the sky." They watched the stars. Then out of nowhere, for no reason at all, Gavrily began to sing in a reedy tenor a few lines of what he called a "baby-song" and this nursery tune—for it was not, Alyx was made to understand, real music—put them all into tears. They sobbed companionably for a little while. It got colder and colder. Gunnar suggested that they pack the snow around them to keep in the heat and Alyx, who had noticed that her buttocks seemed to be the warmest place about her, agreed, so they all built a round wall of snow, with Maudey in the middle of it, and then crawled in around her and pulled the whole thing down on top of them, each packing himself in his own little heap. Then it all had to be disrupted and put right again because the first watch had to climb out. This was Iris. She still seemed very excited, whispering to Alyx "Was I good enough? Will you teach me again?" over and over until somebody poked her and she exclaimed "Ow!" There was yawning, sighing, breathing.

"Will you," said Iris, bending over the little heap of persons, "teach me again? Will you tell me all about yourself? Will you tell me everything? Will you? Will you?"

"Oh, be quiet," said Machine crossly, and Iris took her bow and went a little aside, to sit watch.

It was the eighteenth night.

The nineteenth. The twentieth. The twenty-first. They were very quiet. They were idealizing, trusting, companionable, almost happy. It made Alyx nervous, and the more they looked at her, asked her about her and listened to her the more unnerved she became. She did not think they understood what was happening. She told them about her life with one ear on the sounds about them, instantly alert, ready to spring up, with her crossbow always across her knees; so that they asked her what the matter was. She said "Nothing." She told them legends, fairy tales, religious stories, but they didn't want to hear those; they wanted to hear about her; what she ate, what she drank, what she wore, what her house was like, whom she knew, all the particulars of the business, the alleyways, the gutters, the finest houses and the worst houses in Tyre. She felt it was all being dragged out of her against her will. They were among the mountains now and going very slowly, very badly; they went far into the night now whenever it was clear and as soon as they settled down for the night (everyone had got into the long underwear one clear and frosty morning, hopping about from one bare foot to another, and discovering wrapped within it what they declared to be artificial arches) they bunched up together against the cold, interlacing arms and legs and squirming together as close as they could, saying:

"Tell us about—"

She told them.

On the twenty-fourth night, when she woke Machine to take the dawn watch, he said to her "Do you want to climb it?"

"Climb what?" muttered Alyx. She was chilled and uncomfortable, stirring around to get her blood up.

"Do you want to climb it?" said Machine patiently.

"Wait a minute," she said, "let me think." Then she said "You'd better not use slang; I don't think I'm programmed for it."

He translated. He added—off-handedly—"You don't have to worry about pregnancy; Trans-Temp's taken care of it. Or they will, when we get back."

"Well, no," said Alyx. "No, I don't think I do want to—climb it." He looked, as far as she could tell in the dim light, a little surprised; but he did not touch her, he did not ask again or laugh or stir or even move. He sat with his arms around his knees as if considering something and then he said "All right." He repeated it decisively, staring at her with eyes that were just beginning to turn blue with the dawn;

then he smiled, pulled back the spring on his crossbow and got to his feet.

"And keep your eyes open," she said, on her way back to the snow-heaped nest of the others.

"Don't I always?" he said, and as she turned away she heard an unmistakable sound. He had laughed.

The next day Raydos started to sketch her at every halt. He took out his materials and worked swiftly but easily, like a man who thinks himself safe. It was intolerable. She told him that if anything happened or anyone came he would either have to drop his sketchbook or put it in his pack; that if he took the time to put it into his pack he might die or betray the lot of them and that if he dropped it, someone might find it.

"They won't know what it is," he said. "It's archaic, you see."

"They'll know it's not an animal," she said. "Put it away."

He went on sketching. She walked over to him, took the book of papers and the length of black thing he was using away from him and stowed them away in her own pack. He smiled and blinked in the sunlight. The thing was not real charcoal or gum or even chalky; she considered asking him about it and then she shuddered. She stood there for a moment, shading her eyes against the sun and being frightened, as if she had to be frightened for the whole crew of them as well as herself, as if she were alone, more alone than by herself, the more they liked her, the more they obeyed, the more they talked of "when we get back," the more frightened she would have to become.

"All right, come on," she heard herself say.

"All right, come on.

"Come on!"

Time after time after time.

On the twenty-ninth afternoon Maudey died. She died suddenly and by accident. They were into the pass that Gunnar had spoken of, half blinded by the glare of ice on the rock walls to either side, following a path that dropped almost sheer from the left. It was wide enough for two or three and Machine had charge of Maudey that day, for although her nervous fits had grown less frequent, they had never entirely gone away. He walked on the outside, she on the inside. Behind them Iris was humming softly to herself. It was icy in parts and the going was slow. They stopped for a moment and Machine cautiously let go of Maudey's arm; at the same time Iris began to sing softly, the same drab tune over and over again, the way she had said to Alyx they danced at the drug palaces, over and over to put themselves into trances, over and over.

"Stop that filthy song," said Maudey. "I'm tired."

Iris continued insultingly to sing.

"I'm tired!" said Maudey desperately, "I'm tired! I'm tired!" and in turning she slipped and fell on the slippery path to her knees. She was still in balance, however. Iris had arched her eyebrows and was silently mouthing something when Machine, who had been watching Maudey intently, bent down to take hold of her, but at that instant Maudey's whole right arm threw itself out over nothing and she fell over the side of the path. Machine flung himself after her and was only stopped from falling over in his turn by fetching up against someone's foot—it happened to be one of the nuns—and they both went down, teetering for a moment over the side. The nun was sprawled on the path in a patch of gravel and Machine hung shoulders down over the verge. They pulled him back and got the other one to her feet.

"Well, what happened?" said Iris in surprise. Alyx had grabbed Gunnar by the arm. Iris shrugged at them all elaborately and sat down, her chin on her knees, while Alyx got the rope from all the packs as swiftly as possible, knotted it, pushed the nun off the patch of dry gravel and set Machine on it. "Can you hold him?" she said. Machine nodded. She looped the rope about a projecting point in the wall above them and gave it to Machine; the other end she knotted under Gunnar's arms. They sent him down to bring Maudey up, which he did, and they laid her down on the path. She was dead.

"Well, how is she?" said Iris, looking at them all over her shoulder.

"She's dead," said Alyx.

"That," said Iris brightly, "is not the right answer," and she came over to inspect things for herself, coquettishly twisting and untwisting a lock of her straight silver hair. She knelt by the body. Maudey's head lay almost flat against her shoulder for her neck was broken; her eyes were wide open. Alyx closed them, saying again "Little girl, she's dead." Iris looked away, then up at them, then down again. She made a careless face. She said "Mo-Maudey was old, you know; d'you think they can fix her when we get back?"

"She is dead," said Alyx. Iris was drawing lines in the snow. She shrugged and looked covertly at the body, then she turned to it and her face began to

change; she moved nearer on her knees. "Mo—
Mother," she said, then grabbed at the woman with
the funny, twisted neck, screaming the word "Mother"
over and over, grabbing at the clothing and the limbs
and even the purple hair where the hood had fallen
back, screaming without stopping. Machine said
quickly, "I can put her out." Alyx shook her head.
She put one hand over Iris's mouth to muffle the
noise. She sat with the great big girl as Iris threw
herself on top of dead Maudey, trying to burrow into
her, her screaming turning to sobbing, great gasping
sobs that seemed to dislocate her whole body, just as
vanity and age had thrown her mother about so
terribly between them and had finally thrown her
over a cliff. As soon as the girl began to cry, Alyx put
both arms about her and rocked with her, back and
forth. One of the nuns came up with a thing in her
hand, a white pill.

"It would be unkind," said the nun, "it would be
most unkind, most unkind—"

"Go to hell," said Alyx in Greek.

"I must insist," said the nun softly, "I must, must
insist," in a tangle of hisses like a snake. "I must,
must, I must—"

"Get out!" shouted Alyx to the startled woman,
who did not even understand the words. With her
arms around Iris, big as Iris was, with little Iris in
agonies. Alyx talked to her in Greek, soothed her in
Greek, talked just to be talking, rocked her back and
forth. Finally there came a moment when Iris stopped.

Everyone looked very surprised.

"Your mother," said Alyx, carefully pointing to the
body, "is dead." This provoked a fresh outburst.
Three more times. Four times. Alyx said it again.

For several hours she repeated the whole thing, she did not know how often, holding the girl each time, then holding only her hand, then finally drawing her to her feet and away from the dead woman while the men took the food and equipment out of Maudey's pack to divide it among themselves and threw the body over the path, to hide it. There was a kind of tittering, whispering chatter behind Alyx. She walked all day with the girl, talking to her, arm clumsily about her, making her walk while she shook with fits of weeping, making her walk when she wanted to sit down, making her walk as she talked of her mother, of running away from home—"not like you did" said Iris—of hating her, loving her, hating her, being reasonable, being rational, being grown up, fighting ("but it's natural!"), not being able to stand her, being able to stand her, loving her, always fighting with her (and here a fresh fit of weeping) and then—then—

"I killed her!" cried Iris, stock-still on the path. "Oh my God, I killed her! I! I!"

"Bullshit," said Alyx shortly, her hypnotic vocabulary coming to the rescue at the eleventh instant.

"But I did, I did," said Iris. "Didn't you see? I upset her, I made—"

"Ass!" said Alyx.

"Then why didn't you rope them together," cried Iris, planting herself hysterically in front of Alyx, arms akimbo, "why didn't you? You knew she could fall! You wanted to kill her!"

"If you say that again—" said Alyx, getting ready.

"I see it, I see it," whispered Iris wildly, putting her arms around herself, her eyes narrowing. "Yesss, you wanted her dead—you didn't want the *trouble*—"

Alyx hit her across the face. She threw her down, sat on her and proceeded to pound at her while the others watched, shocked and scandalized. She took good care not to hurt her. When Iris had stopped, she rubbed snow roughly over the girl's face and hauled her to her feet, "and no more trouble out of you!" she said.

"I'm all right," said Iris uncertainly. She took a step, "Yes," she said. Alyx did not hold her any more but walked next to her, giving her a slight touch now and then when she seemed to waver.

"Yes, I am all right," said Iris. Then she added, in her normal voice, "I know Maudey is dead."

"Yes," said Alyx.

"I know," said Iris, her voice wobbling a little, "that you didn't put them together because they both would have gone over."

She added, "I am going to cry."

"Cry away," said Alyx, and the rest of the afternoon Iris marched steadily ahead, weeping silently, trying to mop her face and her nose with the cleaning cloth Alyx had given her, breaking out now and again into suppressed, racking sobs. They camped for the night in a kind of hollow between two rising slopes with Iris jammed securely into the middle of everybody and Alyx next to her. In the dim never-dark of the snow-fields, long after everyone else had fallen asleep, someone brushed Alyx across the face, an oddly unctuous sort of touch, at once gentle and unpleasant. She knew at once who it was.

"If you do not," she said, "take that devil's stuff out of here *at once*—!" The hand withdrew.

"I must insist," said the familiar whisper, "I must, must insist. You do not understand—it is not—"

"If you touch her," said Alyx between her teeth, "I will kill you—both of you—and I will take those little pills you are so fond of and defecate upon each and every one of them, upon my soul I swear that I will!"

"But—but—" She could feel the woman trembling with shock.

"If you so much as touch her," said Alyx, "you will have caused me to commit two murders and a sacrilege. Now get out!" and she got up in the dim light, pulled the pack off every grunting, protesting sleeper's back—except the two women who had withdrawn to a little distance together—and piled them like a barricade around Iris, who was sleeping with her face to the stars and her mouth open. *Let them trip over that*, she thought vindictively. *Damn it! Damn them all! Boots without spikes, damn them! What do they expect us to do, swim over the mountains?* She did not sleep for a long time, and when she did it seemed that everyone was climbing over her, stepping on top of her and sliding off just for fun. She dreamed she was what Gunnar had described as a ski-slide. Then she dreamed that the first stepped on to her back and then the second on to his and so on and so on until they formed a human ladder, when the whole snow-field slowly tilted upside down. Everyone fell off. She came to with a start; it was Gavrily, waking her for the dawn watch. She saw him fall asleep in seconds, then trudged a little aside and sat cross-legged, her bow on her knees. The two nuns had moved back to the group, asleep, sprawled out and breathing softly with the others. She watched the sky lighten to the left, be-

come transparent, take on color. Pale blue. Winter
blue.

"All right," she said, "everyone up!" and slipped
off her pack for the usual handfuls of breakfast food.

The first thing she noticed, with exasperation, was
that Raydos had stolen back his art equipment, for it
was gone. The second was that there were only six
figures sitting up and munching out of their cupped
hands, not seven; she thought *That's right, Maudey's
dead,* then ran them over in her head: *Gunnar,
Gavrily, Raydos, Machine, the Twins, Iris*—

But Iris was missing.

Her first thought was that the girl had somehow
been spirited away, or made to disappear by The
Holy Twins, who had stopped eating with their hands
halfway to their mouths, like people about to pour a
sacrifice of grain on to the ground for Mother Earth.
Both of them were watching her. Her second thought
was unprintable and almost—but not quite—unspeakable, and so instantaneous that she had leapt into the
circle of breakfasters before she half knew where she
was, shoving their packs and themselves out of her
way. She dislodged one of Raydos' eye lenses; he
clapped his hand to his eye and began to grope in
the snow. "What the devil—!" said Gunnar.

Iris was lying on her back among the packs, looking up into the sky. She had shut one eye and the
other was moving up and down in a regular pattern.
Alyx fell over her. When she scrambled to her knees,
Iris had not moved and her one open eye still made
the regular transit of nothing, up and down, up and
down.

"Iris," said Alyx.

"Byootiful," said Iris. Alyx shook her. "Byootiful,"

crooned the girl, "all byootiful" and very slowly she opened her closed eye, shut the other and began again to scan the something or nothing up in the sky, up and down, up and down. Alyx tried to pull the big girl to her feet, but she was too heavy; then with astonishing lightness Iris herself sat up, put her head to one side and looked at Alyx with absolute calm and complete relaxation. It seemed to Alyx that the touch of one finger would send her down on her back again. "Mother," said Iris clearly, opening both eyes, "mother. Too lovely," and she continued to look at Alyx as she had at the sky. She bent her head down on to one shoulder, as Maudey's head had been bent in death with a broken neck.

"Mother is lovely," said Iris conversationally. "There she is. You are lovely. Here you are. He is lovely. There he is. She is lovely. We are lovely. They are lovely. I am lovely. Love is lovely. Lovely lovely lovely lovely—" she went on talking to herself as Alyx stood up. One of the nuns came walking across the trampled snow with her hands clasped nervously in front of her; she came up to the little woman and took a breath; then she said:

"You may kill me if you like."

"I love shoes," said Iris, lying down on her back, "I love sky. I love clouds. I love hair. I love zippers. I love food. I love my mother. I love feet. I love bathrooms. I love walking. I love people. I love sleep. I love breathing. I love tape. I love books. I love pictures. I love air. I love rolls. I love hands. I love—"

"Shut up!" shouted Alyx, as the girl continued with her inexhaustible catalogue. "Shut up, for God's sake!" and turned away, only to find herself looking up at the face of the nun, who had quickly moved about to be in front of her and who still repeated, "You may kill us both if you like," with an unbearable mixture of nervousness and superiority. Iris had begun to repeat the word "love" over and over and over again in a soft, unchanging voice.

"Is this not kinder?" said the nun.

"Go away before I kill you!" said Alyx.

"She is happy," said the nun.

"She is an idiot!"

"She will be happy for a day," said the nun, "and then less happy and then even less happy, but she will have her memory of the All and when the sadness comes back—as it will in a day or so, I am sorry to say, but some day we will find out how—"

"Get out!" said Alyx.

"However, it will be an altered sadness," continued the nun rapidly, "an eased sadness with the All in its infinite All—"

"Get out of here before I alter *you* into the All!" Alyx shouted, losing control of herself. The nun hurried away and Alyx, clapping both hands over her ears, walked rapidly away from Iris, who had begun to say "*I've* been to the moon but *you* won't. *I've* been to the sun but *you* won't, *I've* been to—" and over and over and over again with ascending and descending variations.

"Messing up the machinery," said Machine, next to her.

"Leave me alone," said Alyx, her hands still over her ears. The ground had unaccountably jumped up and was swimming in front of her; she knew she was crying.

"I don't approve of messing up the machinery,"

said Machine softly. "I have a respect for the machinery; I do not like to see it abused and if they touch the girl again you need not kill them. I will."

"No killing," said Alyx, as levelly as she could.

"Religion?" said Machine sarcastically.

"No," said Alyx, lifting her head abruptly, "but no killing. Not my people." She turned to go, but he caught her gently by the arm, looking into her face with a half-mocking smile, conveying somehow by his touch that her arm was not inside an insulated suit but was bare, and that he was stroking it. The trip had given him back his eyebrows and eyelashes; the hair on his head was a wiry black brush; for Machine did not, apparently, believe in tampering irreversibly with the Machinery. She thought *I won't get involved with any of these people*. She found herself saying idiotically "Your hair's growing in." He smiled and took her other arm, holding her as if he were going to lift her off the ground, she hotter and dizzier every moment, feeling little, feeling light, feeling like a woman who has had no luxury for a long, long time. She said, "Put me down, if you please."

"Tiny," he said, "you *are* down," and putting his hands around her waist, he lifted her easily to the height of his face. "I think you will climb it," he said.

"No," said Alyx. It did not seem to bother him to keep holding her up in the air.

"I think you will," he said, smiling, and still smiling, he kissed her with a sort of dispassionate, calm pleasure, taking his time, holding her closely and carefully, using the thoughtful, practiced, craftsmanly thoroughness that Machine brought to everything that Machine did. Then he put her down and simply walked away.

"Ah, go find someone your own size!" she called after him, but then she remembered that the only girl his size was Iris, and that Iris was lying on her back in the snow in a world where everything was lovely, lovely, lovely due to a little white pill. She swore. She could see Iris in the distance, still talking. She took a knife out of her sleeve and tried the feel of it but the feel was wrong, just as the boots attached to their suits had no spikes, just as their maps stopped at Base B, just as Paradise itself had turned into—but no, that was not so. The place was all right, quite all right. *The place*, she thought, *is all right*. She started back to the group of picnickers who were slipping their packs back on and stamping the snow off their boots; some were dusting off the rear ends of others where they had sat in the snow. She saw one of The Heavenly Twins say something in Iris's ear and Iris get obediently to her feet, still talking; then the other nun said something and Iris's mouth stopped moving.

Bury it deep, thought Alyx, *never let it heal*. She joined them, feeling like a mule-driver.

"D'you know," said Gunnar conversationally, "that we've been out here thirty days? Not bad, eh?"

"I'll say!" said Gavrily.

"And only one death," said Alyx sharply, "not bad, eh?"

"That's not our fault," said Gavrily. They were all staring at her.

"No," she said, "it's not our fault. It's mine.

"Come on," she added.

On the thirty-second day Paradise still offered them the semblance of a path, though Gunnar could not find his mountain pass and grew scared and irritable trying to lead them another way. Paradise tilted and zigzagged around them. At times they had to sit down, or slide down, or even crawl, and he waited for them with deep impatience, telling them haughtily how a professional would be able to handle this sort of thing without getting down on his————to go down a slope. Alyx said nothing. Iris spoke to nobody. Only Gavrily talked incessantly about People's Capitalism, as if he had been stung by a bug, explaining at great and unnecessary length how the Government was a check on the Military, the Military was a check on Government, and both were a check on Business which in turn checked the other two. He called it the three-part system of checks and balances. Alyx listened politely. Finally she said:

"What's a——?"

Gavrily explained, disapprovingly.

"Ah," said Alyx, smiling.

Iris still said nothing.

They camped early for the night, sprawled about a narrow sort of table-land, as far away from each other as they could get and complaining loudly. The sun had not been down for fifteen minutes and there was still light in the sky: rose, lavender, yellow, apple-green, violet. It made a beautiful show. It was getting extremely cold. Gunnar insisted that they could go on, in spite of their complaints; he clenched his big hands and ordered them to get up (which they did not do); then he turned to Alyx.

"You too," he said. "You can go on for another hour."

"I'd prefer not to go on in the dark," she said. She

was lying down with her hands under her head, watching the colors in the sky.

"There's light enough to last us all night!" he said. "*Will* you come on?"

"No," said Alyx.

"God damn it!" he said, "do you think I don't know what I'm doing? Do you think I don't know where I'm taking you? You lazy sons of bitches, get up!"

"That's enough," said Alyx, half on her feet.

"Oh no it isn't," he said. "Oh no it isn't! You all get up, all of you! You're not going to waste the hour that's left!"

"I prefer," said Alyx quietly, "not to sleep with my head wedged in a chasm, if you don't mind." She rose to her feet.

"Do I have to kick you in the stomach again?" she said calmly.

Gunnar was silent. He stood with his hands balled into fists.

"Do I?" she said. "Do I have to kick you in the groin? Do I have to gouge your eyes out?

"Do I have to dive between your legs and throw you head foremost on the rocks so you're knocked out?" she said.

"So your nose gets broken?

"So your cheekbones get bloody and your chin bruised?"

She turned to the others.

"I suggest that we keep together," she said, "to take advantage of each other's warmth; otherwise you are bound to stiffen up as you get colder; it is going to be a devil of a night."

She joined the others as they packed snow about

themselves—it was more like frozen dust than snow, and there was not much of it; they were too high up—and settled in against Iris, who was unreadable, with the beautiful sky above them dying into deep rose, into dusty rose, into dirty rose. She did not look at Gunnar. She felt sorry for him. He was to take the first watch anyway, *Though* (she thought) *what we are watching for I do not know and what we could do if we saw it, God only knows. And then what I am watching for . . . What I would do . . . No food . . . Too high up . . . No good . . .*

She woke under the night sky, which was brilliant with stars: enormous, shining, empty and cold. The stars were unrecognizable, not constellations she knew any more but planes upon planes, shifting trapezoids, tilted pyramids like the mountains themselves, all reaching off into spaces she could not even begin to comprehend: distant suns upon suns. The air was very cold.

Someone was gently shaking her, moving her limbs, trying to untangle her from the mass of human bodies. She said, "Lemme sleep" and tried to turn over. Then she felt a shocking draught at her neck and breast and a hand inside her suit; she said sleepily, "Oh dear, it's too cold."

"You had better get up," whispered Machine reasonably. "I believe I'm standing on somebody.

"I'm trying not to," he added solemnly, "but everyone's so close together that it's rather difficult."

Alyx giggled. The sound startled her. *Well, I'll talk to you,* she said. *No,* she thought, *I didn't say it, did I?* She articulated clearly "I—will—talk—to you," and sat up, leaning her head against his knee to wake

up. She pushed his hand away and closed up her
suit. "I'm cross," she said, "you hear that?"

"I hear and obey," whispered Machine, grinning,
and taking her up in his arms like a baby, he carried
her through the mass of sleepers, picking his way
carefully, for they were indeed packed very close
together. He set her down a little distance away.

"You're supposed to be on watch," she protested.
He shook his head. He knelt beside her and pointed
to the watch—Gunnar—some fifteen meters away. *A
noble figure*, thought Alyx. She began to laugh un-
controllably, muffling her mouth on her knees. Machine's shoulders were shaking gleefully. He scooped
her up with one arm and walked her behind a little
wall of snow someone had built, a little wall about
one meter high and three meters long—"Did you—?"
said Alyx.

"I did," said the young man. He reached out with
one forefinger and rapidly slid it down the opening of
her suit from her neck to her—

"Eeeey, it's too cold!" cried Alyx, rolling away and
pressing the opening shut again.

"Sssh!" he said. "No it's not."

"He'll see us," said Alyx, straightening out distrust-
fully.

"No he won't."

"Yes he will."

"No he won't"

"Yes he *will!*" She got up, shook the snow off
herself and immediately started away. Machine did
not move.

"Well, aren't you—" she said, nettled.

He shook his head. He sat down, crossed his legs
in some unaccountable fashion so the feet ended up

on top, crossed his arms, and sat immobile as an Oriental statue. She came back and sat next to him, resting her head against him (as much as she could with one of his knees in the way), feeling soulful, trustful, silly. She could feel him chuckling. "How *do* you do that with the feet?" she said. He wriggled his toes inside his boots.

"I dare not do anything else," he said, "because of your deadly abilities with groin-kicking, eye-gouging, head-cracking and the like, Agent."

"Oh, shut up!" said Alyx. She put her arms around him. He uncrossed his own arms, then used them to carefully uncross his legs; then lay down with her in the snow, insulated suit to insulated suit, kissing her time after time. Then he stopped.

"You're scared, aren't you?" he whispered.

She nodded.

"Goddammit, I've had men before!" she whispered. He put his finger over her lips. With the other hand he pressed together the ends of the thongs that could hold a suit loosely together at the collarbone—first his suit, then hers—and then, with the same hand, rapidly opened both suits from the neck in front to the base of the spine in back and ditto with the long underwear: "Ugly but useful," he remarked. Alyx began to giggle again. She tried to press against him, shivering with cold. "Wait!" he said, "and watch, O Agent," and very carefully, biting one lip, he pressed together the righthand edges of both suits and then the left, making for the two of them a personal blanket, a double tent, a spot of warmth under the enormous starry sky.

"And they don't," he said triumphantly, "come apart by pulling. They *only* come apart by prying!

And see? You can move your arms and legs in! Isn't it marvelous?" And he gave her a proud kiss—a big, delighted, impersonal smack on the cheek. Alyx began to laugh. She laughed as she pulled her arms and legs in to hug him; she laughed as he talked to her, as he buried his face in her neck, as he began to caress her; she laughed until her laughter turned to sobbing under his expert hands, his too-expert hands, his calm deliberateness; she raked his back with her fingernails; she screamed at him to hurry up and called him a pig and an actor and the son of a whore (for these epithets were of more or less equal value in her own country); and finally, when at his own good time the stars exploded—and she realized that *nova* meant—that *nova* meant (though she had closed her eyes a long time before)—someone had said *nova* the other day—she came to herself as if rocking in the shallows of a prodigious tide, yawning, lazily extending her toes—and with a vague but disquieting sense of having done something or said something she should not have said or done. She knew she hated him there, for a while; she was afraid she might have hurt him or hurt his feelings.

"What language were you speaking?" said Machine with interest.

"Greek!" said Alyx, and she laughed with relief and would have kissed him, only it was really too much effort.

He shook her. "Don't go to sleep," he said.

"Mmmmm."

"Don't go to sleep!" and he shook her harder.

"Why not?" she said.

"Because," said Machine, "I am going to begin again."

"All right," said Alyx, complaisantly and raised her knees. He began, as before, to kiss her neck, her shoulders and so on down et cetera et cetera, in short to do everything he had done before on the same schedule until it occurred to her that he was doing everything just as he had done it before and on the same schedule, until she tried to push him away, exclaiming angrily, feeling like a statuette or a picture, frightened and furious. At first he would not stop; finally she bit him.

"What the devil is the matter!" he cried.

"You," she said, "stop it. Let me out." They had been together and now they were sewed up in a sack; it was awful; she started to open the jointure of the suits but he grabbed her hands.

"What is it?" he said, "what is it? Don't you want it? Don't you see that I'm trying?"

"Trying?" said Alyx stupidly.

"Yes, trying!" he said vehemently. "Trying! Do you think that comes by nature?"

"I don't understand," she said. "I'm sorry." They lay silently for a few minutes.

"I was trying," he said in a thick, bitter voice, "to give you a good time. I like you. I did the best I could. Apparently it wasn't good enough."

"But I don't—" said Alyx.

"You don't want it," he said; "all right," and pushing her hands away, he began to open the suits himself. She closed them. He opened them and she closed them several times. Then he began to cry and she put her arms around him.

"I had the best time in my life," she said. He continued to sob, silently, through clenched teeth, turning away his face.

"I had," she repeated, "the best time in my life. I did. I did! But I don't want—"

"All right," he said.

"But I don't," she said. "I don't want—I don't—"

He tried to get away from her and, of course could not; he thrashed about, forgetting that the suits had to be slit and could not be pulled apart; he pushed against the material until he frightened her for she thought she was going to be hurt; finally she cried out:

"Darling, stop it! Please!"

Machine stopped, leaning on his knees and clenched fists, his face stubbornly turned away.

"It's you I want," she said. "D'you see? I don't want a—performance. I want *you*."

"I don't know what you're talking about," he said, more calmly.

"Well, I don't know what *you're* talking about," said Alyx reasonably.

"Look," he said, turning his head back so that they were nose to nose, "when you do something, you do it right, don't you?"

"No," said Alyx promptly.

"Well, what's the good of doing it then!" he shouted.

"Because you want to, idiot!" she snapped, "any five-year-old child—"

"Oh, now I'm a five-year-old child, am I?"

"Just a minute, just a minute, athlete! I never said—"

"Athlete! By God—"

She pinched him.

He pinched her.

She grabbed at what there was of his hair and pulled it; he howled and twisted her hand; then both of them pushed and the result was that he lost his balance and carried her over on to one side with him, the impromptu sleeping-bag obligingly going with them. They both got a faceful of snow. They wrestled silently for a few minutes, each trying to grab some part of the other, Machine muttering, Alyx kicking, Machine pushing her head down into the bag, Alyx trying to bite his finger, Machine yelling, Alyx trying to butt her head into his stomach. There was, however, no room to do anything properly. After a few minutes they stopped.

He sighed. It was rather peaceful, actually.

"Look, dear," he said quietly, "I've done my best. But if you want me, myself, you'll have to do without; I've heard that too often. Do you think they don't want me out there? Sure they do! They want me to open up my" (she could not catch the word) "like a goddamned" (or that one) "and show them everything that's inside, all my feelings, or what they call feelings. I don't believe they have feelings. They talk about their complexities and their reactions and their impressions and their interactions and their patterns and their neuroses and their childhoods and their rebellions and their utterly unspeakable insides until I want to vomit. I have no insides. I will not have any. I certainly will not let anyone see any. I do things and I do them well; that's all. If you want that, you can have it. Otherwise, my love, I am simply not at home. Understood?"

"Understood," she said. She took his face in her hands. "You are splendid," she said thickly. "You are splendid and beautiful and superb. I love your performance. Perform me."

And if I let slip any emotion, she thought, *it will—thank God—be in Greek!*

He performed again—rather badly. But it turned out well just the same.

When Machine had gone to take over the watch from Gunnar, Alyx returned to the sleepers. Iris was sitting up. Not only was it possible to identify her face in the starlight reflected from the snow; she had thrown back her hood in the bitter cold and her silver hair glowed uncannily. She waited until Alyx reached her; then she said:

"Talk to me."

"Did you know I was up?" said Alyx. Iris giggled, but an uncertain, odd sort of giggle as if she were fighting for breath; she said in the same queer voice, "Yes, you woke me up. You were both shouting."

Gunnar must know, thought Alyx and dismissed the thought. She wondered if these people were jealous. She turned to go back to her own sleeping place but Iris clutched at her arm, repeating, "Talk to me!"

"What about, love?" said Alyx.

"Tell me—tell me bad things," said Iris, catching her breath and moving her head in the collar of her suit as if it were choking her. "Put your hood on," said Alyx, but the girl shook her head, declaring she wanted it that way. She said, "Tell me—horrors."

"What?" said Alyx in surprise, sitting down.

"I want to hear bad things," said Iris monotonously. "I want to hear awful things. I can't stand it. I keep slipping," and she giggled again, saying "everybody could hear you all over camp," and then putting one hand to her face, catching her breath, and holding on to Alyx's arm as if she were drowning. "Tell me horrors!" she cried.

"Sssh," said Alyx, "ssssh, I'll tell you anything you like, baby, anything you like."

"My mother's dead," said Iris with sudden emotion. "My mother's dead. I've got to remember that. I've got to!"

"Yes, yes, she's dead," said Alyx.

"Please, please," said Iris, "keep me here. I keep sliding away."

"Horrors," said Alyx. "Good Lord, I don't think I know any tonight."

"It's like feathers," said Iris suddenly, dreamily, looking up in the sky, "it's like pillows, it's like air cushions under those things, you know, it's like— like—"

"All right, all right," said Alyx quickly, "your mother broke her neck. I'll tell you about it again. I might as well; you're all making me soft as wax, the whole lot of you."

"Don't, don't," said Iris, moaning. "Don't say soft. I keep trying, I thought the cold—yes, yes, that's good—" and with sudden decision she began to strip off her suit. Alyx grabbed her and wrestled her to the ground, fastening the suit again and shoving the hood on for good measure. She thought suddenly *She's still fighting the drug.* "You touch that again and I'll smash you," said Alyx steadily. "I'll beat your damned teeth in."

"It's too hot," said Iris feverishly, "too—to—" She relapsed into looking at the stars.

"Look at me," said Alyx, grabbing her head and pulling it down. "Look at me, baby."

"I'm not a baby," said Iris lazily. "I'm not a—a—baby. I'm a woman."

Alyx shook her.

"I am almost grown up," said Iris, not bothered by her head wobbling while she was being shaken. "I am very grown up. I am thirty-three."

Alyx dropped her hands.

"I am thirty-three already," continued Iris, trying to focus her eyes. "I am, I am" (she said this uncomfortably, with great concentration) "and—and Ma—Machine is thirty-six and Gunnar is fifty-eight—yes, that's right—and Maudey was my mother. She was my mother. She was ninety. But she didn't look it. She's dead. She didn't look it, did she? She took that stuff. She didn't look it."

"Baby," said Alyx, finding her voice, "look at me."

"Why?" said Iris in a whisper.

"Because," said Alyx, "I am going to tell you something horrible. Now look at me. You know what I look like. You've seen me in the daylight. I have lines in my face, the first lines, the ones that tell you for the first time that you're going to die. There's gray in my hair, just a little, just enough to see in a strong light, a little around my ears and one streak starting at my forehead. Do you remember it?"

Iris nodded solemnly.

"I am getting old," said Alyx, "and my skin is getting coarse and tough. I tire more easily. I am withering a little. It will go faster and faster from now on and soon I will die.

"Iris," she said with difficulty, "how old am I?"

"Fifty?" said Iris.

Alyx shook her head.

"Sixty?" said Iris hopefully.

Alyx shook her head again.

"Well, how old are you?" said Iris, a little impatiently.

"Twenty-six," said Alyx. Iris put her hands over her eyes.

"Twenty-six," said Alyx steadily. "Think of that, you thirty-three-year-old adolescent! Twenty-six and dead at fifty. Dead! There's a whole world of people who live like that. We don't eat the way you do, we don't have whatever it is the doctors give you, we work like hell, we get sick, we lose arms or legs or eyes and nobody gives us new ones, we die in the plague, one-third of our babies die before they're a year old and one time out of five the mother dies, too, in giving them birth."

"But it's so long ago!" wailed little Iris.

"Oh no it's not," said Alyx. "It's *right now*. It's going on right now. I lived in it and I came here. It's in the next room. I was in that room and now I'm in this one. There are people still in that other room. They are living *now*. They are suffering *now*. And they always live and always suffer because *everything keeps on happening*. You can't say it's all over and done with because it isn't; it keeps going on. It all keeps going on. Shall I tell you about the plague? That's one nice thing. Shall I tell you about the fevers, the boils, the spasms, the fear, the burst blood vessels, the sores? Shall I tell you what's going on right now, right here, right in this place?

"Y—yes! Yes! Yes!" cried Iris, her hands over her ears. Alyx caught the hands in her own, massaging them (for they were bare), slipping Iris's gloves back on and pressing the little tabs that kept them shut.

"Be quiet," she said, "and listen, for I am going to tell you about the Black Death."

And for the next half hour she did until Iris's eyes came back into focus and Iris began to breathe normally and at last Iris fell asleep.

Don't have nightmares, baby, said Alyx to herself, stroking one lock of silver hair that stuck out from under the girl's hood. *Don't have nightmares, thirty-three-year-old baby.* She did not know exactly what she herself felt. She bedded down in her own place, leaving all that for the next day, thinking first of her own children: the two put out to nurse, the third abandoned in the hills when she had run away from her husband at seventeen and (she thought) not to a Youth Core. She smiled in the dark. She wondered if Gunnar had known who was carrying on so. She wondered if he minded. She thought again of Iris, of Machine, of the comfort it was to hear human breathing around you at night, the real comfort.

I've got two of them, she thought, *and damn Gunnar anyway*.

She fell asleep.

The thirty-fifth day was the day they lost Raydos. They did not lose him to the cats, although they found big paw-prints around their camp the next morning and met one of the spotted animals at about noon, circling it carefully at a distance while it stood hissing and spitting on a rocky eminence, obviously unsure whether to come any closer or not. It was less than a meter high and had enormous padded paws: a little animal and a lot of irritation; Alyx dropped to the rear to watch it stalk them for the next three hours, keeping her crossbow ready and making abrupt movements from time to time to make it duck out of sight. Gunnar was up front, leading the way. Its persistence rather amused her at first but she supposed that it could do a lot of damage in spite of its size and was beginning to wonder whether she could risk a loud shout—or a shot into the rocks—to drive it off, when for no reason at all that she could see, the animal's tufted ears perked forward, it crouched down abruptly, gave a kind of hoarse, alarmed growl and bounded awkwardly away. The whole column in front of her had halted. She made her way to the front where Gunnar stood like a huge statue, his big arm pointing up straight into the sky, as visible as the Colossus of Rhodes.

"Look," he said, pleased, "a bird." She yanked at his arm, pulling him to the ground, shouting "Down, everyone!" and all of them fell on to their hands and knees, ducking their heads. The theory was that the white suits and white packs would blend into the snow as long as they kept their faces hidden, or that they would look like animals and that any reading of body heat would be disregarded as such. She wondered if there was any sense to it. She thought that it might be a bird. It occurred to her that distances were hard to judge in a cloudless sky. It also occurred to her that the birds she knew did not come straight down, and certainly not that fast, and that the snow-shoed cat had been running away from something snow-shoed cats did not like. So it might be just as well to occupy their ridiculous position on the ground until whatever it was satisfied its curiosity and went away, even though her knees and elbows hurt and she was getting the cramp, even though things were absolutely silent, even though nothing at all seemed to be happening . . .

"Well?" said Gunnar. There was a stir all along
the line.

"Sssh," said Alyx. Nothing happened.

"We've been down on our knees," said Gunnar a bit
testily, "for five minutes. I have been looking at my
watch."

"All right, I'll take a look up," said Alyx, and
leaning on one arm, she used her free hand to pull
her hood as far over her face as possible. Slowly she
tilted her head and looked.

"Tell us the color of its beak," said Gunnar.

There was a man hanging in the air forty meters
above them. Forty meters up in the sky he sat on
nothing, totally unsupported, wearing some kind of
green suit with a harness around his waist. She
could have sworn that he was grinning. He put out
one bare hand and punched the air with his finger;
then he came down with such speed that it seemed
to Alyx as if he must crash; then he stopped just as
abruptly, a meter above the snow and two in front of
them. He grinned. Now that he was down she could
see the faint outline of what he was traveling in: a
transparent bubble, just big enough for one, a transparent shelf of a seat, a transparent panel fixed to the
wall. The thing made a slight depression in the snow.
She supposed that she could see it because it was
not entirely clean. The stranger took out of his harness what even she could recognize as a weapon, all
too obviously shaped for the human hand to do God
knew what to the human body. He pushed at the
wall in front of him and stepped out—swaggering.

"Well?" said Gunnar in a strained whisper.

"His beak," said Alyx distinctly, "is green and he's
got a gun. Get up," and they all rocketed to their

feet, quickly moving back; she could hear them scrambling behind her. The stranger pointed his weapon and favored them with a most unpleasant smile. He lounged against the side of his ship. It occurred to Alyx with a certain relief that she had known him before, that she had known him in two separate millennia and eight languages, and that he had been the same fool each time; she only hoped mightily that no one would get hurt. She hugged herself as if in fear, taking advantage of the position to take off her gloves and loosen the knives in her sleeves while Machine held his crossbow casually and clumsily in one hand. He was gaping at the stranger like an idiot. Gunnar had drawn himself up, half a head above all of them, again the colossus, his face pale and muscles working around his mouth.

"Well, well," said the stranger with heavy sarcasm, "break my———" (she did not understand this) "I'm just cruising around and what do I find? A bloody circus!"

Someone—probably a nun—was crying quietly in the back.

"And what's *that?*" said the stranger. "A dwarf? The Herculean Infant?" He laughed loudly. "Maybe I'll leave it alone. Maybe if it's female, I'll tuck it under my arm after I've ticked the rest of you and take it away with me for convenience. Some———!" and again a word Alyx did not understand. Out of the corner of her eye she saw Machine redden. The stranger was idly kicking the snow in front of him; then with his free hand he pointed negligently at Machine's crossbow. "What's that thing?" he said. Machine looked stupid.

"Hey come on, come on, don't waste my time,"

said the stranger. "What is it? I can tick you first, you know. Start telling."

"It's a d-d-directional f-f-inder," Machine stammered, blushing furiously.

"It's a what?" said the man suspiciously.

"It's t-to tell direction," Machine blurted out. "Only it doesn't work," he added stiffly.

"Give it here," said the stranger. Machine obligingly stepped forward, the crossbow hanging clumsily from his hand.

"*Stay back!*" cried the man, jerking up his gun. "*Don't come near me!*" Machine held out the crossbow, his jaw hanging.

"Stuff it," said the stranger, trying to sound cool, "I'll look at it after you're dead," and added, "get in line, Civs," as if nothing at all had happened. *Ah yes*, thought Alyx. They moved slowly into line, Alyx throwing her arms around Machine as he stepped back, incidentally affording him the cover to pull back the bow's spring and giving herself the two seconds to say "Belly." She was going to try to get his gun hand. She got her balance as near perfect as she could while the stranger backed away from them to survey the whole line; she planned to throw from her knees and deflect his arm upward while he shot at the place she had been, and to this end she called out "Mister, what are you going to do with us?"

He walked back along the line, looking her up and down—mostly down, for he was as tall as the rest of them; possibly a woman as small as herself was a kind of expensive rarity. He said, "I'm not going to do anything to *you*."

"No," he said, "not to you; I'll leave you here and

pick you up later, Infant. We can all use you." She
looked innocent.

"After I tick these Ops," he went on, "after we get
'em melted—you're going to see it, Infant—then I'll
wrap you up and come back for you later. Or maybe
take a little now. We'll see.

"The question," he added, "is which of you I will
tick first. The question is which of you feather-loving
Ops I will turn to ashes first and I think, after mature
judgment and a lot of decisions and maybe just turning it over in my head, I say I think—"

Gunnar threw himself at the man.

He did so just as Alyx flashed to her knees and
turned into an instant blur, just as Machine whipped
up the crossbow and let go the bolt, just as Gunnar
should have stood still and prayed to whatever gods
guard amateur explorers—just at this moment he
flung himself forward at the stranger's feet. There
was a flash of light and a high-pitched, horrible scream.
Gunnar lay sprawled in the snow. The stranger,
weapon dangling from one hand, bleeding in one
small line from the belly where Machine's bolt had
hit him, sat in the snow and stared at nothing. Then
he bent over and slid onto his side. Alyx ran to the
man and snatched the gun from his grasp but he was
unmistakably dead; she pulled one of her knives out
of his forearm where it had hit him—but high, much
too high, damn the balance of the stupid things!—
hardly even spoiling his aim—and the other from
his neck, grimacing horribly and leaping aside to
keep from getting drenched. The corpse fell over on
its face. Then she turned to Gunnar.

Gunnar was getting up.

"Well, well," said Machine from between his teeth, "what—do—you—know!"

"How the devil could I tell you were going to do anything!" shouted Gunnar.

"Did you make that noise for effect," said Machine, "or was it merely fright?"

"Shut up, you!" cried Gunnar, his face pale.

"Did you wish to engage our sympathies?" said Machine, "or did you intend to confuse the enemy? Was it electronic noise? Is it designed to foul up radar? Does it contribute to the electromagnetic spectrum? Has it a pattern? Does it scan?"

Gunnar stepped forward, his big hands swinging. Machine raised the bow. Both men bent a little at the knees. Then in between them, pale and calm, stepped one of the nuns, looking first at one and then at the other until Gunnar turned his back and Machine—making a face—broke apart the crossbow and draped both parts over his shoulder.

"Someone is hurt," said the nun.

Gunnar turned back. "That's impossible!" he said. "Anyone in the way of that beam would be dead, not hurt."

"Someone," repeated the nun, "is hurt," and she walked back towards the little knot the others had formed in the snow, clustering about someone on the ground. Gunnar shouted, "It's not possible!"

"It's Raydos," said Machine quietly, somewhere next to Alyx. "It's not Iris. He just got the edge. The bastard had put it on diffuse. He's alive," and taking her by the elbow, he propelled her to the end of the line, where Raydos had been standing almost but not quite in profile, where the stranger had shot when his arm was knocked away and up from his aim on Gunnar, when he had already turned his weapon down on Gunnar because Gunnar was acting like a hero, and not tried to shoot Alyx, who could have dropped beneath the beam, twisted away and killed him before he could shoot again. Strike a man's arm up into the air and it follows a sweeping curve.

Right over Raydos' face.

And Raydos' eyes.

She refused to look at him after the first time. She pushed through the others to take a long look at the unconscious man's face where he lay, his arms thrown out, in the snow: the precise line where his face began, the precise line where it ended, the fine, powdery, black char that had been carefully laid across the rest of it. Stirred by their breath, the black powder rose in fine spirals. Then she saw the fused circles of Raydos' eye lenses: black, shiny black, little puddles resting as if in a valley; they still gave out an intense heat. She heard Gunnar say nervously "Put—put snow on it," and she turned her back remarking, "Snow. And do what you have to do." She walked slowly over to the transparent bubble. In the distance she could see some kind of activity going on over Raydos, things being brought out of his pack, all sorts of conferring going on. She carefully kicked snow over the dead body. She reflected that Paradise must know them all very well, must know them intimately, in fact, to find the levers to open them one by one until none of them were left or only she was left or none of them were left. Maudey. She stood aside carefully as Gunnar and Machine carried up something that was lacking a face—or rather, his face had turned lumpy and white—and put him in the transparent bubble. That is,

Gunnar put him in, getting half in with him for the thing would not hold more than the head and arms of another occupant. Gunnar was taping Raydos to the seat and the walls and working on the control board. Then he said, "I'll set the automatic location signal to turn itself off an hour after sundown; he did say he was cruising."

"So you know something," said Machine. Gunnar went on, his voice a little high:

"I can coordinate it for the Pole station."

"So you are worth something," said Machine.

"They won't shoot him down," said Gunnar quickly. "They would but I've set it for a distress call at the coordinate location. They'll try to trap him.

"That's not easy," he added, "but I think it'll work. It's a kind of paradox, but there's an override. I've slowed him down as much as I can without shutting him off altogether, he may last, and I've tried to put in some indication of where we are and where we're headed but it's not equipped for that; I can't send out a Standard call or *they'll* come and pick him up, I mean the others, of course, they must have this section pretty well under control or they wouldn't be sending loners around here. And of course the heat burst registered, but they'll think it's him; he did say—"

"Why don't you write it, you bastard?" said Machine.

"Write?" said Gunnar.

"Write it on a piece of paper," said Machine. "Do you know what paper is? He has it in his pack. That stuff he uses for drawing is paper. Write on it!"

"I don't have anything to write with," said Gunnar.

"You stupid bastard," said Machine slowly, turning Raydos's pack upside down so that everything fell out of it: pens, black stuff, packets of things taped together, food, a kind of hinged manuscript, all the medicine. "You stupid, electronic bastard," he said, ripping a sheet from the manuscript, "this is paper. And this" (holding it out) "is artists' charcoal. Take the charcoal and write on the paper. If you know how to write."

"That's unnecessary," said Gunnar, but he took the writing materials, removed his gloves and wrote laboriously on the paper, his hands shaking a little. He did not seem to be used to writing.

"Now tape it to the wall," said Machine. "No, the inside wall. Thank you. Thank you for everything. Thank you for your heroism. Thank you for your stupidity. Thank you—"

"I'll kill you!" cried Gunnar. Alyx threw up her arm and cracked him under the chin. He gasped and stumbled back. She turned to Machine. "You too," she said, "you too. Now finish it." Gunnar climbed half inside the bubble again and commenced clumsily making some last adjustments on the bank of instruments that hung in the air. The sun was setting: a short day. She watched the snow turn ruddy, ruddy all around, the fingerprints and smears on the bubble gone in a general, faint glow as the light diffused and failed, the sun sank, the man inside— who looked dead—wobbled back and forth as Gunnar's weight changed the balance of the delicate little ship. It looked like an ornament almost, something to set on top of a spire, someone's pearl.

"Is he dead?" said Alyx. Machine shook his head. "Frozen," he said. "We all have it in the packs. Slows you down. He may last."

"His eyes?" said Alyx.

"Why, I didn't think you cared," said Machine, trying to make it light.

"His eyes!"

Machine shrugged a little uncomfortably. "Maybe yes, maybe no," he said, "but" (here he laughed) "one would think you were in love with the man."

"I don't know him," said Alyx. "I never knew him."

"Then why all the fuss, Tiny?" he said.

"You don't have a word for it."

"The hell I don't!" said Machine somewhat brutally. "I have words for everything. So the man was what we call an artist. All right. He used color on flat. So what? He can use sound. He can use things you stick your fingers into and they give you a jolt. He can use wires. He can use textures. He can use pulse-beats. He can use things that climb over you while you close your eyes. He can use combinations of drugs. He can use direct brain stimulation. He can use hypnosis. He can use things you walk on barefoot for all I care. It's all respectable; if he gets stuck in a little backwater of his field, that's his business; he can get out of it."

"Put his sketches in with him," said Alyx.

"Why?" said Machine.

"Because you don't have a word for it," she said. He shrugged, a little sadly. He riffled the book that had come from Raydos's pack, tearing out about half of it, and passed the sheets in to Gunnar. They were taped to Raydos's feet.

"Hell, he can still do a lot of things," said Machine, trying to smile.

"Yes," said Alyx, "and you will come out of this paralyzed from the neck down." He stopped smiling.

"But you will do a lot of things," she said. "Yes, you will get out of it. You will lose your body and Gunnar will lose his—his self-respect; he will make one more ghastly mistake and then another and another and in the end he will lose his soul at the very least and perhaps his life."

"You know all this," said Machine.

"Of course," said Alyx, "of course I do. I know it all. I know that Gavrily will do something generous and brave and silly and because he never in his life has learned how to do it, we will lose Gavrily. And then Iris—no, Iris has had it already, I think, and of course the Heavenly Twins will lose nothing because they have nothing to lose. Maybe they will lose their religion or drop their pills down a hole. And I—well, I—my profession, perhaps, or whatever loose junk I have lying around, because this blasted place is too good, you see, too easy; we don't meet animals, we don't meet paid professional murderers, all we meet is our own stupidity. Over and over. It's a picnic. It's a damned picnic. And Iris will come through because she never lives above her means. And a picnic is just her style."

"What will you lose?" said Machine, folding his arms across his chest.

"I will lose you," she said unsteadily, "what do you think of that?" He caught her in his arms, crushing the breath out of her.

"I like it," he whispered sardonically. "I like it, Tiny, because I am jealous. I am much too jealous. If I thought you didn't like me, I'd kill myself and if I

thought you liked Iris more than me, I'd kill her. Do
you hear me?"

"Don't be an ass," she said. "Let me go."

"I'll never let you go. Never. I'll die. With you."

Gunnar backed ponderously out of the bubble. He
closed the door, running his hands carefully over the
place where the door joined the rest of the ship
until the crack disappeared. He seemed satisfied with
it then. He watched it, although nothing seemed to
happen for a few minutes; then the bubble rose
noiselessly off the snow, went up faster and faster
into the evening sky as if sliding along a cable and
disappeared into the afterglow. It was going north.
Alyx tried to pull away but Machine held on to her,
grinning at his rival as the latter turned around,
absently dusting his hands together. Then Gunnar
groped for his gloves, put them on, absently looking
at the two, at the others who had shared the contents
of Raydos's pack and were flattening the pack itself
into a shape that could be carried in an empty food
container. There was the corpse, the man everyone
had forgotten. Gunnar looked at it impersonally. He
looked at Iris, the nuns, Gavrily, the other two: only
seven of them now. His gloved hands dusted themselves together. He looked at nothing.

"Well?" drawled Machine.

"I think we will travel a little now," said Gunnar;
"I think we will travel by starlight." He repeated the
phrase, as if it pleased him. "By starlight," he said,
"yes."

"By snowlight?" said Machine, raising his eyebrows.

"That too," said Gunnar, looking at something in
the distance, "yes—that too—"

"Gunnar!" said Alyx sharply. His gaze settled on her.

"I'm all right," he said quietly. "I don't care who you play with," and he plodded over to the others, bent over, very big.

"I shall take you tonight," said Machine between his teeth; "I shall take you right before the eyes of that man!"

She brought the point of her elbow up into his ribs hard enough to double him over; then she ran through the powdery snow to the front of the little line that had already formed. Gunnar was leading them. Her hands were icy. She took his arm—it was unresponsive, nothing but a heavy piece of meat—and said, controlling her breathing, for she did not want him to know that she had been running—"I believe it is getting warmer."

He said nothing.

"I mention this to you," Alyx went on, "because you are the only one of us who knows anything about weather. Or about machinery. We would be in a bad way without you."

He still said nothing.

"I am very grateful," she said, "for what you did with the ship. There is nobody here who knows a damn thing about that ship, you know. No one but you could have—" (she was about to say *saved Raydos's life*) "done anything with the control board. I am grateful. We are all grateful."

"Is it going to snow?" she added desperately, "is it going to snow?"

"Yes," said Gunnar. "I believe it is."

"Can you tell me why?" said she. "I know nothing

about it. I would appreciate it very much if you could tell me why."

"Because it is getting warmer."

"Gunnar!" she cried. *"Did you hear us?"*

Gunnar stopped walking. He turned to her slowly and slowly looked down at her, blankly, a little puzzled, frowning a little.

"I don't remember hearing anything," he said. Then he added sensibly, "That ship is a very good ship; it's insulated; you don't hear anything inside."

"Tell me about it," said Alyx, her voice almost failing, "and tell me why it's going to snow."

He told her, and she hung on his arm, pretending to listen, for hours.

They walked by starlight until a haze covered the stars; it got warmer, it got slippery. She tried to remember their destination by the stars. They stopped on Paradise's baby mountains, under the vast, ill-defined shadow of something going up, up, a slope going up until it melted into the gray sky, for the cloud cover shone a little, just as the snow shone a little, the light just enough to see by and not enough to see anything at all. When they lay down there was a pervasive feeling of falling to the left. Iris kept trying to clutch at the snow. Alyx told them to put their feet downhill and so they did, lying in a line and trying to hold each other's hands. Gunnar went off a little to one side, to watch—or rather to listen. Everything was indistinct. Five minutes after everyone had settled down—she could still hear their small readjustments, the moving about, the occasional whispering—she discerned someone squatting at her feet, his arms about his knees, balanced just so. She held out one arm and he pulled her to her feet, putting his arms around her: Machine's face, very close in the white darkness. "Over there," he said, jerking his head towards the place where Gunnar was, perhaps sitting, perhaps standing, a kind of blot against the gray sky.

"No," said Alyx.

"Why not?" said Machine in a low, mocking voice. "Do you think he doesn't know?"

She said nothing.

"Do you think there's anyone here who doesn't know?" Machine continued, a trifle brutally. "When you go off, you raise enough hell to wake the dead."

She nudged him lightly in the ribs, in the sore place, just enough to loosen his arms; and then she presented him with the handle of one of her knives, nudging him with that also, making him take step after step backwards, while he whispered angrily:

"What the hell!

"Stop it!

"What are you doing!

"What the devil!"

Then they were on the other side of the line of sleepers, several meters away.

"Here," she whispered, holding out the knife, "take it, take it. Finish him off. Cut off his head."

"I don't know what you're talking about!" snapped Machine.

"But not with me," she said; "oh, no!" and when he threw her down onto the snow and climbed on top of her, shaking her furiously, she only laughed, calling him a baby, teasing him, tickling him through his suit, murmuring mocking love-words, half in Greek, the better to infuriate him. He wound his

arms around her and pulled, crushing her ribs, her
fingers, smothering her with his weight, the knees of
his long legs digging one into her shin and one into
her thigh; there would be spectacular bruises tomorrow.

"Kill me," she whispered ecstatically. "Go on, kill
me, kill me! Do what you want!" He let her go,
lifting himself up on his hands, moving his weight off
her. He stared down at her, the mask of a very angry
young man. When she had got her breath back a
little, she said:

"My God, you're strong!"

"Don't make fun of me," he said.

"But you are strong," she said breathlessly. "You're
strong. You're enormous. I adore you."

"Like hell," said Machine shortly and began to get
up. She flung both arms around him and held on.

"Do it again," she said, "do it again. Only please,
please, more carefully!" He pulled away, making a
face, then stayed where he was.

"If you're making fun of me—" he said.

She said nothing, only kissed his chin.

"I hate that man!" he burst out. "I hate his damned
'acceptable' oddities and his—his conventional heroism and his—the bloody amateur!

"He's spent his life being praised for individualism," he went on, "*his* individualism, good God! Big
show. Make the Civs feel happy. Never two steps
from trans and ports and flyers. Medicine. High-
powered this. High-powered that. 'Ooooh, isn't he
marvel! Isn't he brave! Let's get a tape and go shooting warts with Gunnar! Let's get a tape and go swimming undersea in Gunnar!' He records his own brain
impulses, did you know that?"

"No," said Alyx.

"Yes," said Machine, "he records them and sells them. Gunnar's battle with the monsters. Gunnar's narrow escape. Gunnar's great adventure. All that heroism. That's what they want. That's why he's rich!"

"Well, they certainly wouldn't want the real thing," said Alyx softly, "now would they?"

He stared at her for a moment.

"No," he said more quietly, "I suppose they wouldn't."

"And I doubt," said Alyx, moving closer to him, "that Gunnar is recording anything just now; I think, my dear, that he's very close to the edge now."

"Let him fall in," said Machine.

"Are you rich?" said Alyx. Machine began to weep. He rolled to one side, half laughing, half sobbing.

"I!" he said, "I! Oh, that's a joke!

"I don't have a damn thing," he said. "I knew there would be a flash here—*they* knew but they thought they could get away—so I came. To get lost. Spent everything. But you can't get lost, you know. You can't get lost anywhere any more, not even in a—a—you would call it a war, Agent."

"Funny war," said Alyx.

"Yes, very funny. A war in a tourist resort. I hope we don't make it. I hope I die here."

She slid her finger down the front of his suit. "I hope not," she said. "No," she said (walking both hands up and down his chest, beneath the long underwear, her little moist palms) "I certainly hope not."

"You're a single-minded woman," said Machine dryly.

She shook her head. She was thoughtfully making the tent of the night before. He helped her.

"Listen, love," she said, "I have no money, either, but I have something else; I am a Project. I think I have cost a lot of money. If we get through this, one of the things this Project will need to keep it happy so it can go on doing whatever it's supposed to do is you. So don't worry about that."

"And you think they'll let you," said Machine. It was a flat, sad statement.

"No," she said, "but nobody ever let me do anything in my life before and I never let that stop me." They were lying on their sides face to face now; she smiled up at him. "I am going to disappear into this damned suit if you don't pull me up," she said. He lifted her up a little under the arms and kissed her. His face looked as if something were hurting him.

"Well?" she said.

"The Machine," he said stiffly, "is—the Machine is fond of the Project."

"The Project loves the Machine," she said, "so—?"

"I can't," he said.

She put her arm around the back of his neck and rubbed her cheek against his. "We'll sleep," she said. They lay together for some time, a little uncomfortable because both were balanced on their sides, until he turned over on his back and she lay half on him and half off, her head butting into his armpit. She began to fall asleep, then accidentally moved so that his arm cut off her breathing, then snorted. She made a little, dissatisfied noise.

"What?" he said.

"Too hot," she said sleepily, "blasted underwear," so with difficulty she took it off—and he took off his—and they wormed it out of the top of the suits where the hoods tied together and chucked it into the snow. She was breathing into his neck. She had half fallen asleep again when all of a sudden she woke to a kind of earthquake: knees in a tangle, jouncing, bruising, some quiet, vehement swearing and a voice telling her for God's sake to wake up. Machine was trying to turn over. Finally he did.

"Aaaaaah—um," said Alyx, now on her back, yawning.

"Wake up!" he insisted, grabbing her by both hips.

"Yes, yes, I am," said Alyx. She opened her eyes. He seemed to be trembling all over and very upset; he was holding her too hard, also.

"What is it?" she whispered.

"This is not going to be a good one," said Machine, "do you know what I mean?"

"No," said Alyx. He swore.

"Listen," he said shakily, "I don't know what's the matter with me; I'm falling apart. I can't explain it, but it's going to be a bad one; you'll just have to wait through it."

"All right, all right," she said, "give me a minute," and she lay quietly, thinking, rubbing his hair—looked Oriental, like a brush now, growing into a peak on his forehead—began kissing various parts of his face, put her arms around his back, felt his hands on her hips (too hard; she thought *I'll be black and blue tomorrow*), concentrated on those hands, and then began to rub herself against him, over and over and over, until she was falling apart herself, dizzy, head swimming, completely out of control.

"Goddamnit, you're making it worse!" he shouted.

"Can't help it," said Alyx. "Got to—come on."

"It's not fair," he said, "not fair to you. Sorry."

"Forgiven," Alyx managed to say as he plunged in, as she diffused over the landscape—sixty leagues in each direction—and then turned into a drum, a Greek one, hourglass-shaped with the thumped in-and-out of both skins so extreme that they finally met in the middle, so that she then turned inside out, upside down and switched right-and-left sides, every cell, both hands, each lobe of her brain, all at once, while someone (anonymous) picked her up by the navel and shook her violently in all directions, remarking, "If you don't make them cry, they won't live." She came to herself with the idea that Machine was digging up rocks. He was banging her on the head with his chin. Then after a while he stopped and she could feel him struggle back to self-possession; he took several deep, even breaths; he opened the suit hoods and pushed his face over her shoulder into the snow; then he opened one side of the little tent and let in a blast of cold air.

"Help!" said Alyx. He closed the suits. He leaned on his elbows. He said "I like you. I like you too much. I'm sorry." His face was wet to her touch: snow, tears or sweat. He said "I'm sorry, I'm sorry. We'll do it again."

"Oh no, no, no," she whispered weakly.

"Yes, don't worry," he said. "I'll control myself, it's not fair. No technique."

"If you use any more technique," she managed to get out, "there'll be nothing left of me in the morning but a pair of gloves and a small, damp spot."

"Don't lie," said Machine calmly.

She shook her head. She plucked at his arms,

trying to bring his full weight down on her, but he remained propped on his elbows, regarding her face intently. Finally he said:.

"Is that pleasure?"

"Is what?" whispered Alyx.

"Is it a pleasure," he said slowly, "or is it merely some detestable intrusion, some unbearable invasion, this being picked up and shaken, this being helpless and—and smashed and shattered into pieces when somebody lights a fuse at the bottom of one's brain!"

"It was pleasure for me," said Alyx softly.

"Was it the same for you?"

She nodded.

"I hate it," he said abruptly. "It was never like this before. Not like this. I hate it and I hate you."

She only nodded again. He watched her somberly.

"I think," he added finally, "that one doesn't like it or dislike it; one loves it. That is, something picked me up by the neck and pushed me into you. Ergo, I love you."

"I know," she said.

"It was not what I wanted."

"I know." She added, "It gets easier." He looked at her again; again she tried to pull him down. Then he remarked "We'll see," and smiled a little; he closed his eyes and smiled. He let his whole weight down on her carefully, saying, "You'll have to scramble out when I get too heavy, Tiny."

"Will."

"And tomorrow night," he added grimly, "I'll tell you the story of my life."

"Nice," she said, "yes, oh that will be . . . nice . . ." and she sank down deliciously into a sleep of feathers, into the swan's-down and duck's-down and peacock's-down that made up the snow of Paradise, into the sleep and snow of Paradise. . . .

The next day Paradise threw hell at them. It was the first real weather. It began with fat, heavy flakes just before dawn so that Gavrily (who had taken the dawn watch) was half buried himself and had to dig out some of the sleepers before he could rouse them; they were so used to the feeling of the stuff against their faces or leaking into their hoods and up their arms that they slept right through it. It turned colder as they ate breakfast, standing around and stamping and brushing themselves; then the snow got smaller and harder and then the first wind blasted around an outcropping of rock. It threw Alyx flat on her back. Gunnar said expressionlessly "You're smaller than we are." The others immediately huddled together. Goggles had not been packed with their equipment. They started out with the wind slamming them from side to side as if they had been toys, changing direction every few seconds and driving into their faces and down their necks stinging grains of rice. Gunnar insisted they were in a pass. They stumbled and fell more often than not, unable to see ten feet on either side, reaching in front of them, holding on to each other and sometimes falling onto hands and knees. Gunnar had faced away from the wind and was holding with both bare hands onto a map he had made from some of Raydos's things. He said "This is the pass." One of the nuns slipped and sprained her back. Gunnar was holding the map close to his eyes, moving it from side to side as if trying to puzzle something out. He said again:

"This is the pass. What are you waiting for?"

"What do you think, you flit!" snapped Iris. She was on one side of the sister and Gavrily on the other, trying to haul the woman to her feet. Gunnar opened his mouth again. Before he could speak, Alyx was at him (clawing at the bottom of his jacket to keep from falling in the wind) and crushing the map into a ball in his hand. "All right, all right!" she shouted through the snow, "it's the pass. Machine, come on," and the three of them plodded ahead, feeling and scrambling over hidden rocks, up a slope they could not see, veiled in snow that whipped about and rammed them, edging on their hands and knees around what seemed like a wall.

Then the wind stopped and Machine disappeared at the same time. She could not see where he had gone for a moment; then the wind returned—at their backs—and blasted the snow clear for a moment, hurrying it off the rock wall in sheets and revealing what looked like a well in the rock and a great, flattened slide of snow near it. It looked as if something had been dragged across it. Then the snow swept back, leaving only a dark hole.

"Chimney!" said Gunnar. Alyx flung herself on the ground and began to inch towards the dark hole in the snow. "I can't see," she said. She went as close as she dared. Gunnar stood back at a little distance, bracing himself against the wall. She risked lifting one hand to wave him closer, but he did not move. "Gunnar!" she shouted. He began to move slowly towards her, hugging the wall; then he stopped where the wall appeared to stop, taking from inside his glove the crumpled map and examining it, bracing himself automatically as the wind rocked him back and forth, and tracing something on the map with one finger as if there were something that puzzled him.

"Gunnar," said Alyx, flattening herself against the ground, "Gunnar, this hole is too broad for me. I can't climb down it."

Gunnar did not move.

"Gunnar," said Alyx desperately, "you're a mountain climber. You're an expert. You can climb down."

He raised his eyes from the map and looked at her without interest.

"You can climb down it," continued Alyx, digging her fingers into the snow. "You can tie a rope to him and then you can climb up and we'll pull him up."

"Well, I don't think so," he said. He came a little closer, apparently not at all bothered by the wind, and peered into the hole; then he repeated in a tone of finality, "No, I don't think so."

"You've got to," said Alyx. He balled up the map again and put it back into his glove. He had turned and was beginning to plod back towards the place where they had left the others, bent halfway into the wind, when she shouted his name and he stopped. He came back and looked into the hole with his hands clasped behind his back; then he said:

"Well, I don't think I'll try that."

"He's dying," said Alyx.

"No, I think that's a little risky," Gunnar added reasonably. He continued to look into the hole. "I'll let you down," he said finally. "Is that all right?"

"Yes, that's all right," said Alyx, shutting her eyes. She considered kicking him or tripping him so that he'd fall in himself but he was keeping a very prudent distance from the edge, and besides, there was

no telling where he would fall or how badly Machine
was hurt. He might fall on Machine. She said, "That's
fine, thanks." She rolled over and half sat up, slipping off her pack; clinging to it, she got out the
length of rope they all carried and tied it under her
arms. She was very clumsy in the wind; Gunnar
watched her without offering to help, and when she
was finished he took the free end and held it laxly in
one hand. "Your weight won't be too much," he said.

"Gunnar," she said, "hold that thing right." He
shook himself a little and took a better hold on the
rope. Coming closer, he said "Wait a minute," rummaged in her pack and handed her a kind of bulb
which she tucked into her sleeve. It looked like the
medicine he had once shown her, the kind they had
used on Raydos. He said "Put it in the crook of his
arm and press it. A little at a time." She nodded,
afraid to speak to him. She crawled toward the edge
of the well where the snow had suddenly collapsed
under Machine, and throwing her arms over the
ground, let herself down into the dark. The rope
held and Gunnar did not let go. She imagined that
he would wait for her to shout and then throw down
his own rope; she wrapped her arms around her
head for the hole was too wide for her to brace
herself and she spun slowly around—or rather, the
walls did, hitting her now and then—until the chimney narrowed. She climbed part of the way down,
arms and legs wide as if crucified. She had once seen
an acrobat roll on a wheel that way. The darkness
seemed to lighten a little and she thought she could
see something light at the bottom, so she shouted
"Gunnar!" up the shaft. As she had expected, a coil
of rope came whispering down, settled about her

shoulders, slid off to one side and hung about her like a necklace, the free end dangling down into the half-dark.

But when she pulled at it, she found that the other end was fastened under her own arms.

She did not think. She was careful about that. She descended further, to where Machine lay wedged like a piece of broken goods, his eyes shut, one arm bent at an unnatural angle, his head covered with blood. She could not get at his pack because it was under him. She found a kind of half-shelf next to him that she could stay on by bracing her feet against the opposite wall, and sitting there, she took from her sleeve the bulb Gunnar had given her. She could not get at either of Machine's arms without moving him, for the other one was twisted under him and jammed against the rock, but she knew that a major blood vessel was in the crook of the arm, so she pressed the nose of the bulb against a vessel in his neck and squeezed the bulb twice. Nothing happened. She thought: *Gunnar has gone to get the others*. She squeezed the medicine again and then was afraid, because it might be too much; someone had said "I've given Raydos all he can take"; so she put the thing back in her sleeve. Her legs ached. She could just about reach Machine. She took off a glove and put one hand in front of his mouth to satisfy herself that he was breathing, and then she tried feeling for a pulse in his throat and got something cold, possibly from the medicine bottle. But he had a pulse. His eyes remained closed. In her own pack was a time-telling device called a watch—she supposed vaguely that they called it that from the watches they had to keep at night, or perhaps they called it that for some other reason—but that was up top. She could not get to it. She began to put her weight first on one leg and then on the other, to rest a little, and then she found she could move closer to Machine, who still lay with his face upward, his eyes shut. He had fallen until the narrow part of the chimney stopped him. She was beginning to be able to see better and she touched his face with her bare hand; then she tried to feel about his head, where he was hurt, where the blood that came out increased ever so little, every moment, steadily black and black. The light was very dim. She felt gashes but nothing deep; she thought it must have been a blow or something internal in the body, so she put the medicine bulb to his neck again and squeezed it. Nothing happened. *They'll be back*, she thought. She looked at the bottle but could not see well enough to tell what was written on it so she put it back into her sleeve. It occurred to her then that they had never taught her to read, although they had taught her to speak. Lines came into her mind, *We are done for if we fall asleep*, something she must have heard; for she was growing numb and beginning to fall asleep, or not sleep exactly but some kind of retreat, and the dim, squirming walls around her began to close in and draw back, the way things do when one can barely see. She put both hands on Machine's face where the blood had begun to congeal in the cold, drew them over his face, talked to him steadily to keep herself awake, talked to him to wake him up. She thought *He has concussion*, the word coming from somewhere in the hypnotic hoard they had put into her head. She began to nod and woke with a jerk. She said softly "What's your name?" but Machine did not move. "No, tell me your name," she persisted gently, "tell me your name," drawing her hands over his face, unable to feel from the knees down, trying not to sink into sleep, passing her fingers through his hair while she nodded with sleep, talking to him, whispering against his cheek, feeling again and again for his hurts, trying to move her legs and coming close enough to him to see his face in the dim, dim light; to put her hands against his cheeks and speak to him in her own language, wondering why she should mind so much that he was dying, she who had had three children and other men past counting, wondering how there could be so much to these people and so little, so much and so little, like the coat of snow that made everything seem equal, both the up and the down, like the blowing snow that hid the most abysmal poverty and the precious things down under the earth. She jerked awake. Snow was sifting down on her shoulders and something snaky revolved in the air above her.

But Machine had stopped breathing some time before.

She managed to wind her own rope loosely around her neck and climb the other by bracing herself against the side of the well: not as smoothly as she liked, for the rope wavered a little and tightened unsteadily while Alyx cursed and shouted up to them to mind their bloody business if they didn't want to get it in a few minutes. Gavrily pulled her up over the edge.

"Well?" he said. She was blinking. The four others were all on the rope. She smiled at them briefly, slapping her gloves one against the other. Her hands were rubbed raw. The wind, having done its job, had fallen, and the snow fell straight as silk sheets.

"Well?" said Gavrily again, anxiously, and she shook her head. She could see on the faces of all of them a strange expression, a kind of mixed look as if they did not know what to feel or show. Of course; they had not liked him. She jerked her head towards the pass. Gavrily looked as if he were about to say something, and Iris as if she were about to cry suddenly, but Alyx only shook her head again and started off behind Gunnar. She saw one of the nuns looking back fearfully at the hole. They walked for a while and then Alyx took Gunnar's arm, gently holding on to the unresponsive arm of the big, big man, her lips curling back over her teeth on one side, involuntarily, horrible. She said:

"Gunnar, you did well."

He said nothing.

"You ought to have lived in my country," she said. "Oh yes! you would have been a hero there."

She got in front of him, smiling, clasping her hands together, saying "You think I'm fooling, don't you?" Gunnar stopped.

"It was your job," he said expressionlessly.

"Well, of course," she said sweetly, "of course it was," and crossing her hands wrist to wrist as she had done a thousand times before, she suddenly bent them in and then flipped them wide, each hand holding a knife. She bent her knees slightly; he was two heads taller and twice as heavy, easily. He put one hand stupidly up to his head.

"You can't do this," he said.

"Oh, there's a risk," she said, "there's that, of course," and she began to turn him back towards the others as he automatically stepped away from her, turning him in a complete circle to within sight of the others, while his face grew frightened, more and more awake, until he finally cried out:

"Oh God, Agent, what will you do!"

She shifted a little on her feet.

"I'm not like you!" he said, "I can't help it, what do you expect of me?"

"He came and got us," said Iris, frightened.

"None of us," said Gunnar quickly, "can help the way we are brought up, Agent. You are a creature of your world, believe me, just as I am of mine; I can't help it; I wanted to be like you but I'm not, can I help that? I did what I could! What can a man do? What do you expect me to do? What could I do!"

"Nothing. It's not your job," said Alyx.

"I am ashamed," said Gunnar, stammering, "I am ashamed, Agent, I admit I did the wrong thing. I should have gone down, yes, I should have—put those things away, for God's sake!—forgive me, please, hate me but forgive me; I am what I am, I am only what I am! For Heaven's sake! For God's sake!"

"Defend yourself," said Alyx, and when he did not—for it did not seem to occur to him that this was possible—she slashed the fabric of his suit with her left-hand knife and with the right she drove Trans-Temp's synthetic steel up to the hilt between Gunnar's ribs. It did not kill him; he staggered back a few steps, holding his chest. She tripped him onto his back and then cut his suit open while the madman did not even move, all this in an instant, and when he tried to rise she slashed him through the belly and then—lest the others intrude—pulled back his head by the pale hair and cut his throat from ear to ear. She did not spring back from the blood but stood in it, her face strained in the same involuntary grimace as before, the cords standing out on her neck. Iris grabbed her arm and pulled her away.

"He came and got us," whispered Iris, terrified, "he did, he did, really."

"He took his time," said Gavrily slowly. The five of them stood watching Gunnar, who lay in a red lake. The giant was dead. Alyx watched him until Iris turned her around; she followed obediently for a few steps, then stopped and knelt and wiped her hands in the snow. Then putting on her gloves, she took handfuls of snow and rubbed them over her suit, up and down, up and down. She cleaned herself carefully and automatically, like a cat. Then she put the knives away and silently followed the four others up the pass, floundering and slipping through the still-falling snow, hunched a little, her fists clenched. At dusk they found a shallow cave at the bottom of a long slope, not a rock cave but soft rock and frozen soil. Gavrily said they were over the pass. They sat as far back against the cave wall as they could, watching the snow fall across the opening and glancing now and again at Alyx. She was feeling a kind of pressure at the back of her neck, something insistent like a forgotten thought, but she could not remember what it was; then she took the medicine bulb out of her sleeve and began playing with it, tossing it up and down in her hand. That was what she had been trying to remember. Finally Iris giggled nervously and said:

"What are you doing with that?"

"Put it in your pack," said Alyx, and she held it
out to the girl.

"*My* pack?" said Iris, astonished. "Why?"

"We may need it," said Alyx.

"Oh, Lord," said Iris uncomfortably, "we've still
got enough to eat, haven't we?"

"Eat?" said Alyx.

"Sure," said Iris, "that's lecithin. From synthetic
milk," and then she clapped both hands across her
mouth as Alyx leapt to her feet and threw the thing
out into the falling snow. It seemed to Alyx that she
had suddenly walked into an enormous snake, or a
thing like one of the things that cleaned up houses in
civilized countries: something long, strong, and elastic that winds around you and is everywhere the
same, everywhere equally strong so that there is no
relief from it, no shifting it or getting away from it.
She could not bear it. She did not think of Machine
but only walked up and down for a few minutes,
trying to change her position so that there would be
a few minutes when it would not hurt; then she
thought of a funnel and something at the bottom of
it; and then finally she saw him. Wedged in like
broken goods. She thought *Wedged in like broken
goods*. She put her hands over her eyes. The same
face. *The same face*. Iris had gotten up in alarm and
put one hand on Alyx's shoulder; Alyx managed to
whisper "Iris!"

"Yes? Yes?" said Iris anxiously.

"Get those damned women," said Alyx hoarsely
for now he was all over the cave, pale, eyes shut, on
every wall, irretrievably lost, a smashed machine
with a broken arm at the bottom of a rock chimney
somewhere. It was intolerable. For a moment she

thought that she was bleeding, that her arms and legs were cut away. Then that disappeared. She put out her hands to touch his face, to stay awake, to wake him up, again and again and again, and then this would not stop but went on and on in a kind of round dance that she could not control, over and over in complete silence with the cold of the rock-chimney and the dim light and the smell of the place, with Machine still dead, no matter what she did, lying on top of his pack and not speaking, wedged into the rock like a broken toy with one leg dangling. It kept happening. She thought *I never lost anything before*. She cried out in her own language.

When the sister came with the pill-box to comfort her, Alyx wrenched the box out of the woman's hand, swallowed three of the things, shoved the box up her own sleeve—above the knife-harness—and waited for death.

But the only thing that happened was that the nuns got frightened and retreated to the other end of the cave.

And Alyx fell aleep almost instantly.

She woke up all at once, standing, like a board hit with a hoe; Paradise—which had been stable—turned over once and settled itself. This was interesting but not novel. She looked outside the cave, forgot what she had seen, walked over to the nuns and pulled one of them up by the hair, which was very amusing; she did it to the other, too, and then when the noise they made had waked up Iris and Gavrily, she said "Damn it, Gavrily, you better be careful, this place has it in for me."

He only blinked at her. She pulled him outside by

one arm and whispered it fiercely into his ear, pulling him down and standing on her toes to do so, but he remained silent. She pushed him away. She looked at his frightened face and said contemptuously "Oh, you! you can't hear," and dropped her pack into the snow; then when somebody put it on her back she dropped it again; only the third time she lost interest. They put it on again and she forgot about it. By then they were all up and facing out onto the plains, a flat land covered with hard snow, a little dirty, like pulverized ice, and a brown haze over the sky so that the sun showed through it in an unpleasant smear: she wanted to look at it and would not go anywhere until someone pushed her. It was not an attractive landscape and it was not an unattractive one; it was fascinating. Behind her Gavrily began to sing:

> "When I woke up, my darling dear,
> When I woke up and found you near,
> I thought you were an awful cutie
> And you will always be my sweetie."

She turned around and shouted at him. Someone gave a shocked gasp. They prodded her again. She found Iris at her elbow, quite unexpectedly pushing her along, and began to explain that her feet were doing that part of the work. She was very civil. Then she added:

"You see, I am not like you; I am not doing anything idiotic or lying in the snow making faces. I haven't lost my head and I'm going on in a perfectly rational manner; I can still talk and I can still think and I wish to the devil you would stop working my

elbow like a pump; it is very annoying, besides being
entirely unnecessary. You are not a nice girl."

"I don't know that language," said Iris helplessly,
"what are you saying?"

"Well, you're young," said Alyx serenely, "after
all."

At midday they let her look at the sky.

She lay down flat in the snow and watched it as
the others ate, through a pair of binoculars she had
gotten from someone's pack, concentrating on the
detail work and spinning the little wheel in the middle until Iris grabbed her hands and hoisted her to
her feet. This made her cross and she bit Iris in the
arm, getting a mouthful of insulated suit. She seriously considered that Iris had played a trick on her.
She looked for the binoculars but they were not
around; she lagged after Iris with her gloves dangling
from her wrists and her bare fingers making circles
around her eyes; she tried to tell Iris to look at that
over there, which is what that which it is, and then a
terrible suspicion flashed into her mind in one
sentence:

You are going out of your mind.

Immediately she ran to Iris, tugging at Iris's arm,
holding her hand, crying out "Iris, Iris, I'm not going
out of my mind, am I? Am I going out of my mind?
Am I?" and Iris said "No, you're not; come on,
please," (crying a little) and the voice of one of the
Hellish Duo sounded, like an infernal wind instrument creeping along the bottom of the snow, in a
mean, meaching, nasty tone, just like the nasty blur
in the brown sky, an altogether unpleasant, excep-
tionable and disgusting tone:

"She's coming out of it."

"How can I come on if I'm coming out?" demanded Alyx, going stiff all over with rage.

"Oh, please!" said Iris.

"How," repeated Alyx in a fury, "can I come on if I'm coming out? How? I'd like you to explain that" —her voice rising shrilly—"that—conundrum, that impossibility, that flat perversion of the laws of nature; it is absolutely and utterly impossible and you are nothing but an excuse, an evasion, a cheap substitute for a human being and a little tin whore!"

Iris turned away.

"But how can I!" exploded Alyx. "How can I be on and out? How can I? It's ridiculous!"

Iris began to cry. Alyx folded her arms around herself and sunk her head on her chest; then she went over to Iris and patted Iris with her mittens; she would have given up even the sky if it made Iris unhappy. She said reassuringly "There, there."

"Just come on, please," said Iris. Subdued, Alyx followed her. A great while after, when she had put down the other foot, Alyx said "You understand, don't you?" She took Iris's arm, companionably.

"It's only the pills," said Iris, "that's all."

"I never take them," said Alyx.

"Of course not," said Iris.

Curiously Alyx said, "Why are you shaking?"

They walked on.

Towards evening, long after the immense day had sunk and even the diffused light died out so that the bottom of the plain was nothing but a black pit, though even then the snow-luminescence glowed about them vaguely, not enough to see by *But enough* (Alyx thought) *to make you take a chance and break*

your neck—she realized that they had been handing her about from one to the other all day. She
supposed it was the pills. They came and went in
waves of unreason, oddly detached from herself; she
dozed between them as she walked, not thinking of
suggesting to the others that they stop, and when
they did stop she merely sat down on the snow, put
her arms around her knees and stared off into the
darkness. Eventually the light from the snow failed.
She felt for the box in her sleeve and laughed a little;
someone near her stirred and whispered "What?
What?" and then yawned. The breathing fell again
into its soft, regular rhythm. Alyx laughed again,
dreamily, then felt something in back of her, then
turned around to look for it, then found nothing. It
was in back of her again. She yawned. The darkness
was becoming uncomfortable. She fought the desire
to sleep. She felt about and nudged the person nearest her, who immediately sat up—to judge from the
sound—and gave out a kind of "Ha!" like a bellows.
Alyx laughed.

"Wha'—huh!" said Gavrily.

"Look," she said sensibly, "about these pills. What
do they do to you?"

"Muh," said Gavrily.

"Well, how many can I take?" said Alyx, amused.

"Take what?"

"Take pills," said Alyx.

"What? Don't take any," he said. He sounded a
little more awake.

"How many," said Alyx patiently, "can I take without hurting myself?"

"None," said Gavrily. "Bad for the liver. Meta—
metabol—give 'em back."

"You won't get them," said Alyx. "Don't try. How many can I take without making a nuisance of myself?"

"Huh?" said Gavrily.

"How many?" repeated Alyx. "One?"

"No, no," said Gavrily stupidly, "none," and he muttered something else, turned over in the dark and apparently fell asleep. She heard him snore; then it was turned off into a strangled, explosive snort and he breathed like a human being. Alyx sat peering keenly into the dark, feeling them come closer and closer and smiling to herself. When the world was about to touch her—and she would not stand for that—she took out her little box. She broke a pill and swallowed half. She came to the surface nonetheless, as one does when breaking the surface of water, blinded, chilled, shocked by the emptiness of air; the snow solidified under her, her suit began to take shape and grate like iron, the sleepers next to her emerged piecemeal out of the fog, grotesquely in separate limbs, in disconnected sounds, there were flashes of realization, whole moments of absolute reality. It simply would not do. She grinned nervously and hugged her knees. She blinked into the darkness as if her eyes were dazzled; she held on to her knees as a swimmer holds on to the piles of a jetty with his fingertips, she who had never been drunk in her life because it impaired the reason. She stuffed the box back up her sleeve. Eventually something happened—she shook her head as if to get rid of a fly or a nervous tic—the water rose. It closed over her head. She yawned. With her mouth wide open, water inside, water outside, she slid down,

and down, and down, singing like a mermaid: *I care for nobody, no, not I*. She slept.
And nobody cares for me.

The false dawn came over the flats, bringing nothing with it. She sat and considered her sins.

That they were vast was undeniably true, a mental land as flat and bare as a world-sized table, and yet with here and there those disturbing dips and slides: concave surfaces that somehow remained flat, hills that slid the other way, like the squares on a chessboard which bend and produce nausea. Such places exist.

Her sins were terrible. She was staring at a pink marble bathtub, full of water, a bathtub in which she had once bathed in the palace of Knossos on Crete, and which now hung on the ceiling overhead. The water was slipping. She was going to be drowned. The ocean stuck to the sky, heaving. In her youth she had walked town streets and city streets, stolen things, been immensely popular; it had all come to nothing. Nothing had come out of nothing. She did not regret a single life lost. In the snow appeared a chessboard and on the chessboard figures, and these figures one by one slid down into squares in the board and disappeared. The squares puckered and became flat. She put her fingers into them but they would not take her, which was natural enough in a woman who had not loved even her own children. You could not trust anyone in those times. The electromagnetic spectrum was increasing. Slowly the plains filled with air, as a pool with water; an enormous racket went on below the cliff that was the edge of the earth; and finally the sun threw up one hand to grasp the cliff, climbed, clung, rose, mounted and sailed brilliantly white and clear into a brilliant sky.

It said to her, in the voice of Iris: "You are frozen through and through. You are a detestable woman."

She fell back against the snow, dead.

When the dawn came, bringing a false truce, Alyx was sitting up with her arms clasped about her knees and watching the others wake up. She was again, as before, delicately iced over, on the line between reason and unreason. She thought she would keep it that way. She ate with the others, saying nothing, doing nothing, watching the murky haze in the sky and the spreading thumbprint in it that was the sun. The landscape was geometric and very pleasing. In the middle of the morning they passed a boulder someone or something had put out on the waste: to one side of it was a patch of crushed snow and brown moss showing through. Later in the day the world became more natural, though no less pleasant, and they stopped to eat once more, sitting in the middle of the plain that spread out to nowhere in particular. Iris was leaning over and eating out of one hand, utterly beautiful as were all the others, the six or seven or eight of them, all very beautiful and the scenery too, all of which Alyx explained, and that at very great length.

"What do you mean!" cried Iris suddenly. "What do you mean you're going to go along without us, what do you mean by that!"

"Huh?" said Alyx.

"And don't call me names," said Iris, trembling visibly. "I've had enough," and she went off and sat by somebody else. *What have you had enough of?*

thought Alyx curiously, but she followed her anyway, to see that she came to no harm. Iris was sitting by one of the nuns. Her face was half turned away and there was a perceptible shadow on it. The nun was saying "Well, I told you." The shadow on Iris's face seemed to grow into a skin disease, something puckered or blistered like the lichens on a rock, a very interesting purple shadow; then it contracted into a small patch on her face and looked as if it were about to go out, but finally it turned into something.

Iris had a black eye.

"Where'd you get that?" said Alyx, with interest.

Iris put her hand over her eye.

"Well, where'd you get it?" said Alyx. "Who gave it to you? Did you fall against a rock?

"I think you're making it up," she added frankly, but the words did not come out quite right. The black eye wavered as it if were going to turn into a skin disease again. "Well?" demanded Alyx. "How'd you get it out here in the middle of the desert? Huh? How did you? Come on!"

"You gave it to me," said Iris.

"Oh, she won't understand anything!" exclaimed one of the nuns contemptuously. Alyx sat down in the snow and tucked her feet under her. She put her arms around herself. Iris was turning away again, nursing the puffy flesh around her bloodshot eye: it was a purple bruise beginning to turn yellow and a remarkable sight, the focus of the entire plain, which had begun to wheel slowly and majestically around it. However, it looked more like a black eye every moment.

"*Me?*" Alyx said finally.

"In your sleep," answered one of the nuns. "You

are certainly a practiced woman. I believe you are a
bad woman. We have all tried to take the pills away
from you and the only issue of it is that Iris has a
black eye and Gavrily a sprained wrist. Myself, I
wash my hands of it.

"Of course," she added with some satisfaction, "it
is too late now. Much too late. You have been eating
them all along. You can't stop now; you would die,
you know. Metabolic balances."

"What, in one night!" said Alyx.

"No," said the other. "Five."

"I think we are running out of food," said Iris.
"We had better go on."

"Come on," she added, getting up.

They went on.

She took command two days later when she had
become more habituated to the stuff, and although
someone followed them constantly (but out of sight)
there were no more hallucinations and her decisions
were—on the whole—sensible. She thought the whole
thing was a grand joke. When the food disappeared
from out of the bottomless bags, she turned them
inside out and licked the dust off them, and the
others did the same; when she bent down, supporting herself on one arm, and looked over the brown
sky for aircraft, the others did the same; and when
she held up two fingers against one eye to take the
visual diameter of the bleary sun and then moved
the two fingers three times to one side—using her
other hand as a marker—to find out their way, so did
they, though they did not know why. There was no
moss, no food, hardly any light, and bad pains in the
stomach. Snow held them up for a day when the sun

went out altogether. They sat together and did not talk. The next day the sky lifted a little and they went on, still not talking. When the middle of the day came and they had rested a while, they refused to get up; so she had to pummel them and kick them to their feet. She said she saw a thing up ahead that was probably the Pole station; she said they had bad eyes and bad ears and bad minds and could not expect to see it. They went on for the rest of the day and the next morning had to be kicked and cuffed again until they got up, and so they walked slowly on, leaving always the same footprints in the thin snow, a line of footprints behind exactly matching the fresh line in front, added one by one, like a line of stitching. Iris said there was a hobby machine that did that with only a single foot, faster than the eye could follow, over and over again, depositing now a rose, now a face, again a lily, a dragon, a tower, a shield. . . .

On the fifty-seventh day they reached the Pole station.

It sprawled over five acres of strangely irregular ground: cut-stone blocks in heaps, stone paths that led nowhere, stone walls that enclosed nothing, a ruined city, entirely roofless. Through their binoculars nothing looked taller than any of them. Nothing was moving. They stood staring at it but could make no sense of it. One of the nuns flopped down in the snow. Gavrily said:

"Someone ought to let them know we're here."

"They know," said Alyx.

"They don't know," he said.

"They know," said Alyx. She was looking through

the binoculars. She had her feet planted wide apart in the snow and was fiddling with the focus knob, trying to find something in the ruins. Around her the women lay like big dolls. She knew it was the Pole because of the position of the sun; she knew it was not a city and had never been a city but something the lieutenant had long ago called a giant aerial code and she knew that if someone does not come out to greet you, you do not run to greet him. She said "Stay here," and hung the binoculars around her neck.

"No, Agent," said Gavrily. He was swaying a little on his feet.

"Stay here," she repeated, tucking the binoculars inside her suit, and dropping to her knees, she began to crawl forward. Gavrily, smiling, walked past her towards the giant anagram laid out on the snow; smiling, he turned and waved, saying something she could not catch; and resolutely marching forward—because he could talk to people best, she supposed, although he was stumbling a little and his face was gray—he kept on walking in the direction of the Pole station, over the flat plain, until his head was blown off.

It was done silently and bloodlessly, in a flash of light. Gavrily threw up both arms, stood still, and toppled over. Behind her Alyx heard someone gasp repeatedly, in a fit of hiccoughs. Silence.

"Iris, give me your pack," said Alyx.

"Oh, no, no, no, no, no, no, no, no," said Iris.

"I want to go away," said someone else, tiredly.

Alyx had to kick them to get the packs off them; then she had to push Iris's face into the snow until the girl stopped grabbing at her; she dragged all four packs over the snow like sleds, and stopping a few feet from Gavrily's body, she dumped all four onto the ground and pulled Gavrily back by the feet. *Marker*, she thought. Cursing automatically, she wrenched the packs open and lobbed a few bottles at the town at random. They vanished in a glitter two meters from the ground. She thought for a moment and then rapidly assembled a crossbow; bolts fired from it met the same fate; the crossbow itself, carefully lifted into the air, flared at the tip and the whole thing became so hot that she had to drop it. Her gloves were charred. Wrapping bandages from one of the packs around the bow, she lifted it again, this time ten paces to one side; again the tip vanished; ten paces to the other side and the same thing happened; crawling forward with her sunglasses on, she held it up in front of her and watched the zone of disappearance move slowly down to the grip. She tried it with another, twenty paces to the left. Twenty paces to the right. Her palms were blistered, the gloves burned off. The thing got closer and closer to the ground; there would be no crawling under it. She retreated to Gavrily's body and found Iris behind it, holding on to one of the packs to keep herself steady, whispering "What is it, what is it, what is it?"

"It's a fence," said Alyx, thrusting her stinging hands into the snow, "and whoever's running it doesn't have the sense to turn it off."

"Oh no, it's a machine," whispered Iris, laying her head against the pack, "it's a machine, it's no use, there's nobody there."

"If there were nobody there," said Alyx, "I do not

think they would need a fence—Iris!" and she began
shaking the girl, who seemed to be falling asleep.

"Doesn't know anything," said Iris, barely audible.
"Idiots. Doesn't care."

"Iris!" shouted Alyx, slapping her, "Iris!"

"Only numbers," said Iris, and passed out. Alyx
pulled her over by one shoulder and rubbed snow on
her face. She fed her snow and put her forefingers
under the girl's ears, pressing hard into the glands
under them. The pain brought the girl around; "Only
numbers," she said again.

"Iris," said Alyx, "give me some numbers."

"I.D.," said Iris, "on my back. Microscopic."

"Iris," said Alyx slowly and distinctly, "I cannot
read. You must count something out for me. You
must count it out while I show those bastards that
there is somebody out here. Otherwise we will never
get in. We are not supposed to be recognized and we
won't be. We are camouflaged. You must give me
some numbers."

"Don't know any," said Iris. Alyx propped her up
against what was left of one of the packs. She dozed
off. Alyx brought her out of it again and the girl
began to cry, tears going effortlessly down her cheeks,
busily one after the other. Then she said "In the
Youth Core we had a number."

"Yes?" said Alyx.

"It was the number of our Core and it meant the
Jolly Pippin," said Iris weakly. "It went like this—"
and she recited it.

"I don't know what those words mean," said Alyx;
"you must show me," and holding up Iris's hand, she
watched while the girl slowly stuck up fingers: six
seven seven, six two, seven six five six. Leaving

Iris with her head propped against the pack, Alyx wound everything she could around the base of one of the crossbows, and lifting it upwards slowly spelled out six seven seven, six two, seven six five six, until everything was gone, when she wound another pack around another bow, leaving the first in the snow to cool, and again spelled out the number over and over until she could not move either hand, both hurt so abominably, and Iris had passed out for the second time.

Then something glittered in the middle of the Pole station and figures in snowsuits came running through the heaps of stone and the incomplete stone walls. Alyx thought dryly *It's about time.* She turned her head and saw the nuns tottering towards her; she thought suddenly *God, how thin!* and feeling perfectly well, she got up to wave the nuns on, to urge them to greet the real human beings, the actual living people who had finally come out in response to Iris's Jolly Pippin. A phrase she had heard sometime during the trip came to her mind: The Old School Yell. She stepped forward smartly and gestured to one of the men, but as he came closer—two others were picking up Iris, she saw, and still others racing towards the nuns—she realized that he had no face, or none to speak of, really, a rather amusing travesty or approximation, that he was, in fact, a machine like the workers she had seen in the sheds when they had first set out on their picnic. Someone had told her then "They're androids. Don't nod." She continued to wave. She turned around for a last look at Paradise and there, only a few meters away, as large as life, stood Machine with his arms crossed over his chest. She said to him "What's a machine?" but he

did not answer. With an air of finality, with the
simplicity and severity of a dying god, he pulled over
his blue eyes the goggled lenses and snout of another
species, rejecting her, rejecting all of them; and tuned
in to station Nothing (twenty-four hours a day every
day, someone had said) he turned and began to walk
away, fading as he walked, walking as he went away,
listening to Trivia between the earth and the air until
he walked himself right into a cloud, into nothing,
into the blue, blue sky.

Ah, but I feel fine! thought Alyx, and walking
forward, smiling as Gavrily had done, she saw under
the hood of her android the face of a real man. She
collapsed immediately.

Three weeks later Alyx was saying goodbye to Iris
on the Moondrom on Old Earth, a vast idiot dome
full of mist and showlights, with people of all sorts
rising and falling on streams of smoke. Iris was going
the cheap way to the Moon for a conventional weekend with a strange young man. She was fashionably
dressed all in silver, for that was the color that month:
silver eyes, silvered eyelids, a cut-out glassene dress
with a matching cloak, and her silver luggage and
coiffure, both vaguely spherical, bobbing half a meter in the air behind their owner. It would have been
less unnerving if the hair had been attached to Iris's
head; as it was, Alyx could not keep her eyes off it.

Moreover, Iris was having hysterics for the seventh time in the middle of the Moondrom because her
old friend who had gone through so much with her,
and had taught her to shoot, and had saved her life,
would not tell her anything—anything—anything!

"Can I help it if you refuse to believe me?" said Alyx.

"Oh, you think I'll tell *him!*" snapped Iris scornfully, referring to her escort whom neither of them had yet met. She was searching behind her in the air for something that was apparently supposed to come out of her luggage, but didn't. Then they sat down, on nothing.

"Listen, baby," said Alyx, "just listen. For the thirty-third time, Trans-Temp is not the Great Trans-Temporal Cadre of Heroes and Heroines and don't shake your head at me because it *isn't*. It's a study complex for archaeologists, that's all it is, and they fish around blindfold in the past, love, just as you would with a bent pin; though they're very careful where and when they fish because they have an unholy horror of even chipping the bottom off a canoe. They think the world will blow up or something. They stay thirty feet above the top of the sea and twenty feet below it and outside city limits and so on and so on, just about everything you can think of. And they can't even let through anything that's alive. Only one day they were fishing in the Bay of Tyre a good forty feet down and they just happened to receive twenty-odd cubic meters of sea-water complete with a small, rather inept Greek thief who had just pinched an expensive chess set from the Prince of Tyre, who between ourselves is no gentleman. They tell me I was attached to a rope attached to knots attached to a rather large boulder with all of us considerably more dead than alive, just dead enough, in fact, to come through at all, and just alive enough to be salvageable. That is, I was. They also tell me that this is one chance in several billion billion so

there is only one of me, my dear, only one, and
there never will be any more, prehistoric or heroic
or unheroic or otherwise, and if you would only
please, please oblige your escort by telling—"

"They'll send you back!" said Iris, clasping her
hands with wonderful intensity.

"They can't," said Alyx.

"They'll cut you up and study you!"

"They won't."

"They'll shut you up in a cage and make you teach
them things!"

"They tried," said Alyx. "The Army—"

Here Iris jumped up, her mouth open, her face
clouded over. She was fingering something behind
her ear.

"I have to go," she said absently. She smiled a
little sadly. "That's a very good story," she said.

"Iris—" began Alyx, getting up.

"I'll send you something," said Iris hastily. "I'll
send you a piece of the Moon; see if I don't."

"The historical sites," said Alyx. She was about to
say something more, something light, but at that
moment Iris—snatching frantically in the air behind
her for whatever it was that had not come out the
first time and showed no signs of doing so the second—
burst into passionate tears.

"How will you manage?" she cried, "oh, how will
you, you're seven years younger than I am, you're
just a *baby!*" and weeping in a swirl of silver cloak,
and hair, and luggage, in a storm of violently crack-
ling sparks that turned gold and silver and ran off the
both of them like water, little Iris swooped down,
threw her arms around her littler friend, wept some
more, and immediately afterward rose rapidly into

the air, waving goodbye like mad. Halfway up to the foggy roof she produced what she had apparently been trying to get from her luggage all along: a small silver flag, a jaunty square with which she blew her nose and then proceeded to wave goodbye again, smiling brilliantly. It was a handkerchief.

Send me a piece of the Moon, said Alyx silently, *send me something I can keep,* and turning away she started out between the walls of the Moondrom, which are walls that one cannot see, through the cave that looks like an enormous sea of fog; and if you forget that it was made for civilized beings, it begins to look, once you have lost your way, like an endless cave, an endless fog, through which you will wander forever.

But of course she found her way out, finally.

At the exit—and it was the right exit, the one with billowing smoke that shone ten thousand colors from the lights in the floor and gave you, as you crossed it, the faint, unpleasant sensation of being turned slowly upside down, there where ladies' cloaks billowed and transparent clothing seemed to dissolve in streams of fire—

Stood Machine. Her heart stopped for a moment, automatically. The fifth or sixth time that day, she estimated.

"God save you, mister," she said.

He did not move.

"They tell me you'll be gone in a few weeks," she said. "I'll be sorry."

He said nothing.

"They also tell me," she went on, "that I am going to teach my special and peculiar skills in a special and peculiar little school, for they seem to think our pilgrimage a success, despite its being full of their own inexcusable blunders, and they also seem to think that my special and peculiar skills are detachable from my special and peculiar attitudes. Like Iris's hair. I think they will find they are wrong."

He began to dissolve.

"Raydos is blind," she said, "stone blind, did you know that? Some kind of immune reaction; when you ask them, they pull a long face and say that medicine can't be expected to do everything. A foolproof world and full of fools. And then they tape wires on my head and ask me how it feels to be away from home; and they shake their heads when I tell them that I am not away from home; and then they laugh a little—just a little—when I tell them that I have never had a home.

"And then," she said, "I tell them that you are dead."

He disappeared.

"We'll give them a run for their money," she said. "Oh yes we will! By God we will! Eh, love?" and she stepped through the smoke, which now contained nothing except the faint, unpleasant sensation of being turned slowly upside down.

Iris may turn out to be surprisingly accurate, she thought, *about the Great Trans-Temporal Cadre of Heroes and Heroines.*

Even if the only thing trans-temporal about them is their attitudes. The attitudes that are not detachable from my special and peculiar skills.

If I have anything to say about it.

But that's another story.

* * *

THE SECOND INQUISITION

If a man can resist the influences of his townsfolk, if he can cut free from the tyranny of neighborhood gossip, the world has no terrors for him; there is no second inquisition.

—*John Jay Chapman*

I often watched our visitor reading in the living room, sitting under the floor lamp near the new, standing Philco radio, with her long, long legs stretched out in front of her and the pool of light on her book revealing so little of her face: brownish, coppery features so marked that she seemed to be a kind of freak and hair that was reddish black but so rough that it looked like the things my mother used for scouring pots and pans. She read a great deal, that summer. If I ventured out of the archway, where I was not exactly hiding but only keeping in the

227

shadow to watch her read, she would often raise her face and smile silently at me before beginning to read again, and her skin would take on an abrupt, surprising pallor as it moved into the light. When she got up and went into the kitchen with the gracefulness of a stork, for something to eat, she was almost too tall for the doorways; she went on legs like a spider's, with long swinging arms and a little body in the middle, the strange proportions of the very tall. She looked down at my mother's plates and dishes from a great, gentle height, remarkably absorbed; and asking me a few odd questions, she would bend down over whatever she was going to eat, meditate on it for a few moments like a giraffe, and then straightening up back into the stratosphere, she would pick up the plate in one thin hand, curling around it fingers like legs, and go back gracefully into the living room. She would lower herself into the chair that was always too small, curl her legs around it, become dissatisfied, settle herself, stretch them out again—I remember so well those long, hard, unladylike legs—and begin again to read.

She used to ask, "What is that? What is that? And what is this?" but that was only at first.

My mother, who disliked her, said she was from the circus and we ought to try to understand and be kind. My father made jokes. He did not like big women or short hair—which was still new in places like ours—or women who read, although she was interested in his carpentry and he liked that.

But she was six feet four inches tall; this was in 1925.

My father was an accountant who built furniture as a hobby; we had a gas stove which he actually fixed once when it broke down and some outdoor tables and chairs he had built in the back yard. Before our visitor came on the train for her vacation with us, I used to spend all my time in the back yard, being underfoot, but once we had met her at the station and she shook hands with my father—I think she hurt him when she shook hands—I would watch her read and wish that she might talk to me.

She said: "You are finishing high school?"

I was in the archway, as usual; I answered yes.

She looked up at me again, then down at her book. She said, "This is a very bad book." I said nothing. Without looking up, she tapped one finger on the shabby hassock on which she had put her feet. Then she looked up and smiled at me. I stepped tentatively from the floor to the rug, as reluctantly as if I were crossing the Sahara; she swung her feet away and I sat down. At close view her face looked as if every race in the world had been mixed and only the worst of each kept; an American Indian might look like that, or Ikhnaton from the encyclopedia, or a Swedish African, a Maori princess with the jaw of a Slav. It occurred to me suddenly that she might be a Negro, but no one else had ever seemed to think so, possibly because nobody in our town had ever seen a Negro. We had none. They were "colored people."

She said, "You are not pretty, yes?"

I got up. I said, "My father thinks you're a freak."

"You are sixteen," she said, "sit down," and I sat down. I crossed my arms over my breasts because they were too big, like balloons. Then she said, "I am reading a very stupid book. You will take it away from me, yes?"

"No," I said.

"You must," she said, "or it will poison me, sure as God," and from her lap she plucked up *The Green Hat: A Romance*, gold letters on green binding, last year's bestseller which I had had to swear never to read, and she held it out to me, leaning back in her chair with that long arm doing all the work, the book enclosed in a cage of fingers wrapped completely around it. I think she could have put those fingers around a basketball. I did not take it.

"Go on," she said, "read it, go on, go away," and I found myself at the archway, by the foot of the stairs with *The Green Hat: A Romance* in my hand. I turned it so the title was hidden. She was smiling at me and had her arms folded back under her head. "Don't worry," she said. "Your body will be in fashion by the time of the next war." I met my mother at the top of the stairs and had to hide the book from her; my mother said, "Oh, the poor woman!" She was carrying some sheets. I went to my room and read through almost the whole night, hiding the book in the bedclothes when I was through. When I slept, I dreamt of Hispano-Suizas, of shingled hair and tragic eyes; of women with painted lips who had Affairs, who went night after night with Jews to low dives, who lived as they pleased, who had miscarriages in expensive Swiss clinics; of midnight swims, of desperation, of money, of illicit love, of a beautiful Englishman and getting into a taxi with him while wearing a cloth-of-silver cloak and a silver turban like the ones shown in the society pages of the New York City newspapers.

Unfortunately our guest's face kept recurring in my dream, and because I could not make out whether she was amused or bitter or very much of both, it really spoiled everything.

My mother discovered the book the next morning. I found it next to my plate at breakfast. Neither my mother nor my father made any remark about it; only my mother kept putting out the breakfast things with a kind of tender, reluctant smile. We all sat down, finally, when she had put out everything, and my father helped me to rolls and eggs and ham. Then he took off his glasses and folded them next to his plate. He leaned back in his chair and crossed his legs. Then he looked at the book and said in a tone of mock surprise, "Well! What's this?"

I didn't say anything. I only looked at my plate.

"I believe I've seen this before," he said. "Yes, I believe I have." Then he asked my mother, "Have you seen this before?" My mother made a kind of vague movement with her head. She had begun to butter some toast and was putting it on my plate. I knew she was not supposed to discipline me; only my father was. "Eat your egg," she said. My father, who had continued to look at *The Green Hat: A Romance* with the same expression of unvarying surprise, finally said:

"Well! This isn't a very pleasant thing to find on a Saturday morning, is it?"

I still didn't say anything, only looked at my food. I heard my mother say worriedly, "She's not eating, Ben," and my father put his hand on the back of my chair so I couldn't push it away from the table, as I was trying to do.

"Of course you have an explanation for this," he said. "Don't you?"

I said nothing.

"Of course she does," he said, "doesn't she, Bess? You wouldn't hurt your mother like this. You wouldn't hurt your mother by stealing a book that you knew you weren't supposed to read and for very good reason, too. You know we don't punish you. We talk things over with you. We try to explain. Don't we?"

I nodded.

"Good," he said. "Then where did this book come from?"

I muttered something; I don't know what.

"Is my daughter angry?" said my father. "Is my daughter *being rebellious?*"

"She told you all about it!" I blurted out. My father's face turned red.

"Don't you dare talk about your mother that way!" he shouted, standing up. "Don't you *dare* refer to your mother in that way!"

"Now, Ben—" said my mother.

"Your mother is the soul of unselfishness," said my father, "and don't you forget it, missy; your mother has worried about you since the day you were born and if you don't appreciate that, you can damn well—"

"Ben!" said my mother, shocked.

"I'm sorry," I said, and then I said, "I'm very sorry, Mother." My father sat down. My father had a mustache and his hair was parted in the middle and slicked down; now one lock fell over the part in front and his whole face was gray and quivering. He was staring fixedly at his coffee cup. My mother came over and poured coffee for him; then she took the coffee pot into the kitchen and when she came back she had milk for me. She put the glass of milk on the table near my plate. Then she sat down again. She smiled tremblingly at my father; then she put her hand over mine on the table and said:

"Darling, why did you read that book?"

"Well?" said my father from across the table.

There was a moment's silence. Then:

"Good morning!"

and

"Good morning!"

and

"Good morning!"

said our guest cheerfully, crossing the dining room in two strides, and folding herself carefully down into her breakfast chair, from where her knees stuck out, she reached across the table, picked up *The Green Hat*, propped it up next to her plate and began to read it with great absorption. Then she looked up. "You have a very progressive library," she said. "I took the liberty of recommending this exciting book to your daughter. You told me it was your favorite. You sent all the way to New York City on purpose for it, yes?"

"I don't—I quite—" said my mother, pushing back her chair from the table. My mother was trembling from head to foot and her face was set in an expression of fixed distaste. Our visitor regarded first my mother and then my father, bending over them tenderly and with exquisite interest. She said:

"I hope you do not mind my using your library."

"No no no," muttered my father.

"I eat almost for two," said our visitor modestly, "because of my height. I hope you do not mind that?"

"No, of course not," said my father, regaining control of himself.

"Good. It is all considered in the bill," said the visitor, and looking about at my shrunken parents, each hurried, each spooning in the food and avoiding her gaze, she added deliberately:

"I took also another liberty. I removed from the endpapers certain—ah—drawings that I did not think bore any relation to the text. You do not mind?"

And as my father and mother looked in shocked surprise and utter consternation—at each other—she said to me in a low voice, "Don't eat. You'll make yourself sick," and then smiled warmly at the two of them when my mother went off into the kitchen and my father remembered he was late for work. She waved at them. I jumped up as soon as they were out of the room.

"There were no drawings in that book!" I whispered.

"Then we must make some," said she, and taking a pencil off the whatnot, she drew in the endpapers of the book a series of sketches: the heroine sipping a soda in an ice-cream parlor, showing her legs and very chic; in a sloppy bathing suit and big grin, holding up a large fish; driving her Hispano-Suiza into a tree only to be catapulted straight up into the air; and in the last sketch landing demure and coy in the arms of the hero, who looked violently surprised. Then she drew a white mouse putting on lipstick, getting married to another white mouse in a church, the two entangled in some manner I thought I should not look at, the lady mouse with a big belly and two little mice inside (who were playing chess), then the little mice coming out in separate envelopes and finally the whole family having a picnic, with some things around the picnic basket that I did not recognize and underneath in capital letters "I did not bring up my children to test cigarettes." This left me blank. She laughed and rubbed it out, saying that it was out of date. Then she drew a white mouse with a rolled-up umbrella chasing my mother. I picked that up and looked at it for a while; then I tore it into pieces, and tore the others into pieces as well. I said, "I don't think you have the slightest right to—" and stopped. She was looking at me with—not anger exactly—not warning exactly—I found I had to sit down. I began to cry.

"Ah! The results of practical psychology," she said dryly, gathering up the pieces of her sketches. She took matches off the whatnot and set fire to the pieces in a saucer. She held up the smoking match between her thumb and forefinger, saying, "You see? The finger is—shall we say, perception?—but the thumb is money. The thumb is hard."

"You oughtn't to treat my parents that way!" I said, crying.

"You ought not to tear up my sketches," she said calmly.

"Why not! Why not!" I shouted.

"Because they are worth money," she said, "in some quarters. I won't draw you any more," and indifferently taking the saucer with the ashes in it in one palm, she went into the kitchen. I heard her voice and then my mother's, and then my mother's again, and then our visitor's in a tone that would've made a rock weep, but I never found out what they said.

I passed our guest's room many times at night that summer, going in by the hall past her rented room where the second-floor windows gave out onto the dark garden. The electric lights were always on brilliantly. My mother had sewn the white curtains because she did everything like that and had bought the furniture at a sale: a marble-topped bureau, the wardrobe, the iron bedstead, an old Victrola against the wall. There was usually an open book on the bed. I would stand in the shadow of the open doorway and look across the bare wood floor, too much of it and all as slippery as the sea, bare wood waxed and shining in the electric light. A black dress hung on the front of the wardrobe and a pair of shoes like my mother's, T-strap shoes with thick heels. I used to wonder if she had silver evening slippers inside the wardrobe. Sometimes the open book on the bed was Wells's *The Time Machine* and then I would talk to the black glass of the window, I would say to the transparent reflections and the black branches of trees that moved beyond it.

"I'm only sixteen."

"You look eighteen," she would say.

"I know," I would say. "I'd like to be eighteen. I'd like to go away to college. To Radcliffe, I think."

She would say nothing, out of surprise.

"Are you reading Wells?" I would say then, leaning against the door jamb. "I think that's funny. Nobody in this town reads anything; they just think about social life. I read a lot, however. I would like to learn a great deal."

She would smile then, across the room.

"I did something funny once," I would go on. "I mean funny ha-ha, not funny peculiar." It was a real line, very popular. "I read *The Time Machine* and then I went around asking people were they Eloi or were they Morlocks; everyone liked it. The point is

which you would be if you could, like being an
optimist or a pessimist or do you like bobbed hair."
Then I would add, "Which are you?" and she would
only shrug and smile a little more. She would prop
her chin on one long, long hand and look into my
eyes with her black Egyptian eyes and then she
would say in her curious hoarse voice:

"It is you who must say it first."

"I think," I would say, "that you are a Morlock,"
and sitting on the bed in my mother's rented room
with *The Time Machine* open beside her, she would
say:

"You are exactly right. I am a Morlock. I am a
Morlock on vacation. I have come from the last
Morlock meeting, which is held out between the
stars in a big goldfish bowl, so all the Morlocks have
to cling to the inside walls like a flock of black bats,
some right side up, some upside down, for there is
no up and down there, clinging like a flock of black
crows, like a chestnut burr turned inside out. There
are half a thousand Morlocks and we rule the worlds.
My black uniform is in the wardrobe."

"I knew I was right," I would say.

"You are always right," she would say, "and you
know the rest of it, too. You know what murderers
we are and how terribly we live. We are waiting for
the big bang when everything falls over and even the
Morlocks will be destroyed; meanwhile I stay here
waiting for the signal and I leave messages clipped to
the frame of your mother's amateur oil painting of
Main Street because it will be in a museum some
day and my friends can find it; meanwhile I read *The
Time Machine*."

Then I would say, "Can I come with you?" leaning against the door.

"Without you," she would say gravely, "all is lost," and taking out from the wardrobe a black dress glittering with stars and a pair of silver sandals with high heels, she would say, "these are yours. They were my great-grandmother's, who founded the Order. In the name of Trans-Temporal Military Authority." And I would put them on.

It was almost a pity she was not really there.

Every year in the middle of August the Country Club gave a dance, not just for the rich families who were members but also for the "nice" people who lived in frame houses in town and even for some of the smart, economical young couples who lived in apartments, just as if they had been in the city. There was one new, red brick apartment building downtown, four stories high, with a courtyard. We were supposed to go, because I was old enough that year, but the day before the dance my father became ill with pains in his left side and my mother had to stay home to take care of him. He was propped up on pillows on the living-room daybed, which we had pulled out into the room so he could watch what my mother was doing with the garden out back and call to her once in a while through the windows. He could also see the walk leading up to the front door. He kept insisting that she was doing things all wrong. I did not even ask if I could go to the dance alone. My father said:

"Why don't you go out and help your mother?"

"She doesn't want me to," I said. "I'm supposed to stay here," and then he shouted angrily, "Bess! Bess!"

and began to give her instructions through the window. I saw another pair of hands appear in the window next to my mother's and then our guest—squatting back on her heels and smoking a cigarette—pulling up weeds. She was working quickly and efficiently, the cigarette between her teeth. "No, not that way!" shouted my father, pulling on the blanket that my mother had put over him. "Don't you know what you're doing! Bess, you're ruining everything! Stop it! Do it right!" My mother looked bewildered and upset; she passed out of the window and our visitor took her place; she waved to my father and he subsided, pulling the blanket up around his neck. "I don't like women who smoke," he mutterd irritably. I slipped out through the kitchen.

My father's toolshed and working space took up the farther half of the back yard; the garden was spread over the nearer half, part kitchen garden, part flowers, and then extended down either side of the house where we had fifteen feet or so of space before a white slat fence and the next people's side yard. It was an on-and-offish garden, and the house was beginning to need paint. My mother was working in the kitchen garden, kneeling. Our guest was standing, pruning the lilac trees, still smoking. I said:

"Mother, can't I go, can't I *go!*" in a low voice.

My mother passed her hand over her forehead and called "Yes, Ben!" to my father.

"Why *can't* I go!" I whispered. "Ruth's mother and Betty's mother will be there. Why couldn't you call Ruth's mother and Betty's mother?"

"*Not that way!*" came a blast from the living-room window. My mother sighed briefly and then smiled a

cheerful smile. "Yes Ben!" and called brightly. "I'm
listening." My father began to give some more
instructions.

"Mother," I said desperately, "why couldn't you—"

"Your father wouldn't approve," she said, and again
she produced a bright smile and called encouragingly
to my father. I wandered over to the lilac trees
where our visitor, in her usual nondescript black
dress, was piling the dead wood under the tree. She
took a last puff on her cigarette, holding it between
thumb and forefinger, then ground it out in the grass
and picked up in both arms the entire lot of dead
wood. She carried it over to the fence and dumped
it.

"My father says you shouldn't prune trees in August," I blurted suddenly.

"Oh?" she said.

"It hurts them," I whispered.

"Oh," she said. She had on gardening gloves, though
much too small; she picked up the pruning shears
and began snipping again through inch-thick trunks
and dead branches that snapped explosively when
they broke and whipped out at your face. She was
efficient and very quick.

I said nothing at all, only watched her face.

She shook her head decisively.

"But Ruth's mother and Betty's mother—" I began, faltering.

"I never go out," she said.

"You needn't stay," I said, placating.

"Never," she said. "Never at all," and snapping
free a particularly large, dead, silvery branch from
the lilac tree, she put it in my arms. She stood there
looking at me and her look was suddenly very se-

vere, very unpleasant, something foreign, like the look of somebody who had seen people go off to battle to die, the "movies" look but hard, hard as nails. I knew I wouldn't get to go anywhere. I thought she might have seen battles in the Great War, maybe even been in some of it. I said, although I could barely speak:

"Were you in the Great War?"

"Which great war?" said our visitor. Then she said, "No, I never go out," and returned to scissoring the trees.

On the night of the dance my mother told me to get dressed, and I did. There was a mirror on the back of my door, but the window was better; it softened everything; it hung me out in the middle of a black space and made my eyes into mysterious shadows. I was wearing pink organdy and a bunch of daisies from the garden, not the wild kind. I came downstairs and found our visitor waiting for me at the bottom: tall, bare-armed, almost beautiful, for she'd done something to her impossible hair and the rusty reddish black curled slickly like the best photographs. Then she moved and I thought she was altogether beautiful, all black and rippling silver like a Paris dress or better still a New York dress, with a silver band around her forehead like an Indian princess's and silver shoes with the chunky heels and the one strap over the instep.

She said, "Ah! don't you look nice," and then in a whisper, taking my arm and looking down at me with curious gentleness, "I'm going to be a bad chaperone. I'm going to disappear."

"Well!" said I, inwardly shaking, "I hope I can

take care of myself, I should think." But I hoped she wouldn't leave me alone and I hoped that no one would laugh at her. She was really incredibly tall.

"Your father's going to sleep at ten," said my mother. "Be back by eleven. Be happy." And she kissed me.

But Ruth's father, who drove Ruth and me and Ruth's mother and our guest to the Country Club, did not laugh. And neither did anyone else. Our visitor seemed to have put on a strange gracefulness with her dress, and a strange sort of kindliness, too, so that Ruth, who had never seen her but had only heard rumors about her, cried out, "Your friend's lovely!" and Ruth's father, who taught mathematics at high school, said (clearing his throat), "It must be lonely staying in," and our visitor said only, "Yes. Oh yes. It is," resting one immensely long, thin, elegant hand on his shoulder like some kind of unwinking spider, while his words and hers went echoing out into the night, back and forth, back and forth, losing themselves in the trees that rushed past the headlights and massed blackly to each side.

"Ruth wants to join a circus!" cried Ruth's mother, laughing.

"I do *not!*" said Ruth.

"You *will* not," said her father.

"I'll do exactly as I please," said Ruth with her nose in the air, and she took a chocolate cream out of her handbag and put it in her mouth.

"You will *not!*" said Ruth's father, scandalized.

"Daddy, you know I will too," said Ruth, serenely though somewhat muffled, and under cover of the dark she wormed over to me in the back seat and passed, from her hot hand to mine, another chocolate cream. I ate it; it was unpleasantly and piercingly sweet.

"Isn't it *glorious?*" said Ruth.

The Country Club was much more bare than I had expected, really only a big frame building with a veranda three-quarters of the way around it and not much lawn, but there was a path down front to two stone pillars that made a kind of gate and somebody had strung the gate and the whole path with colored Chinese lanterns. That part was lovely. Inside the whole first story was one room, with a varnished floor like the high school gym, and a punch table at one end and ribbons and Chinese lanterns hung all over the ceiling. It did not look quite like the movies but everything was beautifully painted. I had noticed that there were wicker armchairs scattered on the veranda. I decided it was "nice." Behind the punch table was a flight of stairs that led to a gallery full of tables where the grown-ups could go and drink (Ruth insisted they would be bringing real liquor for "mixes," although of course the Country Club had to pretend not to know about that) and on both sides of the big room French windows that opened onto the veranda and the Chinese lanterns, swinging a little in the breeze. Ruth was wearing a better dress than mine. We went over to the punch table and drank punch while she asked me about our visitor and I made up a lot of lies. "You don't know anything," said Ruth. She waved across the room to some friends of hers; then I could see her start dancing with a boy in front of the band, which was at the other end of the room. Older people were dancing and people's parents, some older boys and girls. I stayed by the punch table. People who knew my parents came over and talked to me; they asked me how I was and I said I was fine; then they asked me how my father was and I said he was fine. Someone offered to introduce me to someone but I said I knew him. I hoped somebody would come over. I thought I would skirt around the dance floor and try to talk to some of the girls I knew, but then I thought I wouldn't; I imagined myself going up the stairs with Iris March's lover from *The Green Hat* to sit at a table and smoke a cigarette or drink something. I stepped behind the punch table and went out through the French windows. Our guest was a few chairs away with her feet stretched out, resting on the lowest rung of the veranda. She was reading a magazine with the aid of a small flashlight. The flowers planted around the veranda showed up a little in the light from the Chinese lanterns: shadowy clumps and masses of petunias, a few of the white ones springing into life as she turned the page of her book and the beam of the flashlight moved in her hand. I decided I would have my cigarette in a long holder. The moon was coming up over the woods past the Country Club lawns, but it was a cloudy night and all I could see was a vague lightening of the sky in that direction. It was rather warm. I remembered something about *an ivory cigarette holder flaunting at the moon.* Our visitor turned another page. I thought that she must have been aware of me. I thought again of Iris March's lover, coming out to get me on the "terrace" when somebody tapped me on the shoulder; it was Ruth's father. He took me by the wrist and led me to our visitor, who looked up and smiled vaguely, dreamily, in the dark under the colored lanterns. Then Ruth's father said:

"What do you know? There's a relative of yours inside!" She continued to smile but her face stopped moving; she smiled gently and with tenderness at the space next to his head for the barely perceptible part of a moment. Then she completed the swing of her head and looked at him, still smiling, but everything had gone out of it.

"How lovely," she said. Then she said, "Who is it?"

"I don't know," said Ruth's father, "but he's tall, looks just like you—beg pardon. He says he's your cousin."

"*Por nada,*" said our guest absently, and getting up, she shook hands with Ruth's father. The three of us went back inside. She left the magazine and flashlight on the chair; they seemed to belong to the Club. Inside, Ruth's father took us up the steps to the gallery and there, at the end of it, sitting at one of the tables, was a man even taller than our visitor, tall even sitting down. He was in evening dress while half the men at the dance were in business suits. He did not really look like her in the face; he was a little darker and a little flatter of feature; but as we approached him, he stood up. He almost reached the ceiling. He was a giant. He and our visitor did not shake hands. The both of them looked at Ruth's father, smiling formally, and Ruth's father left us; then the stranger looked quizzically at me but our guest had already sunk into a nearby seat, all willowiness, all grace. They made a handsome couple. The stranger brought a silver-inlaid flask out of his hip pocket; he took the pitcher of water that stood on the table and poured some into a clean glass. Then he added whisky from the flask, but our

visitor did not take it. She only turned it aside,
amused, with one finger, and said to me, "Sit down,
child," which I did. Then she said:

"Cousin, how did you find me?"

"*Par chance*, cousin," said the stranger. "By luck."
He screwed the top back on the flask very deliberately and put the whole thing back in his pocket. He
began to stir the drink he had made with a wooden
muddler provided by the Country Club.

"I have endured much annoyance," he said, "from
that man to whom you spoke. There is not a single
specialized here; they are all half-brained: scattered
and stupid."

"He is a kind and clever man," said she. "He
teaches mathematics."

"The more fool he," said the stranger, "for the
mathematics he thinks he teaches!" and he drank his
own drink. Then he said, "I think we will go home
now."

"Eh! This person?" said my friend, drawing up the
ends of her lips half scornfully, half amused. "Not
this person!"

"Why not this person, who knows me?" said the
strange man.

"Because," said our visitor, and turning deliberately away from me, she put her face next to his and
began to whisper mischievously in his ear. She was
watching the dancers on the floor below, half the
men in business suits, half the couples middle-aged.
Ruth and Betty and some of their friends, and some
vacationing college boys. The band was playing the
fox-trot. The strange man's face altered just a little, it
darkened; he finished his drink, put it down, and
then swung massively in his seat to face me.

"Does she go out?" he said sharply.

"Well?" said our visitor idly.

"Yes," I said. "Yes, she goes out. Every day."

"By car or on foot?" I looked at her but she was doing nothing. Her thumb and finger formed a circle on the table.

"I don't know," I said.

"Does she go on foot?" he said.

"No," I blurted suddenly, "no, by car. Always by car!" He sat back in his seat.

"You would do anything," he said conversationally. "The lot of you."

"I?" she said. "I'm not dedicated. I can be reasoned with."

After a moment of silence he said, "We'll talk."

She shrugged. "Why not?"

"This girl's home," he said. "I'll leave fifteen minutes after you. Give me your hand."

"Why?" she said. "You know where I live. I am not going to hide in the woods like an animal."

"Give me your hand," he repeated. "For old time's sake." She reached across the table. They clasped hands and she winced momentarily. Then they both rose. She smiled dazzlingly. She took me by the wrist and led me down the stairs while the strange man called after us, as if the phrase pleased him, "For old time's sake!" and then "Good health, cousin! Long life!" while the band struck up a march in ragtime. She stopped to talk to five or six people, including Ruth's father who taught mathematics in the high school, and the band leader, and Betty, who was drinking punch with a boy from our class. Betty said to me under her breath. "Your daisies are coming loose. They're gonna fall off." We walked through

the parked cars until we reached one that she seemed
to like; they were all open and some owners left the
keys in them; she got in behind the wheel and started
up.

"But this *isn't your car!*" I said. "You can't just—"

"Get in!" I slid in next to her.

"It's after ten o'clock," I said. "You'll wake up my
father. Who—"

"Shut up!"

I did. She drove very fast and very badly. Halfway
home she began to slow down. Then suddenly she
laughed out loud and said very confidentially, not to
me but as if to somebody else:

"I told him I had planted a Neilsen loop around
here that would put half of Greene County out of
phase. A dead man's control. I had to go out and stop
it every week."

"What's a Neilsen loop?" I said.

"Jam yesterday, jam tomorrow, but never jam today," she quoted.

"What," said I emphatically, "is a—"

"I've told you, baby," she said, "and you'll never
know more, God willing," and pulling into our drive-
way with a screech that would have wakened the
dead, she vaulted out of the car and through the
back door into the kitchen, just as if my mother and
father had both been asleep or in a cataleptic trance,
like those in the works of E. A. Poe. Then she told
me to get the iron poker from the garbage burner in
the back yard and find out if the end was still hot;
when I brought the thing in, she laid the hot end
over one of the flames of the gas stove. Then she
rummaged around under the sink and came up with
a bottle of my mother's Clear Household Ammonia.

"That stuff's awful," I said. "If you let that get in your eyes—"

"Pour some in the water glass," she said, handing it to me. "Two-thirds full. Cover it with a saucer. Get another glass and another saucer and put all of them on the kitchen table. Fill your mother's water pitcher, cover that, and put that on the table."

"Are you going to *drink* that?" I cried, horrified, halfway to the table with the covered glass. She merely pushed me. I got everything set up, and also pulled three chairs up to the kitchen table; I then went to turn off the gas flame, but she took me by the hand and placed me so that I hid the stove from the window and the door. She said, "Baby, what is the specific heat of iron?"

"What?" I said.

"You know it, baby," she said. "What is it?"

I only stared at her.

"But you know it, baby," she said. "You know it better than I. You know that your mother was burning garbage today and the poker would still be hot. And you know better than to touch the iron pots when they come fresh from the oven, even though the flame is off, because iron takes a long time to heat up and a long time to cool off, isn't that so?"

I nodded.

"And you don't know," she added, "how long it takes for aluminum pots to become cold because nobody uses aluminum for pots yet. And if I told you how scarce the heavy metals are, and what a radionic oven is, and how the heat can go *through* the glass and the plastic and even the ceramic lattice, you wouldn't know what I was talking about, would you?"

"No," I said, suddenly frightened, "no, no, no."

"Then you know more than some," she said. "You know more than me. Remember how I used to burn myself, fiddling with your mother's things?" She looked at her palm and made a face. "He's coming," she said. "Stand in front of the stove. When he asks you to turn off the gas, turn it off. When I say 'Now,' hit him with the poker."

"I can't," I whispered. "He's too big."

"He can't hurt you," she said. "He doesn't dare; that would be an anachronism. Just do as I say."

"What are you going to *do?*" I cried.

"When I say 'Now,' "she repeated serenely, "hit him with the poker," and sitting down by the table, she reached into a jam-jar of odds and ends my mother kept on the windowsill and began to buff her nails with a Lady Marlene emery stick. Two minutes passed by the kitchen clock. Nothing happened. I stood there with my hand on the cold end of the poker, doing nothing until I felt I had to speak, so I said, "Why are you making a face? Does something hurt?"

"The splinter in my palm," she said calmly. "The bastard."

"Why don't you take it out?"

"It will blow up the house."

He stepped in through the open kitchen door.

Without a word she put both arms palm upward on the kitchen table and without a word he took off the black cummerbund of his formal dress and flicked it at her. It settled over both her arms and then began to draw tight, molding itself over her arms and the table like a piece of black adhesive, pulling her almost down onto it and whipping one end around the table edge until the wood almost cracked. It seemed to paralyze her arms. He put his finger to his tongue and then to her palm, where there was a small black spot. The spot disappeared. He laughed and told me to turn off the flame, so I did.

"Take it off," she said then.

He said, "Too bad you are in hiding or you too could carry weapons," and then, as the edge of the table let out a startling sound like a pistol shot, he flicked the black tape off her arms, returning it to himself, where it disappeared into his evening clothes.

"Now that I have used this, everyone knows where we are," he said, and he sat down in a kitchen chair that was much too small for him and lounged back in it, his knees sticking up into the air.

Then she said something I could not understand. She took the saucer off the empty glass and poured water into it; she said something unintelligible again and held it out to him, but he motioned it away. She shrugged and drank the water herself. "Flies," she said, and put the saucer back on. They sat in silence for several minutes. I did not know what to do; I knew I was supposed to wait for the word "Now" and then hit him with the poker, but no one seemed to be saying or doing anything. The kitchen clock, which I had forgotten to wind that morning, was running down at ten minutes to eleven. There was a cricket making a noise close outside the window and I was afraid the ammonia smell would get out somehow; then, just as I was getting a cramp in my legs from standing still, our visitor nodded. She sighed, too, regretfully. The strange man got to his feet, moved his chair carefully out of the way and pronounced:

"Good. I'll call them."

"Now?" said she.

I couldn't do it. I brought the poker in front of me and stood there with it, holding it in both hands. The stranger—who almost had to stoop to avoid our ceiling—wasted only a glance on me, as if I were hardly worth looking at, and then concentrated his attention on her. She had her chin in her hands. Then she closed her eyes.

"Put that down, please," she said tiredly.

I did not know what to do. She opened her eyes and took the saucer off the other glass on the table.

"Put that down right now," she said, and raised the glass of ammonia to her lips.

I swung at him clumsily with the poker. I was not sure what happened next, but I think he laughed and seized the end—the hot end—and then threw me off balance just as he screamed, because the next thing I knew I was down on all fours watching her trip him as he threw himself at her, his eyes screwed horribly shut, choking and coughing and just missing her. The ammonia glass was lying empty and broken on the floor; a brown stain showed where it had rolled off the white tablecloth on the kitchen table. When he fell, she kicked him in the side of the head. Then she stepped carefully away from him and held out her hand to me; I gave her the poker, which she took with the folded edge of the tablecloth, and reversing it so that she held the cold end, she brought it down with immense force—not on his head, as I had expected, but on his windpipe. When he was still, she touched the hot end of the poker to several places on his jacket, passed it across where his belt would be, and to two places on both of his shoes. Then she said to me, "Get out."

I did, but not before I saw her finishing the job on

his throat, not with the poker but with the thick heel of her silver shoe.

When I came back in, there was nobody there. There was a clean, rinsed glass on the drainboard next to the sink and the poker was propped up in one corner of the sink with cold water running on it. Our visitor was at the stove, brewing tea in my mother's brown teapot. She was standing under the Dutch cloth calendar my mother, who was very modern, kept hanging on the wall. My mother pinned messages on it; one of them read "Be Careful. Except for the Bathroom, More Accidents Occur in the Kitchen Than in Any Other Part of the House."

"Where—" I said, "where is—is—"

"Sit down," she said. "Sit down here," and she put me into *his* seat at the kitchen table. But there was no *he* anywhere. She said, "Don't think too much." Then she went back to the tea and just as it was ready to pour, my mother came in from the living room, with a blanket around her shoulders, smiling foolishly and saying, "Goodness, I've been asleep, haven't I?"

"Tea?" said our visitor.

"I fell asleep just like that," said my mother, sitting down.

"I forgot," said our visitor. "I borrowed a car. I felt ill. I must call them on the telephone," and she went out into the hall, for we had been among the first to have a telephone. She came back a few minutes later. "Is it all right?" said my mother. We drank our tea in silence.

"Tell me" said our visitor at length. "How is your radio reception?"

"It's perfectly fine," said my mother, a bit offended.

"That's fine," said our visitor, and then, as if she couldn't control herself, "because you live in a dead area, you know, thank God, a dead area!"

My mother said, alarmed, "I beg your par—"

"Excuse me," said our visitor, "I'm ill," and she put her cup into her saucer with a clatter, got up and went out of the kitchen. My mother put one hand caressingly over mine.

"Did anyone . . . insult her at the dance?" said my mother, softly.

"Oh no," I said.

"Are you sure?" my mother insisted. "Are you perfectly sure? Did anyone comment? Did anyone say anything about her appearance? About her height? Anything that was not nice?"

"Ruth did," I said. "Ruth said she looked like a giraffe." My mother's hand slid off mine; gratified, she got up and began to gather up the tea things. She put them into the sink. She clucked her tongue over the poker and put it away in the kitchen closet. Then she began to dry the glass that our visitor had previously rinsed and put on the drainboard, the glass that had held ammonia.

"The poor woman," said my mother, drying it. "Oh, the poor woman."

Nothing much happened after that. I began to get my books ready for high school. Blue cornflowers sprang up along the sides of the house and my father, who was better now, cut them down with a scythe. My mother was growing hybrid ones in the back flower garden, twice as tall and twice as big as any of the wild ones; she explained to me about hybrids and why they were bigger, but I forgot it.

Our visitor took up with a man, not a nice man, really, because he worked in the town garage and was Polish. She didn't go out but used to see him in the kitchen at night. He was a thickset, stocky man, very blond, with a real Polish name, but everyone called him Bogalusa Joe because he had spent fifteen years in Bogalusa, Louisiana (he called it "Loosiana") and he talked about it all the time. He had a theory, that the colored people were just like us and that in a hundred years everybody would be all mixed up, you couldn't tell them apart. My mother was very advanced in her views but she wouldn't ever let me talk to him. He was very respectful; he called her "Ma'am," and didn't use any bad language, but he never came into the living room. He would always meet our visitor in the kitchen or sometimes on the swing in the back garden. They would drink coffee; they would play cards. Sometimes she would say to him, "Tell me a story, Joe. I love a good story," and he would talk about hiding out in Loosiana; he had had to hide out from somebody or something for three years in the middle of the Negroes and they had let him in and let him work and took care of him. He said, "The coloreds are like anybody." Then he said, "The nigras are smarter. They got to be. They ain't nobody's fool. I had a black girl for two years once was the smartest woman in the world. Beautiful woman. Not beautiful like a white, though, not the same."

"Give us a hundred years," he added, "and it'll all be mixed."

"Two hundred?" said our visitor, pouring coffee. He put a lot of sugar in his; then he remarked that he had learned that in Bogalusa. She sat down. She

was leaning her elbows on the table, smiling at him.
She was stirring her own coffee with a spoon. He
looked at her a moment, and then he said softly:

"A black woman, smartest woman in the world.
You're black, woman, ain't you?"

"Part," she said.

"Beautiful woman," he said. "Nobody knows?"

"They know in the circus," she said. "But there
they don't care. Shall I tell you what we circus
people think of you?"

"Of who?" he said, looking surprised.

"Of all of you," she said. "All who aren't in the
circus. All who can't do what we can do, who aren't
the biggest or the best, who can't kill a man bare-
handed or learn a new language in six weeks or slit a
man's jugular at fifteen yards with nothing but a
pocketknife or climb the Greene County National
Bank from the first story to the sixth with no equipment. I can do all that."

"I'll be damned," said Bogalusa Joe softly.

"We despise you," she said. "That's what we do.
We think you're slobs. The scum of the earth! The
world's fertilizer, Joe, that's what you are."

"Baby, you're blue," he said, "you're blue tonight,"
and then he took her hand across the table, but not
the way they did it in the movies, not the way they
did it in the books; there was a look on his face I had
never seen on anyone's before, not the high school
boys when they put a line over on a girl, not on
grown-ups, not even on the brides and grooms because all that was romantic or showing off or "lust"
and he only looked infinitely kind, infinitely concerned. She pulled her hand out of his. With the

same faint, detached smile she had had all night, she
pushed back her chair and stood up. She said flatly:

"All I can do! What good is it?" She shrugged. She
added, "I've got to leave tomorrow." He got up and
put his arm around her shoulders. I thought that
looked bad because he was actually a couple of inches
shorter than she was.

He said, "Baby, you don't have to go." She was
staring out into the back garden, as if looking miles
away, miles out, far away into our vegetable patch or
our swing or my mother's hybrids, into something
nobody could see. He said urgently, "Honey, look—"
and then, when she continued to stare, pulling her
face around so she had to look at him, both his
broad, mechanic's hands under her chin, "Baby, you
can stay with me." He brought his face closer to
hers. "Marry me," he said suddenly. She began to
laugh. I had never heard her laugh like that before.
Then she began to choke. He put his arms around
her and she leaned against him, choking, making
funny noises like someone with asthma, finally clapping her hands over her face, then biting her palm,
heaving up and down as if she were sick. It took me
several seconds to realize that she was crying. He
looked very troubled. They stood there: she cried,
he, distressed—and I hiding, watching all of it. They
began to walk slowly toward the kitchen door. When
they had gone out and put out the light, I followed
them out into the back garden, to the swing my
father had rigged up under the one big tree: cushions and springs to the ground like a piece of furniture, big enough to hold four people. Bushes screened
it. There was a kerosene lantern my father had
mounted on a post, but it was out. I could just about

see them. They sat for a few minutes, saying nothing, looking up through the tree into the darkness.
The swing creaked a little as our visitor crossed and
uncrossed her long legs. She took out a cigarette and
lit it, obscuring their faces with even that little glow:
an orange spot that wavered up and down as she
smoked, making the darkness more black. Then it
disappeared. She had ground it out underfoot in the
grass. I could see them again. Bogalusa Joe, the
garage mechanic, said:

"Tomorrow?"

"Tomorrow," she said. Then they kissed each other.
I liked that; it was all right; I had seen it before. She
leaned back against the cushions of the swing and
seemed to spread her feet in the invisible grass; she
let her head and arms fall back onto the cushion.
Without saying a word, he lifted her skirt far above
her knees and put his hand between her legs. There
was a great deal more of the same business and I
watched it all, from the first twistings to the stab-
bings, the noises, the life-and-death battle in the
dark. The word *Epilepsy* kept repeating itself in my
head. They got dressed and again began to smoke,
talking in tones I could not hear. I crouched in the
bushes, my heart beating violently.

I was horribly frightened.

She did not leave the next day, or the next or the
next; and she even took a dress to my mother and
asked if she could have it altered somewhere in town.
My school clothes were out, being aired in the back
yard to get the mothball smell out of them. I put
covers on all my books. I came down one morning to
ask my mother whether I couldn't have a jumper

taken up at the hem because the magazines said it was all right for young girls. I expected a fight over it. I couldn't find my mother in the hall or the kitchen so I tried the living room, but before I had got halfway through the living-room arch, someone said, "Stop there," and I saw both my parents sitting on two chairs near the front door, both with their hands in their laps, both staring straight ahead, motionless as zombies.

I said, "Oh for heaven's sake, what're you—"

"Stop there," said the same voice. My parents did not move. My mother was smiling her social smile. There was no one else in the room. I waited for a little while, my parents continuing to be dead, and then from some corner on my left, near the new Philco, our visitor came gliding out, wrapped in my mother's spring coat, stepping softly across the rug and looking carefully at all the living-room windows. She grinned when she saw me. She tapped the top of the Philco radio and motioned me in. Then she took off the coat and draped it over the radio.

She was in black from head to foot.

I thought *black*, but black was not the word; the word was *blackness*, dark beyond dark, dark that drained the eyesight, something I could never have imagined even in my dreams, a black in which there was no detail, no sight, no nothing, only an awful, desperate dizziness, for her body—the thing was skintight, like a diver's costume or an acrobat's—had actually disappeared, completely blotted out except for its outline. Her head and bare hands floated in the air. She said, "Pretty, yes?" Then she sat cross-legged on our radio. She said, "Please pull the curtains," and I did, going from one to the other and drawing them shut, circling my frozen parents and then stopping short in the middle of the quaking floor. I said, "I'm going to faint." She was off the radio and into my mother's coat in an instant; holding me by the arm, she got me onto the living-room couch and put her arm around me, massaging my back. She said, "Your parents are asleep." Then she said, "You have known some of this. You are a wonderful little pickup but you get mixed up, yes? All about the Morlocks? The Trans-Temporal Military Authority?"

I began to say "Oh oh oh oh—" and she massaged my back again.

"Nothing will hurt you," she said. "Nothing will hurt your parents. Think how exciting it is! Think! The rebel Morlocks, the revolution in the Trans-Temporal Military Authority."

"But I—I—" I said.

"We are friends," she continued gravely, taking my hands, "we are real friends. You helped me. We will not forget that," and slinging my mother's coat off onto the couch, she went and stood in front of the archway. She put her hands on her hips, then began rubbing the back of her neck nervously and clearing her throat. She turned around to give me one last look.

"Are you calm?" she said. I nodded. She smiled at me. "Be calm," she said softly, "*sois tranquille*. We're friends," and then she put herself to watching the archway. She said once, almost sadly, "Friends," and then stepped back and smiled again at me.

The archway was turning into a mirror. It got misty, then bright, like a cloud of bright dust, then almost like a curtain; and then it was a mirror, although all I could see in it was our visitor and myself, not my parents, not the furniture, not the living room.

Then the first Morlock stepped through.

And the second.

And the third.

And the others.

Oh, the living room was filled with giants! They were like her, like her in the face, like her in the bodies of the very tall, like her in the black uniforms, men and women of all the races of the earth, everything mixed and huge as my mother's hybrid flowers but a foot taller than our visitor, a flock of black ravens, black bats, black wolves, the professionals of the future world, perched on our furniture, on the Philco radio, some on the very walls and drapes of the windows as if they could fly, hovering in the air as if they were out in space where the Morlocks meet, half a thousand in a bubble between the stars.

Who rule the worlds.

Two came through the mirror who crawled on the rug, both in diving suits and goldfish-bowl helmets, a man and a woman, fat and shaped like seals. They lay on the rug breathing water (for I saw the specks flowing in it, in and out of strange frills around their necks, the way dust moves in air) and looking up at the rest with tallowy faces. Their suits bulged. One of the Morlocks said something to one of the seals and one of the seals answered, fingering a thing attached to the barrels on its back, gurgling.

Then they all began to talk.

Even if I'd known what language it was, I think it would have been too fast for me; it was very fast, very hard-sounding, very urgent, like the numbers pilots call in to the ground or something like that, like a code that everybody knows, to get things done as fast as you can. Only the seal-people talked slowly, and they gurgled and stank like a dirty beach. They did not even move their faces except to make little round mouths, like fish. I think I was put to sleep for a while (or maybe I just fell asleep) and then it was something about the seal-people, with the Morlock who was seated on the radio joining in—and then general enough—and then something going round the whole room—and then that fast, hard urgent talk between one of the Morlocks and my friend. It was still business, but they looked at *me;* it was awful to be looked at and yet I felt numb; I wished I were asleep; I wanted to cry because I could not understand a word they were saying. Then my friend suddenly shouted; she stepped back and threw both arms out, hands extended and fingers spread, shaking violently. She was shouting instead of talking, shouting desperately about something, pounding one fist into her palm, her face contorted, just as if it was not business. The other Morlock was breathing quickly and had gone pale with rage. He whispered something, something very venomous. He took from his black uniform, which could have hidden anything, a silver dime, and holding it up between thumb and forefinger, he said in perfectly clear English, while looking at me:

"In the name of the war against the Trans-Tempor—"

She had jumped him in an instant. I scrambled up; I saw her close his fist about the dime with her own; then it was all a blur on the floor until the two of them stood up again, as far as they could get from each other, because it was perfectly clear that they hated each other. She said very distinctly, "*I do insist.*" He shrugged. He said something short and sharp. She took out of her own darkness a knife—only a knife—and looked slowly about the room at each person in it. Nobody moved. She raised her eyebrows.

"*Tcha! grozny?*"

The seal-woman hissed on the floor, like steam coming out of a leaky radiator. She did not get up but lay on her back, eyes blinking, a woman encased in fat.

"You?" said my friend insultingly. "You will stain the carpet."

The seal-woman hissed again. Slowly my friend walked toward her, the others watching. She did not bend down, as I had expected, but dove down abruptly with a kind of sidewise roll, driving herself into the seal-woman's side. She had planted one heel on the stomach of the woman's diving suit; she seemed to be trying to tear it. The seal-woman caught my friend's knife-hand with one glove and was trying to turn it on my friend while she wrapped the other gloved arm around my friend's neck. She was trying to strangle her. My friend's free arm was extended on the rug; it seemed to me that she was either leaning on the floor or trying to pull herself free. Then again everything went into a sudden blur. There was a gasp, a loud, mechanical click; my friend vaulted up and backward, dropping her knife and clapping one hand to her left eye. The seal-woman was turning from side to side on the floor, a kind of shudder running from her feet to her head, an expressionless flexing of her body and face. Bubbles were forming in the goldfish-bowl helmet. The other seal-person did not move. As I watched, the water began falling in the seal-woman's helmet and then it was all air. I supposed she was dead. My friend, our visitor, was standing in the middle of the room, blood welling from under her hand; she was bent over with pain and her face was horribly distorted but not one person in that room moved to touch her.

"Life—" she gasped, "for life. Yours," and then she crashed to the rug. The seal-woman had slashed open her eye. Two of the Morlocks rushed to her then and picked up her and her knife; they were dragging her toward the mirror in the archway when she began muttering something.

"Damn your sketches!" shouted the Morlock she had fought with, completely losing control of himself. "We are at war; Trans-Temp is at our heels; do you think we have time for dilettantism? You presume on being that woman's granddaughter! We are fighting for the freedom of fifty billions of people, not for your scribbles!" and motioning to the others, who immediately dragged the body of the seal-woman through the mirror and began to follow it themselves, he turned to me.

"You!" he snapped. "You will speak to nobody of this. Nobody!"

I put my arms around myself.

"Do not try to impress anyone with stories," he added contemptuously, "you are lucky to live," and without another look he followed the last of the Morlocks through the mirror, which promptly disappeared. There was blood on the rug, a few inches from my feet. I bent down and put my fingertips in it, and then with no clear reason, I put my fingers to my face.

"—come back," said my mother. I turned to face them, the wax manikins who had seen nothing.

"Who the devil drew the curtains!" shouted my father. "I've told you" (to me) "that I don't like tricks, young lady, and if it weren't for your mother's—"

"Oh, Ben, Ben! She's had a nosebleed!" cried my mother.

They told me later that I fainted.

I was in bed a few days, because of the nosebleed, but then they let me up. My parents said I probably had had anemia. They also said they had seen our visitor off at the railroad station that morning, and that she had boarded the train as they watched her; tall, frizzy-haired, freakish, dressed in black down to between the knees and ankles, legged like a stork and carrying all her belongings in a small valise. "Gone to the circus," said my mother. There was nothing in the room that had been hers, nothing in the attic, no reflection in the window at which she had stood, brilliantly lit against the black night, nothing in the kitchen and nothing at the Country Club but tennis courts overgrown with weeds. Joe never came back to our house. The week before school I looked through all my books, starting with *The Time Machine* and ending with *The Green Hat;* then I went downstairs and looked through every book in the house. There was nothing. I was invited to a party; my mother would not let me go. Cornflowers grew around the house. Betty came over once and was bored. One afternoon at the end of summer, with the wind blowing through the empty house from top to bottom and everybody away, nobody next door, my parents in the back yard, the people on the other side of us gone swimming, everybody silent or sleeping or off somewhere—except for some-one down the block whom I could hear mowing the lawn—I decided to sort and try on all my shoes. I did this in front of a full-length mirror fastened to the inside of my closet door. I had been taking off and putting on various of my winter dresses, too, and I was putting one particular one away in a box on the floor of the closet when I chanced to look up at the inside of the closet door.

She was standing in the mirror. It was all black behind her, like velvet. She was wearing something black and silver, half-draped, half-nude, and there were lines on her face that made it look sectioned off, or like a cobweb; she had one eye. The dead eye radiated spinning white light, like a Catherine wheel. She said:

"Did you ever think to go back and take care of yourself when you are little? Give yourself advice?"

I couldn't say anything.

"I am not you," she said, "but I have had the same thought and now I have come back four hundred and fifty years. Only there is nothing to say. There is never anything to say. It is a pity, but natural, no doubt."

"Oh, please!" I whispered. "Stay!" She put one foot up on the edge of the mirror as if it were the threshold of a door. The silver sandal she had worn at the Country Club dance almost came into my bedroom: thick-heeled, squat, flaking, as ugly as sin; new lines formed on her face and all over her bare skin, ornamenting her all over. Then she stepped back; she shook her head, amused; the dead eye waned, filled again, exploded in sparks and went out, showing the naked socket, ugly, shocking, and horrible.

"Tcha!" she said, "my grandma thought she would bring something hard to a world that was soft and silly but nice, and now it's silly and not so nice and the hard has got too hard and the soft too soft and my great-grandma—it is she who founded the order—is dead. Not that it matters. Nothing ends, you see. Just keeps going on and on."

"But you can't *see!*" I managed. She poked herself in the temple and the eye went on again.

"Bizarre," she said. "Interesting. Attractive. Stone blind is twice as good. I'll tell you my sketches."

"But you don't—you can't—" I said.

"The first," she said, lines crawling all over her, "is an Eloi having the Go-Jollies, and that is a bald, fat man in a toga, a frilled bib, a sunbonnet and shoes you would not believe, who has a crystal ball in his lap and from it wires plugged into his eyes and his nose and his ears and his tongue and his head, just like your lamps. That is an Eloi having the Go-Jollies."

I began to cry.

"The second," she went on, "is a Morlock working; and that is myself holding a skull, like *Hamlet*, only if you look closely at the skull you will see it is the world, with funny things sticking out of the seas and the polar ice caps, and that it is full of people. Much too full. There are too many of the worlds, too."

"If you'll *stop*—!" I cried.

"They are all pushing each other off," she continued, "and some are falling into the sea, which is a pity, no doubt, but quite natural, and if you will look closely at all these Eloi you will see that each one is holding his crystal ball, or running after an animated machine which runs faster than he, or watching another Eloi on a screen who is cleverer and looks fascinating, and you will see that under the fat the man or woman is screaming, screaming and dying.

"And my third sketch," she said, "which is a very little one, shows a goldfish bowl full of people in black. Behind that is a smaller goldfish bowl full of people in black, which is going after the first goldfish bowl, and behind the second is a third, which is going after the second, and so on, or perhaps they alternate; that would be more economical. Or perhaps I am only bitter because I lost my eye. It's a personal problem."

I got to my feet. I was so close I could have touched her. She crossed her arms across her breast and looked down at me; she then said softly, "My dear, I wished to take you with me, but that's impossible. I'm very sorry," and looking for the first time both serious and tender, she disappeared behind a swarm of sparks.

I was looking at myself. I had recently made, passionately and in secret, the uniform of the Trans-Temporal Military Authority as I thought it ought to look: a black tunic over black sleeves and black tights. The tights were from a high school play I had been in the year before and the rest was cut out of the lining of an old winter coat. That was what I was wearing that afternoon. I had also fastened a silver curling-iron to my waist with a piece of cord. I put one foot up in the air, as if on the threshold of the mirror, and a girl in ragged black stared back at me. She turned and frantically searched the entire room, looking for sketches, for notes, for specks of silver paint, for anything at all. Then she sat down on my bed. She did not cry. She said to me, "You look idiotic." Someone was still mowing the lawn outside, probably my father. My mother would be clipping, patching, rooting up weeds; she never stopped. Someday I would join a circus, travel to the moon, write a book; after all, I had helped kill a man. I had been somebody. It was all nonsense. I took off the curling-iron and laid it on the bed. Then I undressed and got into my middy-blouse and skirt and I put the costume on the bed in a heap. As I walked toward the door of the room, I turned to take one last look at myself in the mirror and at my strange collection of old clothes. For a moment something else moved in the mirror, or I thought it did, something behind me or to one side, something menacing, something half-blind, something heaving slowly like a shadow, leaving perhaps behind it faint silver flakes like the shadow of a shadow or some carelessly dropped coins, something glittering, something somebody had left on the edge of vision, dropped by accident in the dust and cobwebs of an attic. I wished for it violently; I stood and clenched my fists; I almost cried; I wanted something to come out of the mirror and strike me dead. If I could not have a protector, I wanted a monster, a mutation, a horror, a murderous disease, anything! anything at all to accompany me downstairs so that I would not have to go down alone.

Nothing came. Nothing good, nothing bad. I heard the lawnmower going on. I would have to face by myself my father's red face, his heart disease, his temper, his nasty insistencies. I would have to face my mother's sick smile, looking up from the flowerbed she was weeding, always on her knees somehow, saying before she was ever asked, "Oh the poor woman. Oh the poor woman."

And quite alone.

No more stories.

*Here is an excerpt from Book I of THE KING OF YS,
Poul and Karen Anderson's epic new fantasy, coming from
Baen Books in December 1986:*

THE KING OF YS: ROMA MATER
POUL AND KAREN ANDERSON

The parties met nearer the shaw than the city.
They halted a few feet apart. For a space there was
stillness, save for the wind.

The man in front was a Gaul, Gratillonius judged.
He was huge, would stand a head above the centurion when they were both on the ground, with a
breadth of shoulder and thickness of chest that
made him look squat. His paunch simply added to
the sense of bear strength. His face was broad,
ruddy, veins broken in the flattish nose, a scar
zigzagging across the brow ridges that shelved small
ice-blue eyes. Hair knotted into a queue, beard
abristle to the shaggy breast, were brown, and had
not been washed for a long while. His loose-fitting
shirt and close-fitting breeches were equally soiled.
At his hip he kept a knife, and slung across his
back was a sword more than a yard in length. A
fine golden chain hung around his neck, but what
it bore lay hidden beneath the shirt.

"Romans," he rumbled in Osismian. "What the
pox brings you mucking around here?"

The centurion replied carefully, as best he was
able in the same language: "Greeting. I hight Gaius
Valerius Gratillonius, come in peace and good

will as the new prefect of Rome in Ys. Fain would I meet with your leaders."

Meanwhile he surveyed those behind. Half a dozen were men of varying ages, in neat and clean versions of the same garb, unarmed. Nearest the Gaul stood one who differed. He was ponderous of body and countenance. Black beard and receding hair were flecked with white, though he did not seem old. He wore a crimson robe patterned with gold thread, a miter of the same stuff, a talisman hanging on his bosom that was in the form of a wheel, cast in precious metal and set with jewels. Rings sparkled on both hands. In his right he bore a staff as high as himself, topped by a silver representation of a boar's head.

The woman numbered three. They were in ankle-length gowns with loose sleeves to the wrists, of rich material and subtle hues, ornately belted at the waist.

The Gaul's voice yanked him from his inspection: "What? You'd strut in out of nowhere and fart your orders at *me*—you who can talk no better than a frog? Go back before I step on the lot of you."

"I think you are drunk," Gratillonius said truthfully.

"Not too full of wine to piss you out, Roman!" the other bawled.

Gratillonius forced coolness upon himself. "Who here is civilized?" he asked in Latin.

The man in the red robe stepped forward. "Sir, we request you to kindly overlook the mood of the King," he responded in the same tongue, accented but fairly fluent. "His vigil ended at dawn today, but these his Queens sent word for us to wait. I formally attended him to and from the Wood, you see. Only in this past hour was I bidden to come."

The man shrugged and smiled. My name is Soren Cartagi, Speaker for Taranis."

The Gaul turned on him, grabbed him by his garment and shook him. "You'd undercut me, plotting in Roman, would you?" he grated. A fist drew back. "Well, I've not forgotten all of it. I know when a scheme's afoot against me. And I know you think Colconor is stupid, but you've a nasty surprise coming to you, potgut!"

The male attendants showed horror. One of the woman hurried forth. "Are you possessed, Colconor?" she demanded. "Soren's person when he speaks for the God is sacred. Let him go ere Taranis blasts you to a cinder!"

The language she used was neither Latin nor Osismian. Melodious, it seemed essentially Celtic, but full of words and constructions Gratillonius had never encountered before. It must be the language of Ys. By listening hard and straining his wits, he got the drift if not the full meaning.

The Gaul released the Speaker, who stumbled back, and rounded on the woman. She stood defiant— tall, lean, her hatchet features haggard but her eyes like great, lustrous pools of darkness. The cowl, fallen down in her hasty movement, revealed a mane of black hair, loosely gathered under a fillet, through the middle of which ran a white streak. Gratillonius sensed implacable hatred as she went on: "Five years have we endured you, Colconor, and weary years they were. If now you'd fain bring your doom on yourself, oh, be very welcome."

Rage reddened him the more. "Ah, so that's your game, Vindilis, my pet?" His own Ysan was easier for Gratillonius to follow, being heavily Osismianized. " 'Twas sweet enough you were this threenight agone, and today. But inwardly—Ah, I should have known. You were ever more man than woman, Vindilis, and hex more than either."

He swung on Gratillonius. "Go, Roman!" he roared. "I am the King! By the iron rod of Taranis, I'll not take Roman orders! Go or stay; but if you stay, 'twill be on the dungheap where I'll toss your carcass!"

Gratillonius fought for self-control. Despite Colconor's behavior, he was dimly surprised at his instant, lightning-sharp hatred for the man. "I have prior orders," he answered, as steadily as he could. To Soren, in Latin: "Sir, can't you stay this madman so we can talk in quiet?"

Colconor understood. "Madman, be I?" he shrieked. "Why, *you* were shit out of your harlot mother's arse, where your donkey father begot you ere they gelded him. Back to your swinesty of a Rome!"

It flared in Gratillonius. His vinestaff was tucked at his saddlebow. He snatched it forth, leaned down, and gave Colconor a cut across the lips. Blood jumped from the wound.

Colconor leaped back and grabbed at his sword. The Ysan men flung themselves around him. Gratillonius heard Soren's resonant voice: "Nay, not here. It must be in the Wood, the Wood." He sounded almost happy. The women stood aside. Vindilis put hands on hips, threw back her head, and laughed aloud.

Eppillus stepped to his centurion's shin, glanced up, and said anxiously, "Looks like a brawl, sir. We can handle it. Give the word, and we'll make sausage meat of that bastard."

Gratillonius shook his head. A presentiment was eldritch upon him. "No," he replied softly. "I think this is something I must do myself, or else lose the respect we'll need in Ys."

Colconor stopped struggling, left the group of men, and spat on the horse. "Well, will you challenge me?" he said. "I'll enjoy letting out your white blood."

"You'd fight me next!" yelled Adminius. He too had been quick in picking up something of the Gallic languages.

Colconor grinned. "Aye, aye. The lot of you. One at a time, though. Your chieftain first. And afterward I've a right to rest between bouts." He stared at the woman. "I'll spend those whiles with you three bitches, and you'll not like it, what I'll make you do." Turning, he swaggered back toward the grove.

Soren approached. "We are deeply sorry about

this," he said in Latin. "Far better that you be received as befits the envoy of Rome." A smile of sorts passed through his beard. "Well, later you shall be. I think Taranis wearies at last of this incarnation of His, and—the King of the Wood has powers, if he chooses to exercise them, beyond those of even a Roman prefect."

"I am to fight Colconor, then?" Gratillonius asked slowly.

Soren nodded. "In the Wood. To the death. On foot, though you may choose your weapons. There is an arsenal at the Lodge."

"I'm well supplied already." Gratillonius felt no fear. He had a task before him which he would carry out, or die; he did not expect to die.

He glanced back at the troubled faces of his men, briefly explained what was happening, and finished: "Keep discipline, boys. But don't worry. We'll still sleep in Ys tonight. Forward march!"...

It was but a few minutes to the site. A slate-flagged courtyard stood open along the road, flanked by three buildings. They were clearly ancient, long and low, of squared timbers and with shingle roofs. The two on the sides were painted black, one a stable, the other a storehouse. The third, at the end, was larger, and blood-red. It had a porch with intricately carven pillars.

In the middle of the court grew a giant oak. From the lowest of its newly leafing branches hung a brazen circular shield and a sledgehammer. Though the shield was much too big and heavy for combat, dents surrounded the boss, which showed a wildly bearded and maned human face. Behind the house, more oaks made a grove about seven hundred feet across and equally deep.

"Behold the Sacred Precinct," Soren intoned. "Dismount, stranger, and ring your challenge." After a moment he added quietly, "We need not lose time waiting for the marines and hounds. Neither of you will flee, nor let his opponent escape."

Gratillonius comprehended. He sprang to earth,

took hold of the hammer, smote the shield with his full strength. It rang, a bass note which sent echoes flying. Mute now, Eppillus gave him his military shield and took his cloak and crest before marshalling the soldiers in a meadow across the road.

Vindilis laid a hand on Gratillonius's arm. Never had he met so intense a gaze, out of such pallor, as from her. In a voice that shook, she whispered, "Avenge us, man. Set us free. Oh, rich shall be your reward."

It came to him, like a chill from the wind that soughed among the oaks, that his coming had been awaited. Yet how could she have known?

To order any Baen Book by mail, send the cover price plus 75 cents for first-class postage and handling to: Baen Books, Dept. B, 260 Fifth Avenue, New York, N.Y. 10001.

Here is an excerpt from Charles Sheffield's newest novel, The Nimrod Hunt, *to be published in August 1986 by Baen Books:*

They were close to a branch point, where the descending shaft divided to continue as a double descent path. He had not seen that before, or heard of it in any of the records left by Team Alpha. It suggested a system of pathways through Travancore's jungles more complicated than they had realized. Chan looked again at S'greela and Shikari. They were both still engrossed in the Angel's efforts. He strolled slowly down along the sloping tunnel and looked out along each branch in turn.

They were not identical. One continued steadily down towards the surface of Travancore, five kilometers below them. The other was narrower and less steep. It curved off slowly to the left with hardly any gradient at all. If it went on like that the narrow corridor would provide a horizontal roadway through the high forest. Chan took just three or four paces along it. He did not intend to lose sight of the other team members.

After three steps he paused, very confused. There seemed to be something like a dark mist obscuring the more distant parts of the corridor. He shone his light, and there was no answering reflection.

Chan hesitated for a moment, then started to move back up the tunnel. Whatever it was in front of him, he was not about to face it alone. He had weapons with him—but more than those he wanted S'greela's strength, Shikari's mobility, and Angel's cool reasoning powers.

As he turned, he heard a whisper behind him.

"Chan!"

He looked back. Something had stepped forward from the middle of the dark tunnel. He froze.

It was Leah.

Even as Chan was about to call out to her, he remembered Mondrian's warning. *Leah was dead.* What he was seeing was an illusion, something created in his mind by Nimrod.

As though to confirm his thought, the figure of Leah drifted *upwards* like a pale ghost. It hung unsupported, a couple of feet above the floor of the tunnel. The shape raised one white arm. "Chan," it said again.

"Leah! Is it you—really you?" Chan fought back the sudden urge to run forward and embrace the hovering form in front of him.

It did not seem to have heard him. Chan saw the dark-haired head move slowly from side to side. "Not now, Chan," said Leah's voice. "It would be too dangerous now. Say goodbye—but love me, Chan. Love is the secret."

Ignoring all common sense, Chan found that he had taken another step along the tunnel. He paused, dizzy and irresolute.

The figure held up both arms urgently. "Not now, Chan. Dangerous."

She waved. The slim form stepped sharply backwards, and was swallowed up at once in the dark cloud. The apparition was gone.

Chan stood motionless, too stunned to move. At last a sudden premonition of great danger conquered his inertia. He turned and began to stagger and stumble back towards the others.

A voice inside his head was screaming at him. *"NIMROD. Nimrod is active here. A Morgan Construct can produce delusions within an organic brain—it can change what you see and hear. Get back to the others—NOW!"*

He was suddenly back in the part of the tunnel where he had left the other team members. It was totally deserted.

They were gone! To his horror and dismay, there was no sign of the rest of them. *Where was the team?* Surely they would not have left him behind and gone back up the tunnel without him. Had they fallen victim to Nimrod?

Dizzy with fear, emotion, and unanswerable questions, Chan began to run back up the tunnel, back to the sunlight, back to the doubtful safety of the cetent in the upper vegetation layers. As he did so, the face and form of Leah hovered shimmering before his eyes.

AUGUST 1986 • 65582-6 • 416 pp. • $3.50

To order any Baen Book by mail, send the cover price plus 75¢ to cover first-class postage and handling to: Baen Books, Dept. BA, 260 Fifth Avenue, New York, N.Y. 10001.

WE'RE LOOKING FOR
TROUBLE

Well, feedback, anyway. Baen Books endeavors to publish only the best in science fiction and fantasy—but we need you to tell us whether we're doing it right. Why not let us know? We'll award a Baen Books gift certificate worth $100 (plus a copy of our catalog) to the reader who best tells us what he or she likes about Baen Books—and where we could do better. We reserve the right to quote any or all of you. Contest closes December 31, 1987. All letters should be addressed to Baen Books, 260 Fifth Avenue, New York, N.Y. 10001.